Last Call at the Esposito
An Elder Darrow Mystery

For Brooks ...

Best

Last Call at the Esposito
An Elder Darrow Mystery

Richard Cass

Richard J. Cass

Encircle Publications, LLC
Farmington, Maine U.S.A.

Editor: Cynthia Brackett-Vincent
Book design: Eddie Vincent
Cover design and composite illustration by Deirdre Wait, High Pines Creative
Cover images © Getty Images
Author photo by Philip McCarty

Published by: Encircle Publications, LLC
PO Box 187
Farmington, ME 04938

Visit: http://encirclepub.com

Printed in U.S.A.

*If you cannot be grateful for what you have received,
then be thankful for what you have been spared.*
(Yiddish proverb)

Dedication

For Anne, as are they all. And for my parents.

Acknowledgements

As always, many thanks once again to the folks at Encircle Publications, Ed Vincent and Cynthia Brackett-Vincent, for ongoing support and continuing to believe in the long strange saga of Elder Darrow and Dan Burton. And to Deirdre Wait at High Pines Creative for her usual exceptional work in rendering the essence of *Last Call at the Esposito* onto the cover.

Thanks to Brenda Buchanan for an explanation of real estate machinations that turned out to be central to the plot.

Thanks also to important early readers: Kate Flora and John Sheldon for deep attention that helped make the book much better than it might have been. Drinks on the house . . .

Last Call at the Esposito does center around an actual occurrence, the attempt in 2013 and 2014 to bring the Olympic Games to Boston. While the story resides mostly in the background of *Last Call*, you can read a gripping account of the (ultimately unsuccessful) attempt and the amazing bad faith, flim-flammery, and general arrogance of powerful political and business people in the Commonwealth of Massachusetts in *No Boston Olympics* by Chris Dempsey and Andrew Zimbalist. As Margaret Mead said: "Never doubt that a small group of thoughtful, committed citizens can change the world; indeed, it's the only thing that ever has."

I can't say enough how important the encouragement of the Maine literary community and, specifically, the Maine Crime Writing faction, is. It's unusual in my experience to find so many writers devoted to each others' successes, and I am proud and pleased to be part of it. I only hope I give back as much as I receive.

Richard J. Cass

The Maine Writers and Publishers Alliance continues to serve all of Maine's writers with great energy and support.

And I'd be remiss not to acknowledge the importance of our libraries and our independent bookstores in promoting this thing of ours. Maine libraries and librarians, in particular, have been instrumental in raising many of us up.

And for our wealth of bookstores, I give great thanks, especially to those who continue to support all of us. Special thanks to Ari at Longfellow Books in Portland, Josh Christie and Emily Russo Murtagh at Print Bookstore, and Katherine Osborne at Letterpress Books.

Once again, a special thanks to spouses, partners, and friends. We could not, despite what you might think, do it without you.

1

"Randolph Coyne." The dapper gentleman—sharply tailored black suit, handmade brogans, and a drily elegant aftershave— reached his hand over the bar of the Esposito to shake. He bore a long thin nose on a long thin face and a haircut with the sides shaved and the top slicked back like a Spanish soccer player. "I'm an associate of Mr. Maldonado."

"I thought Ricky moved to Miami," I said.

Ricky Maldonado, our neighborhood nickel-and-dime gangster, had developed a spate of health problems a couple years back that made it increasingly difficult for him to manage even the pint-sized fiefdom the city's serious mobsters had left him—they'd tolerated him out of a sense of nostalgia more than anything. But after he lost his chief lieutenant and heir apparent Tommy Cormier in a bomb blast, Ricky retreated to South Florida for his health. Or so the story went.

"I was referring to Mr. Donald Maldonado," Coyne said.

I translated the name in my head.

"Donald Bad Donald?"

Coyne's mouth puckered as if I'd insulted him. The lines radiating out from the corners of his mouth suggested the expression was habitual, that the world perpetually disappointed him.

He was clearly not in the Esposito for the ambience, not that the bar showed itself best at ten o'clock on a Tuesday morning. The bar had come a long way since I bought it: you could drink without getting into a fist fight and step outside to smoke without worrying about being mugged. And the food was better than edible, thanks to Marina.

1

Cleaning up the place had been more work than I expected, but in addition to keeping me more or less sober, it helped me develop an instinct for trouble. And Randolph Coyne was trouble.

He wasn't here for the music, either. Wes Montgomery's *California Dreamin'* flowed like liquid sunshine from the Boston Acoustics speakers mounted up in the corners of the bar. Before Randolph Coyne tip-tapped his way down the twelve steel stairs—who wore Italian loafers in the winter?—I was thinking what a perfect time of year early March was for being somewhere other than Boston. The daytime skies were iron-colored and dull. Slush froze and refroze in masses along the sidewalks and black ice skimmed the streets. There was still another four or five weeks before the first green shoots of spring and even though I could finally afford it, I wasn't going anywhere. I had a bar to run.

"I didn't know Ricky had a brother."

"First cousin," Coyne said. "Once removed."

He placed his hands palms down on the bar top. They were scabbed and scarred, the knuckles knotted from impact and old breakage. Martial arts. Though, smart fist fighters always punched the soft parts.

"Richard signed over control of all his enterprises to Donald," Coyne said. "Effective this date."

I swallowed my amusement. At its apex, Ricky's enterprises comprised a pair of meth-addicted muscle men, a loose and intensely disloyal network of street dealers, and an Apache second-in-command obsessed with business management skills. Tommy Cormier might have been Ricky's only scary asset, but the car bomb had taken him out of the picture and soon thereafter, Ricky quit and left town.

"Ah, Randolph. I'm not sure you know what Ricky was actually doing here in the city, but…"

Coyne raised an index finger, the end of which pointed sideways. There was nothing I liked better than being shushed by a thug, even a well-dressed one.

"Mr. Maldonado is a very astute business person. He has been extremely successful at growing operations in hitherto underserved locations."

Hitherto? Randolph must have checked his word-a-day calendar this morning. It didn't make him any less of a thug.

"I had very little contact with Ricky." I shaded the truth only a little. "Nothing much, either personal or commercial."

Coyne leaned across the bar.

"I know. A shame. Such a wasted opportunity."

My face must have shown that I wasn't impressed, because he bared his teeth and smiled like a wolf. I felt the fear in my backbone—I'd run up against some genuine hardasses in the Esposito's lurch toward respectability, and Randolph rated right up there. I wondered what Mickey Barksdale, the reigning boss of crime right now, would say about him.

"But that is not why I have come here to see you today."

He wasn't using contractions and the rest of his syntax was formal. It sounded memorized rather than learned. My instincts said I didn't want to hear what he had to say. Not yet, anyway.

"I'm not being a very good bartender here. Can I offer you a libation?"

His light gray eyes glinted, as if he thought I might be mocking his diction.

"Do you stock Fernet-Branca?"

I didn't even know what it was.

"Sorry."

"No matter, we should maintain our focus on the business at hand. I believe you have had the acquaintance of a young woman named Kathleen Crawford."

Hearing her name out loud spiked the hair on the back of my neck. She and I had had a too-brief encounter recently enough that I hadn't gotten over it yet. She'd worked in a local bank and owned a house in Cambridge, and while I'd thought we might have had something serious going, my cop buddy Burton had found out she was a thief. She'd disappeared, leaving me a cryptic video about being pursued by one of her victims.

"Don't believe I've heard the name."

Coyne slapped a black and white picture down on the bar, a fuzzy still from a surveillance camera: the angle of the shot was from high over her head. In the picture, the woman's hair was chopped very short and so blond it glowed in the photo. And she wore no earrings. When she'd been here with me, Kathleen had long black hair threaded with silver and she favored long dangly pendants that caught the light when she moved her head. The shape of her skull looked familiar, but that wasn't enough to identify her to Coyne.

He held up his hand, as if to stop me from saying anything. I didn't want to lie to him outright until I was sure it wouldn't cause me any trouble.

"I might have met her once or twice," I said. "A lot of women come into the bar."

Coyne's long face twitched.

"I believe you two were much better acquainted than that. But no matter. I have no interest in your private life."

Wes finished up *California Dreamin'* and segued into *Road Song*, one of my recent favorites. I'd started to hear it as a personal call, to think about doing something new.

"And why would you be looking for this Ms. Crawford?"

Coyne nodded to himself, as if I'd admitted something, and sat down on a stool.

"Excellent. I much prefer that we do not dance around the truth." He folded his gnarled hands on top of the bar, as if offering a prayer. "Your lady friend is a very accomplished professional thief."

I kept my expression flat, something I'd gotten better and better at the longer I stood behind the bar and listened to the stories and confessions that alcohol freed from the mouths of my customers. Kathleen had told me her father financed large-scale criminal activities in New England. He'd been the man to see if you needed weapons, explosives, vehicles, or heavy equipment to take on a job. And before I'd found out she was a thief, she'd shown me flashes of an outlaw personality. It was probably why I'd been attracted to her.

"Really? News to me."

I grabbed a rag and started to polish the pristine beer taps. Coyne held up his hand to stop me, as if aware I was doing it because I was nervous. He inclined his head.

"Be that as it may. Your Ms. Crawford is in possession of

something Mr. Maldonado desires."

"Not something he owned?"

Coyne coughed drily. I poured him a glass of club soda and he nodded his thanks.

"Let us just say 'ownership' is a mutable concept in the case of this item."

"Possession not counting as nine-tenths of the law?"

"Perhaps not. But insofar as a right to possession exists? It accrues to Mr. Maldonado. Ms. Crawford's appropriation of the item was adverse."

He leaned forward to set the glass back on the bar, having barely sipped. The jacket of the black suit gapped open, not incidentally displaying a black nylon shoulder holster and harness, the butt of a pistol. He buttoned the jacket, having made whatever point he was making.

I concentrated on steady breathing. He was a much higher level of threat than I was used to dealing with, higher than, say, a drunken stockbroker heckling the band.

"And you are here because you think I know her? I'm not sure how I can help."

"Ms. Crawford is not to be found in any of her usual venues, Mr. Darrow. I—we—wondered if she'd perhaps been in contact."

Other than that video, telling me she was sorry she had to disappear, I hadn't heard from her. But even if I hadn't still been harboring feelings for her, I wasn't going to deliver her to Randolph Coyne and Icky Ricky's cousin.

"You've tried the house in Cambridge? I can give you the address."

I realized I'd confirmed that I knew her, but hoped being accommodating would help. Coyne shook his head.

"I believe I said we have looked in all her usual haunts. The place has been sold."

My stomach dropped. Even though I hadn't expected to hear from her, I'd hoped she might come back once she resolved her problems. The fact she'd sold the house confirmed she wasn't returning.

"Then I guess I can't help you."

Coyne's lips crept back from his teeth.

"As a writer once said, 'Wouldn't it be pretty to think so?' I'm afraid, Mr. Darrow, that Mr. Maldonado had designated you the responsible party. You represent the most likely path to Ms. Crawford and to the recovery of Mr. Maldonado's property."

I shook my head, but Coyne talked over what I was about to say.

"And I need not draw you a portrait of the consequences of failure, do I? You do have a great deal of your capital invested in the Esposito, don't you?"

He raised his hand and flicked a plastic lighter, the flame rising six inches into the air.

All I had invested was the last of my money, my pride, a shitload of work, and my continued sobriety. Hardly a thing.

I picked up the glass of club soda and sluiced its contents at the lighter, dousing the flame and soaking the fine Italian wool of Randolph Coyne's sleeve.

"No one in this neighborhood responds very well to threats, Randolph. You might tell Mr. Maldonado that."

He didn't flinch, or even show surprise. He dropped the lighter on the bar with a clatter.

"Now I think you'd better leave," I said.

He squeezed the water out of his sleeve onto the floor.

"It has been a pleasure meeting you, Mr. Darrow." His eyes looked past me, to somewhere remote and cold. "This time, at least."

2

Nina shivered underneath the unlined canvas barn coat that was all the Boston Pre-Release Center provided for the inmates who had to work outside. The sun was the color of weak lemonade in a washed-out blue sky, but at least the wind wasn't blowing in off the water any more. She'd almost frozen on the boat ride over to Rinker Island.

Standing at the edge of a hole maybe six feet deep, eight feet long, and fifteen feet wide, Nina smelled the cold minerality of the fresh-turned dirt. She nudged the huge pale mountain of a woman beside her, who was holding her own coat closed across her bulging belly with a clutch of fingers the size of carrots, her bleached thinning hair held back under a nonregulation do-rag.

"Alberta," Nina said. "At least it isn't us. Am I right?"

"This time, maybe." Somewhere between a very hard forty years old and a merely rough sixty, Alberta spit on the gravel path at their feet.

Nina volunteered for the paupers' grave detail because it was a way to get out of the facility and into the fresh air for a few hours. The stress of living with a couple hundred other women making the transition back to civilian life was more of a strain than she'd expected. For people who'd been incarcerated for any length of time, the prospect of pure freedom apparently fostered all kinds of uncertainty that a regimented schedule, a secure place to sleep, and regular meals kept suppressed. She smelled it in the disinfectant-bathed hallways of the center, the mildewed shower rooms. She only had a couple weeks left to go and time outside meant she couldn't get in trouble inside. And she hadn't been such a model prisoner that she'd gotten used to living without sunshine and fresh air.

Or sex. She hadn't been inside long enough to be tempted by anything but solo options, being a strictly hetero girl herself. And that made her think of Elder, their short intense collision—she wondered what he'd thought when she disappeared on him. She regretted not being able to explain it to him, but it was safer for him that way. If Donald ever found his way to Elder, at least Elder wouldn't be able to give her up.

"Here they come, honey chile." Alberta liked to sprinkle Southern phrases into her speech like chocolate jimmies on an ice cream cone, though Nina was pretty sure the woman had never been out of South Boston.

Alberta loved this detail because she'd been a lay minister out in the world once, with a Sunday following and a storefront church, until she cold-cocked a DSS investigator who asked her if she'd ever heard of birth control. Unfortunately, the bureaucrat had a thin skull and died from the impact with a wooden door frame.

Nina shoved all thoughts of the free and outside word to the back of her mind as the stake body truck rolled up the hill from the boat landing. She tried to set herself into a respectful frame of mind, knowing what they were here to do for people who had no one else to do it for them.

"Y'all mind your ways, little girl," Alberta said. "Or you'll find yourself getting planted out here one day."

"I know, Alberta. I know."

Not too fucking likely, once she was back out in the world. She had safe deposit boxes chocked with cash in four New England states. She might die young, but she wasn't going to end up in a pauper's grave.

But she also owed Alberta some respect. When Nina—neé Kathleen Crawford—decided to hide out from Donald Maldonado in jail, she'd thought a short sentence in South Middlesex would be a snap. But the minimum risk facility allowed all kinds of visitors to come and go, and the quantities of drugs, bad behavior, and general craziness made the outside world seem safer. Nina hadn't been as tough as she thought she was and Alberta had seen her as a project in salvation.

The truck groaned to a stop, the brakes squealing.

"Shoot," Alberta said. "I was hoping he'd stay down with the boat, send someone else up."

Trick Randisi—no one knew his real name—had an in-facility reputation as a leerer and a groper. He was short, with thick shoulders and a pigeon chest, and wore glasses with colorless frames. None of the women Nina talked to inside had heard of him trying for anything more than a quick grab, but all of them knew how often lines got crossed.

"He doesn't bother you, does he?" Nina said.

Alberta gave a phlegmy chuckle.

"He told me once I was too fat for him. Said he'd have to roll me in flour and look for the wet spot. I told him if he finds one, it's because I'm pissing on him."

Nina winced.

"What was the name of your church again?"

"Climb on." Trick grouchoed his eyebrows from the open window. "Got us some stiffies to take care of here."

The back of the truck bore a seat with a small crane and a winch, the hook dangling out over the cargo. It was a light load today, only seven plain pine coffins. Nina didn't know if that meant the economy was getting better or fewer people were dying on the streets. It had been a warmer winter than usual.

She walked around the truck so she didn't have to ride on the running board with her face near Trick's. He knew better than to fuck around with Alberta.

He reversed the truck and backed it to the lip of the common grave. A small Kubota tractor idled on the other side, its driver eying Nina's ass as she climbed down, mildly embarrassed that the lines of her state-provided granny panties showed. Two more weeks and she'd treat herself—La Perla, maybe.

Trick climbed the narrow ladder alongside the cab and sat down behind the crane's controls. Alberta pulled on white cotton gloves and handed a pair to Nina, the only concession to respect she'd been

9

able to wring from prison administration. The tractor driver climbed down into the pit to guide the coffins into a line that would fit the hole.

"Let us pray." Alberta placed both hands on the unstained wood of the nearest box. "Heavenly father..."

Nina kept her eyes open, focused on the black steel Phillips-head screws holding the coffins together. She'd never met a heavenly father and her childhood had soured her on organized religion from puberty onward.

Trick snorted, but held his peace.

"Amen," Alberta said.

"Amen." Nina always supported her friend.

Trick grunted and raised the crane arm, shook loose the heavy canvas straps with the clips on the end.

Lighter and more agile than Alberta, Nina clambered up and onto the back of the truck. The coffins were stacked with two by four spacers, leaving room to run the straps underneath, an unusual display of forethought. She secured the canvas bands and stepped to the other side of the truck, raised her hand to Trick.

The first four coffins settled into their final resting places fine. Trick was practiced enough with the crane to keep any undignified swinging of the pine boxes to a minimum. And Nina liked feeling useful, not that she intended to take this up on the outside. She did feel a bleak satisfaction in helping the poor disconnected people the coffins represented receive a respectful exit from earth.

Alberta, after pawing at one of the coffins trying to guide it, stood aside and closed here eyes, her lips moving.

"Looking good." The tractor driver down in the pit called up as he slotted the fourth coffin into place. He leaned back against the earth wall to wait for the next one and surveyed Nina, who felt a flash of intense horniness. It worried her that a redneck in a dirty white T-shirt, oily black ball cap, and grubby jeans could stir her up. Two more weeks.

As she ran the fraying straps under and around the fifth coffin, she noticed the shiny nail heads. Hadn't the other coffins all been fastened with screws? She almost said something to Trick, but he didn't like anything that interrupted the flow of the task. And once the box was down in the hole, it wouldn't matter. She cinched the buckle and signaled Trick.

The crane's motor whirred, then ground as if something inside had jammed. She smelled burning wire, then a jolt caused a nick in the farthest strap to rip. It didn't give way altogether, but the outward end of the coffin bounced hard against the steel tailgate and the square wooden end popped off and fell over the side onto the ground.

"Shit!" Trick yelled.

"Jesus Christ." Alberta crossed herself in the wrong direction, touching her shoulders right to left.

Nina's gorge rose, choking off a cry. The body slid out of the sleeve of the coffin like a missile, straight into the grave.

"Incoming!" The redneck down in the pit ducked to the right.

Nina sidestepped as the unweighted pine box swung back toward her head.

"Fuck!" Trick yelled, trying to gain control by yelling at the thing.

Nina suspected he was angry because he was going to have to climb his fat ass down out of the seat.

Alberta stepped up to the edge of the grave, hands up to her mouth. Nina seemed to be the only one who remembered how to move. She jumped down off the back of the truck, hearing the seat of her coverall split.

"Jesus," she muttered.

She stepped up beside Alberta, who was keening under her breath like an old-country Irish woman. The tractor driver slipped his hand into his pocket, not looking at Nina, even with her underwear showing.

"Dude doesn't exactly come off poor, does he?" she said to him.

The body sprawled across the tops of the four coffins was male, at least three hundred pounds, in a three-piece beige suit with a royal purple shirt and a black four-in-hand tie with airplanes flying across it. He wore two thick gold rings, a band on the traditional wedding finger and a coin-shaped one that winked off his left pinkie. His left hand showed a pale mark where he'd worn a big watch.

11

Nina gave the redneck a hard look as she scrambled down the short ladder into the grave.

"I saw that."

"Good luck getting anyone to believe you." He grinned, his breath the odor of old meat.

She bent to look at the corpse: well-fed, definitely, good teeth, and an expensive pair of photo-sensitive glasses only slightly askew. He had dull blue eyes and a soft man's tan, lotioned and smooth. The only obvious damage was the bullet hole centered above the bridge of his nose. Small caliber, and though she wasn't CSI, the skin around the wound was charred, speckled with burnt gunpowder. A close-in shot. And he was definitely starting to smell.

"Guess this guy got on the wrong ride," the redneck said.

Trick got down off the back to stand at the edge of the pit. He balanced his phone in one hand, as if weighing the chances this would all go away.

"Price of that suit would have paid for a whole lot of funerals," Nina said. "Not to mention the bling."

The redneck took the hint and climbed up out of the pit. Nina had a flash of wondering if he might use his tractor to bury her, make his problem go away.

"Trick, for god's sake." She cracked the whip in her voice. "Call your boss. This man should not be here."

He sighed—she could hear him down here—and started poking at his phone buttons. Alberta conquered her shock enough to try and do something useful.

"Honey, you come up out of there right now, before any of that old gangster's death essence crawls over to you. Come here now."

Nina stepped to the ladder, took one last look down at the well-dressed corpse. Not really a gangster. For one thing, he wore cheap shoes—Rockports—and his thick black hair looked like it had been cut at home. A pinkie ring didn't make you a mobster.

"Coming, Mommy."

But Nina was glad there were witnesses here. Something like this could have a very bad effect on her smooth release and she didn't want to be tied to this any more than she already was.

As she stepped out onto the rim of the grave, the tractor driver eyed her from the seat of his machine, smoking a cigarette. She was tempted to flip him off, but refrained.

"I don't care," Trick whined into his phone. "Give me your boss, then. Tell him the grave detail just found a body."

3

I couldn't decide whether to mention Randolph Coyne's visit to Burton. My good friend on the Boston police force had almost gotten fired in the fallout from the Antoine Bousquet case, and only being flex-cuffed to a baseball field dugout and poked at with a knife had convinced his bosses he'd been a victim, that he hadn't gone rogue. It looked for a little while as if I might have to take him on as a bartender—a fox in the hen house prospect—but the various boards and committees that regulate police behavior laboriously passed him through, with only a short suspension.

No one in the BPD would say such a complimentary thing to his face, but we both knew he owned the highest homicide clearance rate in the city, and that the Suffolk County District Attorney could always count on getting a case from Burton that was built like a rock wall. All the same, watching the bullshit he went through made me very glad I only had one boss. And if the boss acted like an asshole, I had nobody to blame but myself.

"Still haven't heard anything from your sweetheart Kathleen?" Burton said.

He tapped the bottom of his Heineken bottle on the bar top in rhythm with the drummer backing Eubie Blake. Both his disposition and his finances had improved after he cut loose his ex-wife, and his big celebration was to drink better beer.

"Keep it up, I'll start serving plastic bottles." I didn't understand why he kept poking at the semi-open wound that Kathleen Crawford had left. I'd almost forgotten about her until Randolph showed up.

"I told you there was something off about her."

14

Like a couple other cops I knew, Burton claimed a certain clairvoyance about people that he wouldn't indulge in others. Of course, he'd run the background check on her that revealed she was a fairly high-end thief.

I held up my hands. It was only eleven in the morning, another gray, bleak, raw winter Wednesday. It had snowed three or four inches overnight, and as I walked down to the Esposito from my apartment, I'd seen the lawn chairs and traffic cones marking the parking spaces people had shoveled out. I wondered if there'd be fistfights over those parking spaces—which happened in some parts of the city—though this snow would probably be gone by noon.

"It's done," I said. "It's over. And I'm done talking about it."

He rapped the bottle harder on the bar, his signature impolite request for a refill. I swapped in a fresh glass and let him pour his own. He'd never been much of a tipper.

"Whatever," he said. "I'm just saying your skills in the romantic side of life might need a little brushing up."

"Keep it up and you'll start paying for your beer."

Ever since he and Marina had reconciled, he'd been acting like he was smarter than Dr. Phil.

He grunted and spread the *Globe* wide on the bar. I moved down to the far end to finish restocking the beer cooler. The last few months had given us plenty to be touchy about, but things were slowly rebounding. Unless he was doing his heavy drinking elsewhere, he wasn't as deep into the booze as he had been. And I was still sober, mostly trying to figure out what to do with the money my father had left me.

"Hey!" He traced a drawing in the newspaper, a shaded diagram of streets and blocks. "Isn't this you?"

I looked at it upside down. The picture was a map of the neighborhood including Mercy Street, the Esposito's location.

"What the fuck?"

"'The four-block section is under consideration for the velodrome.' Fuck is a velodrome?" Burton said.

I turned the newspaper around and oriented myself, tapped a spot two blocks in from the edge of the shaded part of the map.

"This is the bar. What's the map all about? Why would someone want a bicycle racing venue down here?"

Burton chugged a couple inches of beer.

"Apparently you haven't been paying much attention to the newspapers?"

"Funny papers mostly, a couple of the sports columnists to remind me what dicks people can be. Baseball."

Other than that, I figured I'd hear about anything else big. Witness whatever this was.

"You don't have a clue the city's putting together a bid to host the Olympics?"

"The *real* Olympics? The every-four-years ones?"

Eubie's showboating was starting to annoy me. I reset the playlist to a section that included Brad Mehldau, Charlie Haden, and Brubeck.

"You ought to try out satellite radio," Burton said.

"The station with the twenty tune playlist?" I shook my head. "Like listening to wallpaper. Are they serious? Where the hell would you put the Olympics in Boston?"

Burton tapped the newspaper.

"In this neighborhood, for one. The whole thing is a fucking travesty." Flush rose into his pale cheeks and higher, almost to his hairline. "There's about a dozen boosters who want it bad. It means new construction, hotels, venues, an Olympic village. Of course, these assholes all live out in Concord and Lexington. Their neighborhoods aren't the ones that are getting fucked up."

"That's the stupidest thing I've ever heard. Can't you see thousands of tourists in rental cars on the Southeast Expressway, trying to find the ping pong venue?"

"Get this—the Olympic committee requires the host city to designate traffic lanes for visitors and athletes only."

"Jesus. Ping pong matches at Mechanics' Hall in Worcester."

"Tie-ups in the Ted." Burton raised his glass. "Still. Could happen. Mayor's behind it. All the heavy hitters."

"Mumbles would have never inflicted this on us." Tom Menino, Boston's much-loved previous mayor.

"You better keep track of it, though. You know there's nothing the

BRA likes better than a little eminent domain. And this part of town doesn't exactly represent the ideal of New Boston. You remember how urban renewal went?"

I wasn't that old, but my father's bank had funded a good deal of the construction. In the fifties, the old Boston Redevelopment Authority decided to raze the city's West End—a set of ethnic neighborhoods—under the guise of spiffing up the city. The newspapers conspired with the politicians and bureaucrats to designate large swaths of the West End as slums, true only if you were a Brahmin or Irish-come-lately and believed that poor Poles and Italians were dirty and disease-ridden. Developers and the BRA bought buildings condemned by the city, paying fire sale prices to landlords and small business people. What replaced the vibrant neighborhoods was a clutch of high rise office buildings, pay parking lots, and strip malls. Not too long ago, the BRA had actually apologized publicly for the project, though far too late for the thousands forced to relocate.

"I don't know," I said. "Lots of yuppies, puppies, and yummy mummies living down here now. They must have some pull. And they're all mostly white, which still counts in Boston, if not out loud."

"Shit," Burton said. "You starting to sound like you're running for President. Money talks, and it talks loudest to a politician. You know the mayor's never going to have a better job than the one he's got."

Randolph Coyne's visit—could that be connected to the Olympic development somehow? I shook my head. That idea was too paranoid even for me. He was focused exclusively on Kathleen, and she and I had been keeping company long before the idea of an Olympic bid came up.

"You know that Icky Ricky had a cousin?" I said.

Burton looked up from an intense focus on the stock market pages, which I knew he was faking. He didn't own a share of anything, and the only interest he had in the world was solving murders.

"Now there's a name I hoped I'd never hear again. Ricky Maldonado. Didn't he relocate his bulbous self to South Beach?"

17

"Theoretically. I had a visit yesterday."

Burton looked up from the paper, only half-interested.

"From this cousin?"

"Factotum-type character. Very suave, nice suit, smooth line in attempted intimidation."

Burton's countenance shifted and I saw how he got people—his suspects, even—to talk to him, by an intense kind of listening. No way to tell if the interest was sincere, of course.

"You can't still owe Ricky anything. Protection racket?"

"That's what I thought at first."

I wasn't thinking clearly when I brought it up. I wanted to talk to him about Randolph Coyne, but that would open him up to shoot some more arrows about Kathleen, whom he'd never liked or trusted.

"What?" he said as I paused.

"Nothing."

"Horseshit. If you're not going to buy me another beer, at least tell me a story."

"He was looking for Kathleen."

I uncapped another bottle and started pouring it into his glass. He grabbed the bottle.

"The old gal pal. Really?"

I recognized his flat tone, part I-told-you-so, part concern.

"Not so old," I said. "He claimed she had something of his boss's that the boss wanted back."

"She stole something?" Burton worked his eyebrows. "From Ricky's cousin? I'm shocked."

"Cousin's name is Donald."

"You know I never say I told you so, Elder, but…"

He inspected the head on his beer.

"I know you're not surprised," I said.

"And you still haven't heard from her?"

I shook my head. What I didn't tell him was that Randolph's visit made me worry about Kathleen more than I had before. I could accept that she'd left Boston to avoid facing me or turning me down, but now it looked as if she'd been running from an actual threat. Oddly, that gave me a jolt of hope.

"Couple months now," I said.

"Three and a half. And counting. Look, if she were dead, I would have heard about it."

That was Burton's idea of comforting me.

"That doesn't make me feel any better."

"She's probably hiding out somewhere."

She was probably tougher than I thought, certainly tougher than I was. I wondered if she might come back and we could pick up the relationship, see if it was worth keeping on.

"I hope so, for her sake. You run her through the system recently?"

I would never have asked him to do it, but he did look out for me.

"And you didn't find anything," I said. "Because you would have been happy to share."

"Come on, Elder. The woman's a fucking ghost." He took a deep breath. "She has no history before 1998. And you know damn well she's older than twenty-nine."

Kathleen and I hadn't had time to trade much personal history, though mine was more public than hers: family in Boston since the Revolution, me a prep school graduate and Harvard dropout, recovering drunk, and struggling bar owner. Struggling less now that I'd hauled the Esposito into the black. And had a few extra dollars in the bank. Several million, to be exact.

"No, we never traded stories."

Burton drank the last inch in his glass. The music shifted into something upbeat, and I started thinking about getting ready for the lunch rush.

"I'd kiss her right off, I were you," Burton said. "A gangster taking interest in a woman never bodes too well."

I hadn't said anything about Randolph Coyne's insistence that I find her for Maldonado. There wasn't much Burton could do to help me there.

"Out of my hands. So. The Olympics? Seriously?"

Burton rolled his eyes, letting me know that he'd seen me changing the subject. As he pulled the newspaper back in front of him, his phone buzzed.

"Shit," he said. "I'm supposed to be off today."

Hence the eleven a.m. beers. But I was glad to have his attention diverted, the tension over Kathleen dissipated. What was not a good thing was that a phone call to Burton meant someone in the city had died, and not of natural causes.

He backed off the stool and headed for the stairs, yammering into the phone. Halfway up, he raised his hand and waved goodbye.

I refolded the newspaper and slipped it under the bar, and walked back into the kitchen to be sure Marina had everything ready for lunch.

4

D an Burton was a city boy all the way, Charlestown born and
brought up, and he did not believe that city boys belonged on
boats. As the Harbor Patrol's Boston Whaler bounced across the
whitecaps of the harbor, he held his head down between his knees,
choking down a nausea that threatened to erupt with every hard-
bottomed thump on the water.

"No need to hurry," he yelled at the pilot, a bright-eyed clean-
shaven young Harbor Patrol cop in full blue uniform and an orange
life vest, grinning like a Labrador retriever in full romp. "The dude's
still going to be dead when I get there."

"What?" Captain Whatever cupped his hand around one ear, his
teeth white in the sun.

If Burton wasn't so close to losing his breakfast, he would have
cold-cocked the happy little shit. As it was, it was all he could do
to keep his head up as they approached the island. The engine noise
deepened as the boat slowed.

The ride smoothed out, and with a loud clunk as the motor dropped
out of gear, forward motion stalled and the boat drifted sideways
in toward the dock. The harbor cop leaped out and Burton had the
panicky feeling the son of a bitch was abandoning him, letting him
float back out to sea, until he noticed the officer also held onto a
length of rope, which he wound around an upright pole and knotted.

"Toss out those bumpers, will you?"

Burton scowled. He hated not knowing what he was doing.

"Those big white puffy things?" The harbor cop's tone dripped
with the sarcasm of an expert for the rookie. "They keep my pretty

21

boat from getting all scratched up."

He considered pulling the kid down into the water when he reached a hand down to help. Burton ignored the offer and vaulted up onto the dock, pulling a groin muscle when the boat shifted underneath him. He started up the steep ramp covered in old roof shingles.

"Hey!"

The harbor cop was looking at his watch, one of those underwater five dial shockproof jobs that did everything but make soup.

"How long you going to be? I'm supposed to be off at three."

Burton grinned, back on his own field of play.

"As long as it takes, Bucko. Stand tight."

His mood improved as he limped off the top of the ramp toward a rock staircase that led up the hill. He'd known about Rinker Island in a back-of-the-mind way—occasionally a homicide victim without family or money had to be interred out here. It was the first time he'd been here, though.

At the top of the stairs, he paused to catch his breath. The wind, stronger over the naked plain than out on the water, slapped at his face. At least it blew away the last of his nausea.

He buttoned his sport coat and started overland on a narrow gravel path between sections of the cemetery, toward a small truck with a crane arm jutting off the top and four people, two of them in orange inmate jumpsuits and brown canvas coats. Each headstone he passed was inscribed with a number, no names or dates, and he found that unbearably sad.

A fireplug in a half-assed guard's uniform stood with his back to the two prisoners. The guy lounging in the seat of the small tractor next to the truck looked like a once or future meth head: sunken cheeks, gray teeth, and the duck-away don't-hit-me look down pat. Burton was about to shout to get the guard's attention when he got close enough to recognize the smaller of the two female inmates.

"Well, hello there," he said.

Kathleen Crawford—short-haired and blonde as a beach girl now, looking tired and used as female inmates tended to—gave him a pleading look, shook her head. It didn't take a Phi Beta Kappa to figure out what she wanted. When he'd done the latest background check for Elder, he would have found her if she was here under her own name. She clearly did not want him to out her.

He'd give her what she wanted, but not as a favor to her. Any time he knew something no one else did, he held onto it until he figured out what it meant. In this case, the homicide might be easy to solve. A dead body in the presence of a known criminal. Not a coincidence.

"Hey!" he said.

The guard was tapping at his phone with both thumbs and when he didn't turn around, Burton laid a hand on his shoulder. The guard twisted, an ugly sneer pulling at his mouth, and the hand without the phone bunched up and headed for Burton's face.

Burton stepped back out of the way and let the fist pass by, then stepped in and rammed the heel of his hand against the idiot's nose. No crunch, but a definite creak of the cartilage. And blood, lots of blood, all of a sudden.

The phone clattered to the ground, the screen starring on a rock. The guard cupped his hands around his face as if he could hold in all his precious bodily fluids that way.

"You broke my nodze," he snuffled.

"Nah. Just tweaked it a little," Burton said, showing him his credentials. "Why would you want to take a swing at a cop, anyway?"

The guard's eyes went exophthalmic.

"Homicide? I thought you were the mechanic they were sending up." He tipped his head toward the truck and winced. "To fix the crane?"

Burton looked down at his sport jacket, charcoal pants, white shirt, and tie. Not as nice as the suits he wore off duty, and not Joseph Abboud, but still. A mechanic?

Someone snorted behind him. He looked over his shoulder to see Kathleen fighting a smile. He glared at her.

"Where's the body?"

The guard ignored Burton, sat down on the truck's running board with a handkerchief to his nose. The other prisoner, a mountain of a woman holding what he thought was a fistful of rosaries until he saw the feathers and bones, stepped forward.

"His earthly essence is down in the pit," she said in a sing-song voice that made him think of grade school nuns and steel rulers. "Me and Nina here were just saying a prayer over him. I'm Sister Alberta."

He assumed Sister Alberta was naming herself metaphorically, until she made the sign of the cross over the grave. Kathleen stood in the other woman's shadow as if trying to stay unnoticed. Nina?

The hole was wide and long. He'd never thought about whether they planted multiple coffins in one hole—they hadn't always, if the headstones were any proof—but he supposed it could be a money-saving measure.

"Why women-inmates?" he said to the guard, who'd recovered enough to come and stand with them to look down into the hole.

"These were all supposed to be female corpses." The man spoke with a nasal whistle he hadn't woken up with this morning. "Gives a little respect."

And a male guard/truck driver and a male heavy equipment operator. Typical bureaucratic response: small and symbolic.

"You." He pointed at the guard.

"My name is Trick."

"Of course it is."

Burton cycled through a mental list of nicknames for him—dirty, cheap, hat—then decided not to provoke things any more. Dark blood was crusting up the rims of Trick's nostrils and he was going to have a headache. Lucky he wasn't a hemophiliac.

"Yes, you, Trickster. I want you to climb down there and hold the ladder steady for me."

"I don't care for enclosed spaces," Trick said.

"None of us do." Burton pushed him lightly toward the hole. "Go."

He turned to Kathleen, standing in Sister Alberta's considerable shade.

"What do you know about this, Nina? Did you kill this guy?"

He doubted it, but he wanted her to understand up front that knowing who he was didn't buy her anything.

For the bulky type, Trick was pretty agile. He scrambled down into the hole, braced one of his boots against the bottom rung of the ladder.

"All set."

The tractor guy shut down his engine, and the wind seemed louder in the silence. Kathleen and Alberta moved into the lee of the truck.

Tell the truth, Burton didn't like holes, either. He'd worked one summer in a seventy foot deep pit in South Station, laying conduit for underground utilities, and that was as close to hell as he hoped he'd ever get. He backed down the ladder, careful of his slick leather soles, and maneuvered around Trick.

The corpse was laid out flat on top of the coffins they'd already set into the hole, as out of place as a beached whale in a corn field. The man had taken a very wrong turn to end up in the women's section of a paupers' graveyard, and Burton made a mental note to find out how hard it was to get the schedule for the boat runs out to Rinker. And the coffin truck's route, for that matter.

He stepped in close to the body, hands in his pockets, though the man clearly hadn't been killed here. The crime scene techs weren't going to find shit.

Beyond the fact that he was male, the dead man was too prosperous-looking to be here. His tan suit was a decent grade of wool and relatively new, no stains or signs of wear. The purple shirt—not something Burton would wear—was silk, though. And he was obviously well-fed. Burton guessed he'd go two-sixty, which meant they better hurry up and fix that crane if they were going to get him out of the hole. A pale mark on his left wrist showed where he'd normally worn a watch. He'd have to get a matron to search Kathleen for it—she was the only thief on the scene that he knew about.

"Anyone been down in the hole with him?"

Trick put his hands up.

"Not me. Like I said, too close to being underground." He frowned as he thought, as if this were a math final. "Nina. And the tractor guy."

"Hmm."

Burton returned to his inspection of the body: heavy-set male Italian or Greek, curly black hair, maybe dyed, and those big-lensed glasses that changed with the amount of light. They paled as Burton's shadow cast over the body, revealing staring blue eyes. The shirt and tie would have been fashion-forward at a goombah's picnic, that and

25

the hole in the middle of his forehead.

"Anyone actually touch the body?"

Trick flinched infinitesimally, signifying a lie coming.

"I didn't get down in here before you arrived."

Burton caught the evasion, wondered what else Nina/Kathleen had stolen while she was down here.

It was against all crime scene protocol for him to mess with the body before the forensics kids got here, but he needed to know who lay dead in front of him before he could begin to find out who'd killed him or why. He folded back the lapel of the man's suit coat with two fingers and saw a small leather folder, the size of a passport wallet, sticking up out of the inside pocket.

"Hey," Trick said. "Are you supposed to be doing that?"

Burton, stretching on a nitrile glove, raised an eyebrow.

"Doing what?"

Trick headed for the ladder and climbed out.

"I guess you don't need me down here."

Burton opened the wallet, which held ten or twelve credit cards, including a black American Express and a driver's license for one Constantine Boustaloudis, DOB 8/25/1967. And lying like a bastard about his weight—he hadn't seen two-ten since junior high.

The sound of an engine starting up on the ground level startled him. He thought at first the tractor driver had restarted the rig, then realized he was hearing a gasoline engine, not a diesel.

Burton compounded his breach of protocol by pocketing the wallet and climbing up the ladder.

"Fuck!" Trick yelled as he ran back toward the truck, zipping up his pants.

The truck engaged gear and rumbled away.

"They take off on you?" Burton stepped up beside an unhappy Trick, sounding more sympathetic than he felt. The inmates weren't his problem, though Kathleen's taking off confirmed his suspicion she had something more to do with this than he knew.

"Fucking bitches," Trick said.

Burton noticed he wasn't making any move to chase the truck. The tractor driver was smiling.

"We're on an island, Trick. They won't get far."

Though he wasn't too sure the harbor cop down on the dock would be smart enough to stop them. He looked across the field of headstones at the truck chugging along in slow motion, as if the driver couldn't find her way out of first gear. Burton sighed.

"We go across country," he said. "We can probably cut them off."

And he took off at a run, his soles slipping on the gravel until he found a stiff-legged gait he could maintain. Trick turned out to be something of an athlete, getting out in front right away and leading Burton toward the rock stairway at a ground-eating lope.

The truck accelerated over the crest of the hill a good half minute before they reached the top of the steps. Burton bent over, hands on his knees, his chest heaving.

When he looked down, he saw the truck at the dock, both doors wide open. Trick was halfway down the stairs. As Burton jogged to follow him, the Boston Whaler roared away from the dock, trailing a long rope, and sped off toward the city skyline. Two orange figures stood behind the windshield, facing forward.

Burton shook his head. When he caught up to Trick on the dock, he was cutting the plastic ties off the harbor cop's wrists.

"Fuck me," the cop said.

"Exactly."

Burton held back his smile, but only because he needed the harbor guy to get him off this island. Kathleen was involved in this somehow and that made him feel better. That ought to cure Elder of his desire for some happy reunion.

5

I wasn't convinced an espresso machine was a great idea, but my lunch business with people who worked in the neighborhood was picking up. A couple of my middle-aged regulars, refugees from Seattle, convinced me a nice cappuccino would enhance the Esposito experience for people who couldn't or wouldn't drink at lunch. I wasn't a coffee hound myself, though Burton had picked up the habit—mostly I didn't like the connotation that it was an alternate drug of choice for alcoholics trying to stay sober. So I wouldn't have thought of it on my own. But today was the day.

The chromed-metal hulk crouched in an alcove I'd had carpentered and plumbed especially. The name Rancilio marched across the matte steel front and I heard the loud ticks as the brass boiler heated up, expanding.

"You use any kind of this machine before?" The voice at my elbow was dry and cracked.

"I've seen them in the shops. Fairly simple, yes?"

It didn't look that complicated—three buttons, a set of switches, a wand for steam—but there were apparently subtleties I didn't know about.

The machine's distributor in the North End had sent along a technician, a tiny middle-aged lady in a pristine white jump suit, like a mechanic at a high-end Mercedes garage, to train me on the new monster. Mrs. Mal'occhio's gray hair was braided so tightly she had stretch marks on her forehead, the braids coiled and pinned on top of her head.

She fiddled with a black-handled chunk of iron she called the gruppa, packing it with ground coffee and tamping it down like a pipe full of tobacco she intended to smoke.

"It's an art," she said. "Size of the grind, weight of the tamp, and length of the pull must all be in balance."

I'd already judged her as a fanatic, and though I always liked people who got absorbed in their work, I was worried I might have to hire a kid with a nose ring and sleeve tattoos to run the beast. It was more work for a shot of coffee than I'd thought it was going to be and the profit margin on draft beer was a hell of a lot higher.

"*Scusi*," she rasped. "You are paying me attention?"

She slammed the gruppa up into the machine and twisted it home. I found myself focusing on a dime-sized wen on the point of her chin with three long black hairs sprouting out of it. The Chinese called them 'lucky hairs,' but all I wanted to do was pluck them out.

"Sure," I said. "Grind, tamp, pull."

I stepped down the bar for a moment to pour another Drambuie for Donnie Bartlett, one of my last reliable pre-lunch drinkers. He rolled his eyes at me as Mrs. Mal'occhio hissed.

"*Rampicoglioni*," she said under her breath.

"Sorry," I said. "I am trying to run a business here, too. What else?"

She slapped the button to start the pump that expressed the water through the coffee grounds. It was conveniently labeled with a drawing of white drops falling into a tiny white cup.

"When everything is correct." She turned the small porcelain cup under the twin yellow-brown streams. "The flow should be the radius of a mouse's tail."

"I think you mean diameter."

The flow quit. She handed me the cup. I supposed if I didn't taste it, she would curse me some more.

"Very good," I said. "What was that word you used?"

She flushed a strange sallow shade.

"I was cursing the machine."

"*Rampico* ... something."

"*Rampicoglioni*. It means something that hurts a man's parts."

"Ah. Ball breaker." I set the cup down and shook her small bony hand. "Very good espresso. Thank you for the lesson."

Steps rang on the steel stairs, up by the street door. When I looked up and saw who it was, my chest locked up.

"I have eleven more items on the checklist," Mrs. Mal'occhio said. "We don't want you dissatisfied."

"That's all I have time for today. I have your number if I run into any problems."

She rolled up her tools in a canvas wrap and tied it shut with a fierce jerk, then stalked out through the kitchen to the back door and the alley where she'd parked her van.

"*Rampicoglioni*," I said to myself as I brushed past the end of the bar to get to the stairs. I'd have to try that one on Burton. "And where the hell have you been?"

I might have tried hugging her if I hadn't still been so angry about how she'd disappeared in the first place. Kathleen had lost some weight she couldn't afford, and her hands and face looked dry and weathered. She wore a pair of khaki pants too big in the seat and rolled up at the ankles and a Black Watch tartan flannel shirt. Her hair had been cropped short and dyed blonde, and not in a salon. My stomach flipflopped. I didn't care how she looked.

"Nice to see you again, too, Elder." She looked up and down the bar, then at the door to the kitchen. "Burton isn't around, is he?"

"No. Why?"

Then I remembered Randolph Coyne and wondered whether he'd followed her here.

She took hold of my forearms and leaned in to kiss me on the cheek. She smelled of Ivory Soap and fruity shampoo, not her usual elegant scents.

"Can we go out back? I need a favor."

Donnie was staring at us.

"Of course."

I led her out through the kitchen, where Marina was chopping vegetables.

"Call me if anyone comes in, OK?" I said to her.

She gave me that darkly unhappy Mediterranean stare and slammed her knife down on the cutting board. Inheriting the money from my father hadn't made her any easier to work with—she was a fine cook, but she needed to hear it every day.

"Hi, Marina," Katherine said, and got a grunt in return.

I led her back to what passed for my office, a drywalled cubicle with a small desk, rolling chair, a couple of clipboards hanging from nails in the wall board. Her legs trembled.

"Sit down. You look like you're about to fall over."

Under the rough exterior, she was unhealthily pale, as if she hadn't been eating or sleeping well. She seemed to deflate into the chair, as if being upright had exhausted her.

"Have you eaten?"

She gestured with her hand as if to say that wasn't important.

"I need a favor."

I'd always considered myself an easygoing person, but she'd disappeared for the better part of six months and then showed up without an explanation. And the first thing she does is ask me for a favor?

"Just like that," I said.

She felt my unhappiness and turned her face up to try a smile on me.

"I'm sorry, Elder. I can't explain it right now, but I will. I have to get off the street."

She looked nervous and unhappy, but I doubted it was on my behalf.

"This has something to do with your being a thief, I suppose?"

Randolph's menace hadn't been unfounded.

"I just need to get cleaned up, eat, get a little rest," she said. "Do I still have any clothes left at your place?"

When it looked as if we might be more than a one-nighter, I'd made space in one of my closets, but she'd only ever brought a couple outfits over. I'd stored them, finally, rather than keep looking at them.

"In a plastic box in the hall closet."

"Look, I'm sorry to do this to you. Really. I'll explain everything when I can."

I still felt a pull to her, but I was reasonably sure I didn't want to know any details or even be involved again, beyond granting this one favor. Though I was curious about where she'd been all this time. I picked up my key ring.

"Wait. You know where the spare key is, don't you?"

I realized I didn't want to hand over my key ring, with the bar and car keys on it, too. I'd come home one night to find her sitting in my living room with a pizza and a six-pack, before she knew me well enough to find out I didn't drink.

"No," she said.

She was trying to be polite. I didn't believe her.

"Fake rock in the front flower bed, by the Rose o' Sharon. You might have to dig around in the slush a little."

She stood up, put her hands on my shoulders as if to calm herself, and kissed me on the lips. Lingering.

"Thank you, thank you."

"So you'll come back here after you clean up and let me feed you? Bring me up to date?"

"Of course."

But her look slipped to one side—fifty/fifty proposition at best. I had to wonder why my chest still ached when I hadn't seen her in so long.

"Can I go out the back door?"

"I'd rather you did."

That snapped her head up and she gave me a hurt look. But I had the distinct sense I was talking myself into an interpretation of her that wasn't true.

"Great."

She pecked my cheek and started for the alley door, stopped.

"I wasn't running away from you, Elder. It's just, well, complicated."

And with that apology, true or not, I was back in her corner.

"Don't disappear on me again," I said, as the brass handle of the fire door clanged open.

"No worries." She breezed out into the afternoon, letting the door slam behind her and leaving me with nothing but worries.

6

Burton had learned enough about wrangling the Internet that he no longer had to pass off his research questions to one of the administrative types who seemed to be reproducing themselves at D-4 these days. He actually found it restful to click through the electronic ether looking for background on the corpse who'd been sent out to an anonymous grave on Rinker Island.

He'd called into the mainland for a patrol unit to pick up the escapees at the main dock of the South Boston Yacht Club, their likeliest landfall, and left it to Dispatch to organize the arrest. He'd stayed on the island until the scene-of-crime people and everyone else who attended a homicide showed up, then took a much larger boat back to civilization. He wouldn't find the answer to the killing of Constantine Boustaloudis on Rinker Island.

The whole cock-up after Kathleen and her oversized sidekick escaped in the Harbor Patrol's boat was being downplayed. Trick, who'd receive most of the shit rained down from above, wasn't a cop and the harbor guy wasn't either, really. Both of them had been embarrassed enough that Burton didn't think he'd hear from them again.

Though he had an actual cubicle of his own at D-4, he preferred to do his Google searching in someone else's space, where his electronic droppings wouldn't automatically trace back to him. He always practiced safe surfing, but especially in the politicized and pressurized environment of the department. He did not believe the bean counters' assurances that they only monitored Internet usage for obvious offenses like watching porn or cat videos. Discretion was a prudent investment in self-protection.

Constantine Boustaloudis. The name rang a tiny bell, but Burton was the first to admit that very little about what went on in the city that didn't have to do with murder stuck in his brain. He couldn't deny something that had fucked up his marriage and skidded him off the flat edge of Planet Drunk more than once.

Ah. He clicked through. Boustaloudis had been the nominal leader of a grassroots organization trying to convince the good people of the Commonwealth of Massachusetts not to support a bid to bring the Olympic Games to Boston. It was a shoestring operation without much traction to speak of, but Burton knew the media in Boston well enough to guess it would slobber all over a controversy that pitted the common folk against the moneyed and powerful.

Not that that constituted a reason to murder Boustaloudis. And if it had, why try to dump his body in an unmarked grave? Anyone who wanted to make a point about resisting the idea of the Olympics would have wanted his fate to be public.

Burton paged through the autobiographical detail, taking notes. Boustaloudis owned a drug store on the corner of Hyde Park Avenue near Cleary Square, and that part of the city was as ethnically tense as Charlestown and Southie, if in a quieter way. In the sixties and seventies, Hyde Park High School was a hot spot for bussing-related violence. As a rookie, Burton had heard the stories of the raw feral anger of the neighborhood's white residents, the ill-hidden fear of black kids shoved around the city in the name of a dubious equality. The emotions weren't all that different now, a testament to the success of the political solution.

"Whaddaya got on this latest thing?"

A puff of garlic-clam pizza and old cigarette smoke announced Dennis Martines, Burton's nominal superior. A politician-cop—ten years younger than Burton, he was two ranks higher—Martines had, against Burton's expectations, turned out to be a decent boss. He had done serious police work in his career, undercover narcotics, and while Burton didn't love working for anyone, they managed to avoid each other's hot buttons. It was unusual for him to check in on an investigation that had barely started.

"Someone trying to push my good friend Dennis around?" Burton said.

"None of your lip. What's happening?"

"I assume we're discussing our little Greek friend?"

Martines sniffed and his fingers twitched. Burton read the signs. The lieutenant was on his way out for a smoke and didn't want too detailed a story.

"Not so little, I understand."

"So far, the one thing I'm sure of is, he's dead," Burton said. "And probably at someone else's hand."

"'Probably?' The best you can tell me is it wasn't a suicide?"

"ME will confirm. But the angle's wrong. You can't shoot yourself that straight-on unless you have help."

Martines shrugged, slipped his hand into the shirt pocket where the blocky shape of the Marlboro box rested.

"Well, that's too bad."

"What? We're rooting for people to off themselves now?"

"This thing has all the makings of a serious ratfuck. You knew he was head of this anti-Olympics thing, right?"

"You think he got popped on account of that? It's pretty small-time."

"Stranger things," Martines said. "And there's a shitload of money on the line here. And a large number of swinging dicks."

Burton mostly tried to ignore the politics, but it looked like he was going to have to clue himself in. The Olympic bid was clearly in his lane now.

"Who knows the most about it? In house, I mean. Are the F & F boys working on any of it?"

Finance and Fraud were the whitest of the white-collar cops, focused solely on crimes of greed, that universal human desire for more.

"Try Farnsworth in E-6. Supposedly he went to Amos Tuck."

The business school at Dartmouth. Burton didn't show Martines what he thought of that—the lieutenant had graduate degrees, too.

Martines's desire for nicotine overrode his managerial impulses at exactly the moment Burton ran out of things to tell him. The lieutenant loped in the direction of the back stairway and down toward the ground floor. Burton jotted Farnsworth's name on a sticky note, then turned back to the research on Boustaloudis, printing out some of the pages to read later.

He stacked the papers and rooted in the drawer for a binder clip. A shadow darkened the beige wall of the cubicle and he swiveled in his chair, fast.

"Do not fucking sneak up on me like that."

The harbor cop, last seen morose on the dock at Rinker Island, filled the opening to the cubicle. Outdoors, he hadn't seemed so big. He rubbed at his wrists, as if seeing Burton had reminded him of the plastic cuffs he'd been bound with.

"Sir."

Burton's heart rate eased.

"I'm not your boss, Scout. What's the problem?"

He was not in the kid's chain of command, so if he had to guess, the Harbor Patrol was looking for a way to weasel in on his case. The sea cops were always defensive about the petty kinds of crime they mostly worked. But this kid looked seriously upset.

"They were unable to intercept the fugitives, sir. We stayed at the yacht basin until 1700 hours and no one showed."

Five PM exactly, Burton noted.

"Well, you gave it a shot, right? Thanks for the report."

Mr. Sea Hunt wasn't done.

"What else?" Burton said, clipping his stack of papers.

"We recovered the boat farther up the beach."

"M Street?"

"Right outside the Curley Center. They stole clothes from the lockers and changed there."

Orange jumpsuits being a little hard for people out in the world to miss. And then, the two women had disappeared into the wilds of South Boston, where no one loved cops. He wondered if Kathleen Crawford had friends there. Or maybe her traveling companion, Woman Mountain Dean.

"Best we could do." He didn't want to torch the kid, but he wasn't going away.

"Sir?"

"Not me. Burton is fine. Or Dan."

"I'd like to stay involved."

The sea dog had had his pride manhandled. Woman-handled, actually. Of course he wanted payback.

"Sure. Give me your card."

"Actively, Detective Burton."

Burton shook his head.

"You must not have been here long. The police divisions in this city are like the Sunnis and the Shiites. Best I can do is let you know if something breaks."

"I've been working that island run for a while. They bring the coffins across on a barge, bigger than my boat. But I run the prisoners back and forth."

Burton sat back in his chair, mildly interested.

"And?"

"I think I know how they got the dead guy onto the island."

7

Marina would never say anything directly to me about Kathleen, but when I walked back past her toward the bar, she shot me a sideways look more eloquent than a curse.

"What?"

"Nothing, Elder."

The soup she was building smelled rich, tomatoes and garlic and herbs.

"Marina?"

"None of my business," she said.

The relationship between us had shifted subtly when she found out about the money from my father. She was a little more inclined to push back on decisions, at least ones having to do with the kitchen and food. It didn't buy her a vote on my personal life, though.

"You're absolutely right."

The Esposito was never too busy on Thursday nights, one of the unintended side effects of upgrading my clientele. Fewer and fewer of my customers started their weekends early these days, so I could count on a little quiet time before some of the neighborhood regulars rolled in. This was also school vacation week, which meant some of my workweek customers had left town with their kids.

The quiet seemed to make it hard to get the music right, too. I'd started out with some old acoustic blues, Mississippi John Hurt, thinking I'd build a little narrative out of the music, the kind of arc you got on a good radio show. But tonight all I was doing was casting a lot of disconnected tunes out into the world without tying anything together. It didn't happen that often, but I was actually relieved when last call came and I could turn up the lights and turn off the sound system.

Walking up Commonwealth Ave. in the direction of my building, I realized the uncertainty had something to do with Kathleen coming back into my orbit. We'd had our moments, but that was months ago now, and she'd left me with nothing more personal than a goodbye video. I didn't really care where she'd been or what she'd been up to, and I particularly didn't want to know what she'd stolen to attract the attention of Randolph Coyne and Donald Maldonado.

At the bottom of the stoop, I looked up at my windows. No lights showed. She'd probably fallen asleep on the couch.

I mounted the granite stairs and saw deep gouges where someone had levered the street door open. When I pushed, the heavy door floated inward.

"Shit."

My building had been burgled more than once, and I'd had to get Mrs. Rinaldi, my other tenant, used to the idea that she had to lock both doors, the building's and her apartment's, to be safe.

The blackness in the foyer had a still-empty quality that made my gut clutch. I flicked the switch and the light came on, a dim smear from the forty-watt bulb I'd been meaning to replace with an LED. I started up the stairs.

The door to my third-floor apartment was closed, but the knob turned. The door swung inward, the squeak of hinges reminding me of one of those cheesy horror films where a man with a chain saw and a leather mask waited in the dark. The intelligent thing would have been to call 911, but I couldn't call any of this an emergency. Yet. Kathleen had forgotten to relock the door. Or she was inside, hurt or dead, real possibilities if Coyne had found her.

"Kathleen?"

I fumbled on the lights, ducking down in case anyone was inside thinking about shooting or throwing things. There were signs of disturbance: the captain's chair in the corner by the window lay on its side, the framed poster from the '98 Montreal Jazz Festival tilted left, and a crumpled wad of clothing, the flannel shirt and pants she'd been wearing when she came into the bar this afternoon.

My breathing slowed down. The chair was the only sign anything violent might have happened, but Kathleen was perfectly capable of knocking it over by accident and leaving it there.

I walked down the short hall to the bathroom, where wet towels puddled on the floor. The tub was wet, too, and the mirror showed beads of condensation.

My bedroom was untouched, but when I walked back into the living room, I saw the blood behind the sofa, a patch the color of a rare steak against the pale yellow carpet. And once I saw it, I smelled it, a raw-iron stench that thickened the air.

The stain was small enough to cover with a dish towel. I wished I knew enough forensics to know if it represented a life-threatening loss, though I didn't think so. And Kathleen knew there was a first aid kit hanging in the kitchen. She'd made fun more than once of my propensity to plan ahead. It hadn't been opened.

I set the chair back up on four legs, straightened the poster. Though I wanted to believe everything was fine and she'd only disappeared once more, the blood made it unlikely.

My land line, one of the last in the city no doubt, had no dial tone. I tugged the cord up from behind the table and found the plastic connector snapped. Someone had yanked the wire out of the wall. I pulled out my cell.

It was after two, but Burton would be awake. He'd been cutting back on the alcohol and that meant he was drinking a lot of coffee. When he complained about sleeping poorly, he blamed it on everything but that, and I'd given up trying to convince him. I didn't feel a twinge about calling him this late at night anyway—over the years, he'd phoned me at any number of odd hours, drunk and sober.

Tonight, he sounded sober.

"Elder. Who died?"

Social graces aside, his one-pointed mind was both remarkable and annoying. It was one of the reasons it had taken him and Marina so long to make it work, even after he'd eased up on the drinking. He was a homicide-solving machine. Everything else was secondary.

"Need you to come over and take a look at something."

"Personal or professional?"

"Not sure. Maybe both."

"Close enough. You're at home?"

"Yep."

"Ten, fifteen minutes."

* * *

Ten minutes to my apartment from Charlestown was pushing it, but it was late at night and Burton could always flash his badge if he got stopped. I heard the downstairs door squeak open and reminded myself to fix the jamb. I stepped out into the hallway and half-whispered down the stairs.

"Quiet," I said. "I don't want to wake Mrs. Rinaldi up."

He took the stairs two at a time, puffing by the time he reached the top. He'd thrown on a pair of paint-stained khakis, a T-shirt from the Harley-Davidson store in North Conway, and deck shoes without socks. His brown leather bomber jacket was cracked and dry, old as he was.

"That nice old lady is deaf as a haddock." He rounded up onto the landing next to me. "What's the problem?"

"Maybe nothing. I could be wrong."

I had to admit to myself that having him here calmed me down. Our friendship had been strained by the relationship with Kathleen, which he did not approve of and had actively tried to sabotage. And he'd finally cut loose from Sharon, his ex-wife, which meant he hit the bottle hard for a while until he and Marina got back together. He'd been a good friend since I opened the Esposito, all the way back to the days of Alison Somers, and I was glad to feel him back on my side.

We walked into the living room. He noticed the blood behind the couch first thing. Then he did something I'd never seen a CSI on TV do, drop to his hands and knees and sniff the reddish patch.

"Yup. Blood," he said. "Not yours?"

"No. But it might be Kathleen Crawford's."

He came up off the floor like he was spring-loaded.

"Say what? Kathleen was here? In your apartment? Today?"

41

The violence of his reaction surprised me, but I read it as surprise that she'd reappeared.

"Yeah. She showed up at the bar, said she needed a place to get cleaned up and rest. No explanation."

"Anyone with her? Like a big Amazon woman?"

I shook my head.

"Why?"

"And you didn't call me?"

"Why would I? You not being one of her greatest fans."

"Did she say anything about where she'd been hiding out?"

"Burton. What?"

"I've already seen your girlfriend once this week. Yesterday morning, in fact."

It was my turn to be irritated.

"And you didn't call *me*?"

"I happened to be doing my job. Which, you recall, is working a homicide."

A weight dropped in my stomach.

"She's involved in a murder? How?"

"Jesus." Burton rotated his head like his neck was stiff. "Make me some coffee and I'll tell you."

"What about the blood?"

He sniffed.

"Maybe enough for a serious nosebleed. Nothing life-threatening. But my guess is you don't want me to call anyone in about it."

His skepticism reminded me that he considered every other cop in the department a separate species; their value was what they could do to support him in solving murders.

"I don't see why not. They could at least check the blood type, see if it was hers."

Burton started for the kitchen.

"That's not very likely. And you'll see why when I tell you. Are we going to have coffee or not?"

* * *

42

I didn't have any myself because I was holding onto the slim hope I might get to sleep afterwards. Burton, on the other hand, drank a cup so fast it might have been medicine, then refilled his mug. I was still absorbing the story.

"She's been in jail all this time?"

"Soft jail," he said. "Like the semi-jail you get sent to before you go out to a halfway house. There's a wicked overcrowding problem."

"For shoplifting."

"Leather jacket out of Louis'. I went back and looked at the arrest report. She walked in, grabbed it off the rack, strolled out. No attempt to get away."

"She wanted to get caught?"

None of which squared with anything I knew about her. The criminal history Burton had found on her described Kathleen Crawford as a sophisticated and careful thief, one who took high-value low-risk jobs only. She'd also been particular about paying her own way when we dated, to the point I expected her to pull out a calculator. I put it down to a desire for control.

I picked up the remote and turned on the little Bose radio, though at this time of night, my only chance for jazz would be one of the little college radio stations. Burton stared at me with the fierce focus that said he was on the job.

"I need to find her, Elder. She was at a murder scene where I was working and I need to know why. What she saw."

"You don't think she killed anybody?"

He pushed his mug back across the table at me.

"I don't. But I purely hate coincidence. And she was right there in the same place with a corpse that shouldn't have been there."

I was doubly irked now, that she'd use me and the Esposito as some kind of safe harbor, without hinting she might be a fugitive or involved in a murder. I'd been going to ask her about Randolph Coyne and Donald Maldonado when I saw her tonight, but she wasn't here now.

I didn't want to protect her, but I wondered if telling Burton about Randolph Coyne might not put her in more jeopardy. Maybe that had nothing to do with his murder case.

"How hard would it be to get a blood type?" I gestured back at the living room. "Find out if it's hers?"

His eyebrows went up.

"Lot of effort for a woman who's using you. To what end?"

"What if someone came and grabbed her?"

"You're talking about Ricky's cousin? You're reaching."

"How hard?"

"Well, we're not doing it through the department. You'd have to pay for a private company. And I doubt it would tell you anything useful."

Burton's sentences started clipping, like he thought I was trying to protect her. He was right—it was a stupid idea.

"Maybe I just need to figure out how to get it out of the carpet." I tried to joke his mood back to normal.

"Salt. And cold water."

"Look, Burton. I get it. You're pissed off. But I didn't know she was on the run, or that she was tangled up in something else that's threatening her. Besides Donny, I mean. Is it the mob?"

"Local? You're talking about Mickey."

The local mob had been mostly a joke since the seventies, a procession of revenge killings, arrests, and Federal stings that left the remaining disorganized crime activity in the hands of third-raters like Ricky Maldonado. Until a few years ago, that is, when Burton's childhood friend Mickey Barksdale had gathered the few remaining shreds and started reweaving an organization.

"Not sure. Are Coyne and Donald connected locally?" I said. "Through Ricky maybe?"

Burton frowned.

"Unlikely. This Coyne, though. He mentioned Kathleen by name?"

I nodded. "And that she had stolen something that belonged to Maldonado. Donald."

"Well, we do know she's a thief."

"Shoplifter." I still hadn't convinced myself that the history Burton showed me about her was accurate.

He drummed on the table with his thumbs.

"Try this. She knew that Donald Maldonado, not being from

44

around here, wouldn't have any support system. Anyone with local connections would have thought to look for her in South Middlesex. She wouldn't have been able to hide there. Too many snitches."

"Is that the only reason Donald's here, then? None of Ricky's enterprises were particularly profitable."

"Looking for her might give him an excuse to be here. Nose under the tent. But I still need to talk to her."

He was giving me the full-on blue-eyed nasty homicide dick stare, but I'd seen it before.

"I do not know where she is. Seriously. She borrowed my keys. I figured I'd find out what was going on when I got home."

Burton's seriousness didn't slip.

"You hear one word from her, the next one to hear it is me."

He beat out a rhythm on the table with his thumbs again.

"I have no interest in interfering with the workings of the law."

Burton scoffed, carried his mug to the sink, and washed it out. He turned it upside down on the drain board and looked at me.

"OK. Look. I don't think she killed that guy. But she was there when the body was found. She might have seen or heard something."

"I get it."

He frowned again, like he didn't believe I was serious. I was rapidly losing my desire to protect Kathleen from anything, least of all him.

"This other thing—where Maldonado threatened you?"

"Yeah."

"Nothing I can do about that without a crime. But you know you can call me if it heats up again."

"Assuming I'm able to." I was only half-joking. Randolph Coyne chilled me.

"Assuming," he said. "But don't let it get that far. All right?"

8

Burton woke up the next morning in his third-floor apartment in Charlestown, the late winter sun trying hard to warm up the bedroom through the uncurtained windows. He'd managed a solid five hours' sleep after coming back from Elder's, which was about as good as it got these days.

He pulled on a pair of nylon basketball shorts and a Boston Tech High School sweatshirt, and walked out to the kitchen to start the hot water. Java had turned out to be an unlikely savior from the hard-drinking nights, though he was slightly embarrassed by how deeply he'd dropped into the coffee culture: Japanese water kettles, roasting his own beans, mastering the pour-over.

He was brewing Sulawesi Toraju this morning, an air-roasted bean with herbal overtones. It had given him a sour stomach yesterday morning, but he was using bottled water today, in case the city's old pipes were imparting any strange elements into the water. He snorted at his own pretension, but at least he was keeping the obsession private. He could imagine how Elder would react if he knew.

The leather chair by the bay window was warm from the sun. Usually he was up and out fast when he had a case to work, but he needed to think a little about how Kathleen and her semi-Amazon friend fit in here. Could it really have been a coincidence they'd been there when Boustaloudis's body showed up? Or had Kathleen had something to do with it somehow? She'd bolted pretty quickly when she saw he was going to be involved, and he'd checked: she only had another two weeks until she went free.

What was as important as why Boustaloudis had been killed,

though, was why his killer had wanted to conceal the fact by burying him with a bunch of anonymous corpses. The harbor cop's ideas hadn't been much help—he'd only had a half-assed guess as to how an extra coffin, occupied, had gotten onto the island.

His iPhone burbled and he looked down at the display: Martines. Burton didn't report into the precinct that regularly when he was working a case and that worked fine with most of his bosses: he cleared his cases and he worked a lot of unpaid overtime. But Martines had aspirations to bureaucratic heights beyond his current station—twin girls thinking about college—and so he was trying to regularize things in his command. Wouldn't be smart not to answer.

"Burton."

"You coming in to work today?"

"I am working." He stretched his legs out over the arm of the chair.

"I've only got Schmidt and Henrickson on the board if something comes in."

"I'm on my way out to Hyde Park. On this Boustaloudis thing."

"The stiff from the poor farm?"

Burton indulged in as much dark and raunchy cop humor as anyone, but he would never call a victim a stiff.

"His name was Boustaloudis." He felt his voice freeze. "And it might have something to do with the Olympic bid."

As soon as he said that out loud, he wished he hadn't. Any political element, anything more complicated than one hood offing another, was bound to make Martines sweat. The department's upper levels still belonged to Boston's traditional ethnic cliques— mainly the Irish—and the lieutenant was always calculating how his command's performance might play there. He didn't like complications.

"The Olympics? You sure? Based on what?"

"Not completely sure of the connection yet, Dennis. What I'm doing this morning, trying to connect it up. Boustaloudis supposedly headed up some citizen's group against the bid."

"You sure there's a connection?"

Hadn't he just said he wasn't?

47

"This is why we call it an investigation, Dennis."

"You're saying there are people who don't want the Olympics to come here?"

Burton frowned into the phone. At a minimum, someone who worked for the city ought to read the newspaper once in a while. The movement hadn't gained a lot of traction, but it had been written about and discussed in the press.

"Grassroots effort, Loo. All Facebook and social media right now. They're worried the traffic will get worse, the effort will drain money from things like fixing the T, and they know the taxpayers will foot the bill. The only people in favor besides the mayor are the construction unions and the real estate developers—more cake and pie for them."

"In other words, business as usual in the hub of the universe."

"Gotta go, Loo. You know the laws about cell phones while you're driving."

"Sure. Don't forget to check in. Today."

Burton clicked off. The politics meant Martines would be paying more attention than usual, but as long as he didn't get inspired to be actively involved, Burton could manage him.

He was shaved, showered, and dressed, out the door of his building and into the Jeep in fifteen minutes. The department allowed him an unmarked, but he preferred to drive his own vehicle, a smallish SUV that didn't scream 'cop' everywhere he drove. He made a mental note to file for his mileage reimbursement—he needed to buy some more coffee.

He cut down Bunker Hill Street to Vine and Chelsea, then jumped on 93 and headed south. Traffic was no worse than usual and once he was through the city, he was traveling against the flow. He took Gallivan Boulevard to River Street, then turned left onto Hyde Park Ave., where he saw the sign for Connie's Corner Drugs. The Boustaloudis name must have been too long for the sign.

He backed into a parking spot around the corner and laid the Police Business placard on the dash. In Charlestown, it would get his vehicle vandalized, but maybe the Hyde Park meter maids were a kinder, gentler bunch.

Despite the forty degree temperatures, the door to the drug store was propped open. He stopped in the entryway, blocked by the oversized black-clad rear end of a woman scrubbing the floor. She looked back over her shoulder at him.

"Sorry. Not open yet." Her accent was noticeable, something European.

He noticed shards of glass on the floor, the open pane in the door.

"I'm from the police, ma'am."

"It's about time. I called you three hours ago. Isn't the police station right up the street? Or am I losing my mind?"

"Called about what? I'm here to talk to you about your husband's death."

He assumed from her age she was Boustaloudis's wife. Her face closed and tears came to her eyes, supporting his conclusion.

"Connie? They already told me all about that. What I want to know is what you're going to do about this."

She waved her hand around the store.

Connie's Corner Drugs funneled back from the street in a compressed triangle, one wall following the acute angle of the side street cutting back from Hyde Park Ave. Even at its deepest, at the door to the back room, you could reach out and touch the shelves on both sides.

Which someone clearly had done. Beyond where Mrs. Boustaloudis had been scrubbing the floor, the cracked green and white linoleum was strewn with boxes of aspirin, travel-sized shaving cream, mouthwash, and shampoo, razors and blades, energy drinks, bags of chips, nuts, and candy bars. Magazines. It was a mess, though not as bad as it could have been—no one had pissed or shit in the mess.

"This happened when?"

She gave a pulmonary gasp, aggravation or asthma.

"Last night. You're not from Hyde Park?"

Burton shook his head, pulling out his phone.

"No. But let me get someone down here."

He called back to D-4 and had the admin patch him through to E-6, where he assured the desk sergeant that all beneficence would redound to his children and their offspring if he would dispatch someone here forthwith to take a report.

He helped Mrs. Boustaloudis pick up the mess until a surly detective arrived to fill out a report. Once he'd left, Burton sat down with her in the back room to discuss why he'd actually come here.

The command center from which the Boustaloudises ran their empire was a largish storeroom stacked with merchandise, including a very large number of small electric appliances like coffeemakers and hair dryers. A green metal school desk butted against one wall, three chairs around it, and a large travel poster of Corfu covered the wall by the exit.

Burton focused on the vandalism first—the timing, right after Boustaloudis's death, seemed suspicious.

"Have you had this kind of trouble before?" he said. "Local kids, anything like that?"

Mrs. Boustaloudis—"Call me Dorris, two R's"—slumped in a folding chair with an open can of Red Bull. Absent the furious work of cleaning up the mess out front, she seemed shrunken and sad.

"I don't think so." Her eyes welled up again, but did not overflow. She took a sip from the can and shuddered. "It was like this when I came in this morning. My Kenny was supposed to open up, but his car wouldn't start."

"Kenny."

She looked sadder, if that was possible.

"Our—my—son. He's going to the Mass. College of Pharmacy."

Burton couldn't ignore the click of a connection: young male, drugstore, pharmacy school. The smarter class of drug dealers all over the country were educating themselves, learning the legal possibilities in operating in the pharmaceutical business.

He didn't want to get tunnel vision, though. He already had a likely reason for Constantine Boustaloudis to get killed.

"Tell me about Connie's work with this anti-Olympic group."

Dorris slammed down the can, spurting a geyser of amber liquid out the top.

"Ridiculous. He was the whole group, almost. He ran the meetings, sent all the emails, made the phone calls. While I worked here in the store, forty, fifty hours a week."

Burton, whose mother had done the books for his father's auto repair shop after being on her feet all day at Jordan Marsh, was not sympathetic.

"But why? Was he active in local politics? Neighborhood committees and all that?"

Burton had found no evidence of it, but neighborhood activism tended to stay local. You might not hear about it on the other side of town.

"Franklin Park." Dorris said it with such a bitter flavor Burton could tell it had been the topic of argument around the Boustaloudis table.

"Yes."

He knew now he was going to have to get up to speed on his whole Olympic thing. All he really knew was that there were small pockets of resistance around the city.

"Connie, he grew up in Jamaica Plain." Her voice softened, into memory. "You probably thought we came off the boat."

Burton shook his head.

"I don't care about that, Mrs. Boustaloudis. We were all immigrants at some point."

Dorris eyed him suspiciously.

"Connie's parents came over right after the war. His mother and mine were best friends."

He didn't want to trek too far down memory lane or he'd wind up with her whole genealogy.

"Franklin Park," he said.

"High school football games, they played in White Stadium, you know. And Connie's *papu*, every Saturday afternoon in the summer time, eighteen holes at George Wright."

"The Olympics were going to take over George Wright?"

She lifted her chin, her dark eyes angry on behalf of her husband.

"They were going to close it off for a year and redo the stadium for the Games. Run horse races up and down the golf course."

Jesus Christ. No wonder the neighbors were bullshit. Franklin Park was the largest of the pieces in Boston's Emerald Necklace, Frederic Law Olmstead's chain of open spaces around the city that included the Common, the Public Garden, the Fens, and Arnold Arboretum.

51

It contained the golf course, tennis and basketball courts, ball fields, and the second largest zoo in New England. Burton himself had run in the city cross-country championships there in high school. Closing it down for a year would have irked a hundred different interest groups.

Nothing in Boston that Burton knew of, not dope or greed or street crime, unhinged people the way local politics did, especially in a city with such a long history of municipal corruption.

Dorris snorted as she polished off the Red Bull.

"*Feh*. A Facebook page, email list, some meetings. You think a Greek doesn't know how politics works?"

"I wouldn't know anything about that. So, no one in particular was angry at your husband?"

She leaned across the table, dark eyes glittering with suspicion.

"You heard about this Vault thing?"

Burton all but rolled his eyes. Recent Boston history ascribed an outsized influence on civic and political affairs to a semi-mythological group of business leaders and politicians who'd supposedly created an agenda for the city's development into the 21st century and beyond. Burton's experience told him the movers and shakers you never heard about were the ones you had to worry about.

"I have."

"They don't have the kind of power they used to." She tapped the side of her nose. "But some of them, the sons and daughters . . ."

"You think they're making a comeback? That they had something to do with your husband's death?"

"People love power," she said.

"But there wasn't a specific person or group Mr. Boustaloudis was fighting with?"

"Call him Connie. Everyone did."

"The pushback was general?"

Dorris had a dreamy look, as if the Red Bull had an opposite effect on her and calmed her down.

"You know, the old Mayor, he was from Hyde Park. This would never have happened, he was still in office."

The dead and gone mayor, Burton thought: well-loved and as much a grandmaster of neighborhood politics as any of them.

"You're probably right," he said.

"He got people thinking power was easy, he did so good."

"Are you saying Connie had problems with some of the local politicians? Someone from Hyde Park?"

She was dancing around something and he wished she'd just say it.

"These Chamber of Commerce types," she said. "All of them wanted a piece of it." She rubbed her thumb and fingers together in the universal sign.

"But no one specific."

She picked up the empty Red Bull can as if she wanted to crush it.

"Maybe this one fellow, one of a pair of brothers…"

A crash out front interrupted her.

"Ma!"

Scuffling, then footsteps crunched on what must have been a leftover piece of glass. The door to the back room flew open and a tall good-looking kid—styled dark hair, pressed cotton pants, a dark blue linen shirt with the sleeves rolled up—burst in, looking wild. He wore clear plastic braces on his teeth.

"Why didn't you call me right away?"

Dorris rose out of her chair easily, given her bulk, and allowed herself to be enfolded in a hug. The boy, maybe twenty, squeezed his eyes shut and hung on as if they were adrift in Boston Harbor and she was his life jacket.

Dorris caught Burton's eye over her son's shoulder and smiled proudly.

"My son Kenny," she said.

"Why didn't you call me?" Kenny said tearily. "You weren't going to tell me my father had been murdered?"

Now Burton had two things bothering him: why the kid was just finding out his father was dead, and why Dorris had come in to open the store up the next day.

9

The sky outside was a pale blue and the sun could not coax any warmth out of the ground. I had to drag myself out of bed and then the apartment to get down to the Esposito. Burton had convinced me not to worry about the bloodstain, and I was irked enough by Kathleen's most recent disappearance that I didn't know if I would help her again if I could. I was still trying to grapple with the idea she'd gone to jail deliberately to hide from Donald Maldonado.

The transition from March into April was always too slow for me, a hard slog through the slush and the sleet toward warmer times. As I unlocked the bar's steel door and pegged it open with a wedge—every bar needs a good airing out in the morning—I found myself looking forward to next week, when some of the regulars would be back. I'd scheduled my first live music show of the year for a week from Saturday, and that always raised my spirits.

I rattled down the steel stairs, wondering for the hundredth time if I ought to replace them with something less industrial. But I'd already sunk some serious dollars into the place, and now that we ran in the black, if barely, I needed to be judicious in how much I upgraded. Inheriting the money from my father gave me too many options, but I didn't want to spend any more of it than I had to.

I turned up the lights and switched on the sound system, the speakers popping. Before WGBH screwed him over, I'd been prescient enough to record a couple hundred hours of *Eric in the Evening*, and as I heard Tommy Flanagan dip into that ethereal cover of "Peace," I breathed in satisfaction. If only for the moment, I was where I wanted to be, doing what I wanted to do. If I'd still been drinking, I would have lifted a glass to myself and to Eric Jackson and all the great music he'd brought to Boston over the last thirty years. And all the other subtle beauties and beasts that made this city such a great place to live.

I flicked on the espresso machine, figuring I needed more practice with it before I started charging people for the coffee. Out in the kitchen, I flipped on the overheads and turned on the gas burner under a pot of stock Marina wanted hot when she came in at ten. Some kind of complicated stew for the lunch menu.

A light down in my office spilled into the hallway. I frowned. Turning that off was the last thing I did every night before I let myself out.

A match sizzled and I smelled smoke. Cigar, not cigarette.

"Who's there?"

No answer. I grabbed an eight-inch chef's knife and edged down the hallway.

"I'm armed," I called. "Come out here where I can see you."

No sound but the soft shushing of exhaled smoke.

I wasn't too worried—anyone who'd wanted to hurt me could have waited out in the bar and picked me off as I came down the stairs. Though that begged the question of how anyone got in. Had I left the fire exit unlocked? One of the homeless guys sneaking in? I doubted I could stab anyone, but I could scare them at least.

I turned the corner into the door way, and *wham!* Stiff knuckles popped against my breastbone and stunned me, breathless. I thought my heart had stopped until I realized I was choking on saliva I'd inhaled, whooping for air. Gagging, I felt lightheadedness wash through me like a gray fog.

A pair of strong hands held me upright, away from what I wanted to do, which was curl up in a fetal position and die.

"Slow and deep, my friend. Breathe easy."

The only other time in my life I'd been hit that hard was in my single prep school try at playing rugby, long before the sport became the darling of high-testosterone college boys and girls. None of us had known what we were doing, beyond running into each other as hard as we could.

Achingly slowly, breath fought its way back through my throat. The point of impact on my breastbone ached like I'd been shot. I straightened up as well as I could and sidestepped like a drunken old man to the closest chair. Not the fancy ergonomic leather one behind the desk, which Randolph Coyne had reclaimed.

"That wasn't necessary." I grunted, shifting around in a quest for a position where I could breathe without pain.

"Oh, my friend. But you made it so."

He turned the desk lamp away so his face melted into shadows, not before I caught a strangely sated look, as if he'd met his minimum daily requirement of violence on others.

"Because not only did you lie to me, you failed to do what I asked you to do."

He picked up a ballpoint pen from the desk and held it loosely in a fist.

"She showed up and then she was gone again." I didn't like the whine in my voice. "I don't know where she went."

"I'm afraid I'm not going to be able to take your word for it, Elder."

The soft sound of my name in his mouth was chilling. He held up the pen, his thumb over one end.

"I understand microsurgery can do wonderful things these days. Even repair an eardrum."

For some reason, maybe my love for music, the prospect of losing my hearing frightened me in a way a punch in the mouth did not. Which meant Randolph Coyne was more consciously and thoughtfully evil than my gut had told me. I tensed, ready to fight.

"I might have been able to tell you what I knew if I had a way to get in touch with you."

Total Hail Mary on my part, but Randolph paused, contemplated the steel point of the pen, and stared at me in mock surprise.

"Truly? I think you're lying to me, Elder Darrow. But I suppose it wouldn't be quite cricket of me to punish you, in that case. Give me your arm."

I was giving him nothing. He dropped the pen to clatter on the desk.

"Your arm or your eardrum. Your choice."

He reached into his pants pocket and extracted a small square folding knife that he thumbnailed open. Then he grabbed my wrist and pulled the arm out straight.

"Can you remember the area code 504?" he said. "That will make less work for me."

And with the delicacy of a miniaturist—I thought of Mrs. Rinaldi, my tenant who built set models for the Boston Opera Company—he traced the seven digits of a phone number into my forearm with the tip of the knife. The numbers seeped red.

I was incapable of speech—the frigid cruelty of the act stunned me. I'd dealt with some rough customers in the past few years, but not, I saw now, any true sociopaths.

He wiped the blade clean on the sleeve of my shirt, refolded the knife, and stowed it.

"I'm glad we straightened that out," he said. "Now you won't have any trouble contacting me. When she returns."

"You do know I have friends in the police?"

It was lame, third grade playground lame, but I sensed not resisting at all might put me in worse danger.

"Of course. The inimitable Detective Burton. I understand he's with Homicide, though. Do we really need to escalate to the point where you'll attract that kind of attention?"

It shouldn't have surprised me that he knew about Burton. The current Maldonado organization was a good deal more competent than the previous version.

"We are friends, Randolph. Maybe the concept is familiar? He's operated outside of his job description before."

Randolph remade his sour-pickle mouth.

"Let's get back to the topic at hand, shall we? What do you know that you haven't told me?"

I checked the clock. Twenty to ten. I wanted him gone before Marina showed up.

"Look. The woman waltzed in, borrowed my keys to take a shower, then disappeared all over again." The fact that he hadn't mentioned the blood meant it hadn't been his doing. "She's an escaped prisoner. From the county jail. She's hiding out somewhere else."

Randolph's long face lit as if I'd handed him a hundred dollar bill.

"Ah, so that's where she's been hiding. Very clever." He turned those deep brown eyes on me again. "She left you no notes? No billets-doux or packages? No 'see you soon'?"

"Not a word." Maybe I was going to get out of this without further damage.

"She's traveling with someone. Another woman."

Coyne rubbed his hands together.

"Now we're talking, aren't we. Who is she?"

I tried to remember what Burton had told me.

"Big woman. Tall. Maybe with a religious bent."

He shook his head regretfully.

"That's not terribly helpful. But I do believe you've told me everything you know."

The depth of my relief at hearing that unnerved me. Randolph Coyne was a threat I couldn't shed fast enough.

"I'm not going to be able to check back on you soon. Out of town business." He pointed to my scratched forearm. "But you do know how to contact me."

I nodded, relieved that he was getting ready to leave without further damage.

"Let me leave you with a small reminder, though."

And without a windup, he drove his knuckles into my side, about eight inches under the armpit. Bone gave way and I felt a crack.

"So, call me if you hear anything, Elder. Will you?"

10

Kathleen glanced across the bench seat of the F-150 she'd hotwired in the garage on Commonwealth Avenue. The foot well on the passengers' side was ankle deep in fast food trash, and Alberta had her feet up on the dash as if she thought there might be snakes down there. Kathleen was more worried about the wet bloody handkerchief her traveling companion held to her nose.

"Did it stop yet, Alberta? You need another rag?"

She'd grabbed a stack of handkerchiefs from Elder's bureau on the way out of the apartment, feeling a warm burst of affection at the idea of a man so old-fashioned he carried a cloth in his pocket to blow his nose in.

"I can't help it." Alberta whined. "I always get them when I get nervous."

"It's all right, honey. We just have to get us off the street for a while. We'll take you to a doc-in-the-box."

Kathleen was regretting the impulse she'd had on Rinker to steal Trick's truck, then drop the zipper on her jumpsuit long enough to distract the harbor cop, tie him up, and steal his boat. It had blown the plan to get herself released on time and disappear to bits, but Burton was looking for a way to blame the fat man's death and near-burial on her, she was sure. The escape had also saddled her with a partner who was about thirteen years old mentally, and as agile as a three-legged bear. If Alberta hadn't launched herself off the dock into the boat at the last possible minute, Kathleen would have escaped without her.

All this was Burton's fault, for sure. She'd suppressed her thoughts about Elder as long as she'd been in South Middlesex, but wondered now if there was any chance they'd be together again. Burton had killed that possibility once, and she might have reinforced it last night. Donny D and his asshole buddy Randolph had dug up her connections easily enough. It was better that Elder didn't get hurt.

She backed the truck into a space at the upper end of Mattapan Square, across the street from the pastel sign for a MediRX Center. This was close enough to the rougher suburbs that she didn't anticipate a lot of questions. You'd need a gunshot wound to raise an eyebrow around here.

She helped Alberta get checked in, then patted her leg.

"You OK for now? I have to make a phone call."

Alberta, snuffling into the bloody handkerchief, nodded tearfully.

"Back in a bit, hon. Really."

Kathleen stepped out onto the corner of Blue Hill Avenue and Babson Street and looked around for a pay phone, considering whether she ought to just leave Alberta here. The corrections system would catch up with Alberta eventually—she was a convicted murderer—and she would be safer in jail than running around with a thief who had gangsters chasing her ass.

Elder, bless him, had kept a stack of twenties in his handkerchief drawer. She broke one in a bodega and eyed the burner phones. Better to wait and see how much cash she needed on the run. The bodega's pay phone hung on the wall in the back, the instructions in Spanish.

"Esposito. This is Elder."

"It's Kathleen. Please don't say my name out loud."

"Don't worry. Burton's not here."

She heard his bitterness. He must know it all now. Fucking Burton.

"That's not the only set of ears I'm worried about."

"Randolph Coyne? I met him, too."

She sucked in a breath. Her wish for him not to get pulled in had been in vain.

"I'm sorry, Elder."

He was silent. She thought he'd hung up.

"I have to say I'm not too crazy about being blown off. Are you the one who bled all over my rug?"

Alberta's nosebleed. Shit. She hadn't noticed.

"No. I'm traveling with someone."

"Really."

"Do I hear jealousy? Really?"

"No."

"Look," she said. "I didn't know what I was getting into with these guys. But I'll get it straightened out. On my own."

"Could Burton help?"

She barked a laugh.

"You don't know your friend very well if you think so. His world view wouldn't allow it."

"He's a friend, Kathleen. I might be able to talk to him about it."

She softened at the desire in his voice, the urge to help, to mitigate the chaos.

"I don't think it will matter. But let me think about it."

"And you owe me some money. And six cotton handkerchiefs."

She thought she heard a smile in his voice. Could he be that forgiving?

"I always pay my debts, Elder." She looked out the bodega's front window to see Alberta shuffling out of the care center. "Gotta go."

She wanted to say something more, but hung up before she dug herself in any deeper.

* * *

Kathleen was doing her best to convince Alberta to turn themselves in. They sat in a Subway three blocks up Blue Hill Ave. from the clinic, and while it was almost empty right now, noon was coming.

"Look, honey. We have no resources, no place to stay. They'll catch up to us sooner or later, and that will make it worse when they do. We go back voluntarily, it's a slap on the wrist."

Kathleen doubted anyone was looking for her in a serious way, a thief with two weeks left on her sentence. Alberta was another story. And Kathleen's plan did not include turning herself in.

Alberta smelled of singed hair and flesh. The so-called doctor at the clinic had cauterized both nostrils to stop the bleeding. Kathleen wouldn't have paid the butcher the hundred dollars if he hadn't looked like the type who'd call the police.

"I thought you knew that guy on the cops," Alberta said, chewing on the end of a tuna sub. "Couldn't he help us out?"

When had Kathleen said anything like that? She knew Burton only as a friend of Elder's, a friend who'd been extremely skeptical of her place in Elder's life. She wouldn't have put it past the cop mind to run her name through a bunch of law enforcement databases, which meant he'd have a lot of questions about her past.

"Not me. Look, Alberta. We can't survive out here if we have to look over our shoulders every minute."

She didn't want Alberta to think she was trying to abandon her, at least not until after it happened.

"You don't want me around, do you?"

The large woman dripped tears onto the table top. Kathleen mopped them up automatically with a napkin.

"Of course I do. We'll go back in together. Then it'll be like having a clean slate."

Alberta scowled at her.

"But I'm a life sentence," she said.

The only other customer in the place, a ferrety kid with an oversized soda cup and a cell phone on the table in front of him, stared at them with intent, maybe smelling some kind of score. Kathleen glared at him and shook her head, handed Alberta the clutch of napkins.

"Dry it up, honey. We're going to go do this, and it will be fine."

"Will you still pray with me, Nina?"

Kathleen shrugged. Anything to get her to shut up.

"Of course. Just not here. Let's go, while you're still being brave about it."

The B-3 substation—what its close neighbors and habitués called Mat-Dot for Mattapan-Dorchester—backed onto Blue Hill Ave., though the front door had a lovely view of the Mobil station on the other side of Morton Street. Kathleen felt as if she were dragging a small child up the stairs on the first day of school, holding Alberta's hand tightly so she wouldn't bolt.

"Come on now." She tried not to sound impatient, which would only intensify Alberta's resistance. "They'll probably have us back to South Middlesex in time for dinner. Chocolate pudding, maybe."

Kathleen saw the desk officer watching through the heavy glass doors as they climbed the stairs. Must have been a slow law enforcement day in Mattapan. The foyer was a wide open space with no chairs or tables, probably to discourage loitering. Happy posters of neighborhood events, school opening warnings, a portrait of the governor, and generic prints of farm and forest adorned the calming beige walls.

Alberta stopped short on the blue industrial carpet, a third of the way to the glass window behind which the young male uniformed officer sat, waiting placidly for them to advance and state their business.

Alberta started to sob.

"Come on," Kathleen said. "It's not that bad."

"But I liked being free."

Then Alberta took in a deep breath, and Kathleen, guessing what she was about to do, caught the officer's eye and pointed at the ladies' room. He pressed a button under the desk and the lock clicked. As she ducked into the surprisingly spacious restroom, Alberta loosed her first scream. Kathleen heard the glass window slide open.

"Ma'am!" The young cop, a noncombatant who sat at his desk all day long, probably dreaming of shootouts and takedowns, sounded nervous and irked. "Are you all right?"

"Nooooo." Alberta's voice muffled under snuffles and sobs. "I don't want to go back. I can't, Nina."

Kathleen waited for the sound of the security door opening and the officer's voice coming out from the desk.

"It's OK, miss. Come inside and sit down for a minute and I'll get you some water."

Water? Why did people think a glass of water solved everything?

Kathleen cracked the ladies' room door and watched the cop, one hand in the middle of Alberta's back, conduct her into the inner office. Before the door closed behind them, she glimpsed a couple of upholstered chairs and a complicated telephone switchboard.

She turned sideways and slipped out through the smallest space in the restroom doorway she could manage, covering the five yards between it and the outside door with noiseless steps, but as she pushed open the glass door, the young cop yelled out at her.

"Hey! Miss? Your friend is in here."

* * *

Kathleen sat on the commode in the ladies' room of the Mobil station, counting the remaining money she'd borrowed from Elder. Two hundred seventy dollars, nowhere near enough to get her to New Orleans so she could retrieve a new set of IDs and the item she'd stolen from Donald Maldonado. Maybe he would let her get on with her life if she returned it.

She felt slightly guilty about leaving Alberta to the mercies of the Boston Police, but it was the best thing for her, really. The woman was only a little smarter than a child and not at all inconspicuous. Staying partnered with her would have made it impossible to resolve her problem with Donny.

She shook off the feeling, concentrating on how she was going to finance herself. It had been a half an hour since she dumped Alberta, and if the cops had come looking for her—doubtful—they were finished by now. She needed to get herself moving.

She wasn't going to be able to mug anyone—she didn't have a weapon, and no one would believe a five-foot-six skinny little blonde could kick their ass, even if she had learned some moves at South Middlesex. Guilt and slyness would have to do.

A fist thumped on the door and she almost peed.

"Come on out of there," a bass voice thundered. "I don't know what you're up to in my restroom, but I want you out of there."

She ran some water in the sink and rubbed her eyes so it would look like she'd been crying.

"Wait. Please." She made her voice quaver.

Then she scrunched up her face a few times and rubbed her cheeks, opened one more button down the front of her flannel shirt, and opened the door.

"I'm sorry, I'm sorry, I'm sorry." She sobbed as she fell through the doorway toward the tall skinny man in the dark blue mechanic's overall.

He was surprised enough to put his arms up to catch her, exactly the reaction she'd hoped for. When she cannoned into him, she moved her hand around his waist, and as they banged off the door jamb, she used the impact to lift the wallet out of his pocket and shove it under her waistband, feeling it drop. For the first time, she was grateful for the ample room in her state-issued underpants. No unsightly bulges.

"Whoa. Easy now." He grabbed her arms and steadied her. "Are you all right? Do I need to call the EMTs?"

He glanced at the crook of her elbows, then into her eyes. Up at this end of Mattapan, he probably thought she was shooting up in his bathroom.

"I'm OK, I'm OK." She panted. "I'm sorry. I just, I lost my mom and I… I…"

To her horror, actual tears spilled from her eyes, disgusting her. Apparently she was even more of a liar and a manipulator than she thought.

He ripped a paper towel from the dispenser and handed it to her.

"I'm really sorry," she said.

"I heard you. Can we step outside?"

She dabbed at the tears with the rough paper and followed him outside.

"It just got over on me all of a sudden."

The name tag over his pocket read "Ted." He was all one width from his shoulders to his hips, but his forearms were muscled and lightly freckled. She'd always had a thing for forearms. He was dark-complected, Italian or Greek, with a strong nose and curly black hair.

"It's all right, hon."

She allowed him the "hon," considering he was at least fifteen years older than she was.

"I lost my dad, I stared out the window for two weeks. You get through it however you can. You sure you don't want the paramedics? Maybe they could give you something."

65

"It was kind of a panic attack," she said. "I've had them before." She was anxious to get away from him, see what she'd scored. "I'm fine. Really."

She held out her hands, flat and steady. A car pulled in for gas, ringing a bell. Ted's attention diverted.

Go, go, she said to herself.

"If you're sure." He was already leaning toward the front of the station.

A horn honked.

"Really," she said. "Go. And thank you."

He turned, then snapped his fingers and turned around, a sly smile on his stubbled face. She was two steps into walking away.

"One thing, though? You want to give me back my wallet? Or make me go in after it?"

She put her foot down and sprinted off up into the neighborhood behind the station. He cursed, then the horn honked again, more insistently. She ran as hard as she could, without looking back.

11

I slammed the receiver down so hard the bell jangled. I couldn't remember the last time I was so angry I wanted to break things. Kathleen had a maddening way of stating something as a *fait accompli*, then shutting down discussion.

I stepped out of the office to find Marina peering down the short corridor at me, light glinting off the cleaver in her hand. In silhouette, she looked like a comic book Mayan warrior queen.

"Jesus," she said, a prayer more than a curse. "Is it ever going to quiet down around here?"

"Sorry."

I loved my cook to death, but the rough things she'd been through getting back with Burton had convinced her she was a better judge of how to run my love life than I was.

"That must have been your Kathleen, yeah? No one else riles you up like that."

"I don't want to talk about it."

"You should be telling Burton you're talking to her."

"You two are actually communicating now?"

Her confidence was brittle, easy to shatter, and I was ashamed of myself. But I did hate being told what to do.

"That isn't your business."

"My point exactly."

We'd been getting testier with each other since my father's money had been disbursed and I feared we were going to come to a parting soon. She didn't need to sling hash in a dive bar any more.

She retreated to the kitchen, stepped back behind the work surface, and poked her knife at the mess of onions she'd been chopping.

"What's on the menu for lunch?" I tried to make peace.

"Nothing you're likely to eat." She didn't look up.

My unadventurous taste in food was a running joke. I hoped that meant we were going to drop the subject of Kathleen Crawford.

"I'll make you something if you're hungry."

"Cheeseburger with a fried egg on it?"

She sniffed, but went to the near refrigerator, pulled out a patty, and threw it on the grill. When she turned back, though, concern made her frown.

"She's a burglar, Elder."

"A thief, actually." Though I wasn't sure what the technical difference was.

"Burton said she has arrest warrants out on her all over Florida and Texas."

"She must not be very good at it, then. If she keeps getting arrested."

She frowned at me—I suppose defending Kathleen on the grounds of her incompetence was backwards.

The smell of cooking meat made my stomach growl. I'd only had coffee for breakfast. I bent my attitude. Marina had a right to worry about me, even if it was for the wrong reason. She flipped the burger.

"I appreciate it. But right now, Kathleen needs help."

"But she escaped from jail. You help her, you're going against Burton. He'll take it personally."

"I don't think so. He knows she got herself arrested on purpose. It's not like she killed anyone."

Marina topped my sandwich with the fried egg.

"So she says, right? She was where there was a body. Burton can't give her any breaks until he knows she's innocent."

It sounded like she was quoting Burton.

"I didn't realize you were his assistant." My voice rose in frustration. "It was a coincidence she was on the island."

She shook her head, ignoring my jab.

"You know how he hates coincidence."

I took my plate from her and turned my back on the topic, though behind me, I felt the evil eye she'd learned from her mother. Out behind the bar, I poured myself some club soda and picked up the burger. It could be that Kathleen was going to be my rock and Burton my hard place.

12

Pete Fountain was playing "A Closer Walk with Thee." He'd died not too long ago, and every time another of my jazz heroes passed, I tried to create a musical tribute in the bar. We seemed to have lost a lot of the good ones recently—Dave Brubeck, most notably—and I wasn't feeling the upcoming generation of jazz musicians. A lot of the music seemed corporate: composed, burnished, and recorded in ways that said the marketing and the A & R people had as much to say as the players.

"This a church or a bar?" yelled Pedey Thomas, as he clanged down the stairs.

"I thought this was your church."

He walked up and tossed a scuffed leather satchel on the bar.

"Cute," he said. "What happened to your arm? You lose your address book?"

I glanced at the scabbed-over digits.

"Memory aid."

Pedey lifted a bushy gray eyebrow.

"You say so. I think I'll just sit here until my personal yardarm gets crossed."

Never before four, was his motto, and I recognized the way degenerate drinkers tried to convince themselves they had it all under control. It was a bitter knowledge—I'd been there many times myself.

Nowadays, the programs, the support, the public recognition of alcoholism were stronger than when I started my drinking career. I wondered sometimes if my life would have unfolded differently if a knowledgeable adult had recognized the egg of the snake in me and taken me in hand. Probably not. Most of us don't hear a message until we're ready.

And envy wasn't a cause discussed at AA meetings. I started drinking to hide my envy, at the easy way my peers lived their lives, with confidence and assurance they were worth what they'd been given. I wanted to make myself appear as one of them. I didn't know what Pedey Thomas's particular lack was, but I understood its genesis.

"Bingo," he said, as the minute hand on the bog schoolhouse clock ticked over to the 12.

I set up a rocks glass with a generous pour of Johnny Walker Black and a single ice cube, pushed it across the bar.

"First one's on me today."

"Says the pusher." He picked up the glass, and I could see him will himself not to nuzzle it as he sipped. The tremor in his fingers faded. "Presents and Jesus music. Christmas come late this year and nobody told me?"

"Are you still working the Metro section? Or did they bury you in the back room to update the obituaries?"

A black look flashed across his face and his cheek twitched. Shit. I'd touched something raw.

"Still in Metro. For the moment." He stared past my shoulder at himself in the mirror. "Oldest living artifact."

He drank the rest of the Scotch as if it were milk and placed the empty glass on the bar. My minimal remaining moral sense gave me a twinge. Given how hard I worked to stay sober, how did I justify feeding other people's addictions?

"Why?" he said. "And double that up this time."

I pushed back my qualms and poured. He was a grownup.

"What do you know about the state of the Olympic bid?"

He sipped more slowly, having sanded off the rough edge.

"Don't you read the newspaper?" He sighed. "Wait. Check that. No one does any more. Which is the problem."

I wanted to remind him that at least he still had a job, that any number of people of his age and experience were trying to freelance, or writing for free for mushy-news outfits like the *Huffington Post* for

71

the exposure. And some of the wood-pulp companies were starting to learn the Internet. There would always be readers in the world, but I knew better than to try and argue with a drunk with a notion.

"I just want to know who in the hell thinks bringing the games here is a good idea," I said.

"Beside every local pol, the unions, and the real estate developers? The politicians are thinking legacy, the union jobs, the developers—no surprise—smell money. What else is new in the hub of the universe?"

The conventional wisdom in the Commonwealth was that Boston was a corrupt city. It had such a history all the way back to the Revolution that included fleecing Connecticut soldiers, a mayor whose tenure was interrupted by five months in a Federal prison, and a local FBI Special Agent whom local gangsters had controlled for most of his career.

But growing up in my father-the-investment-banker's home, I never heard of undue pressure to do anything except make good deals. And he'd been grooming me to take over the business, so it would have been part of my education, if the corruption were true. I doubted that the city had any more or less lawlessness than other cities its size.

"Union guy would be Dougie Ryan, right?"

That was the only prominent name I could think of, other than the mayor's.

Pedey shook his head, glass to his lips.

"Karen Jansky. They pushed Dougie out six or seven months ago."

"A woman? Not a typical choice for the brotherhood."

"She's a ballbuster: five-one, drop-dead gorgeous, gigunda kadoobas, and hard as cement. She performed a hostile takeover of the union membership and an orchiectomy on Dougie."

"Hmmm. So the mayor is in favor. And Putnam, of course. Who else?"

Peter Putnam, our local representative, would have some goodies to hand out if they were planning on taking four blocks of his district for a velodrome.

"Murray Carton and Harry Feinberg are the major developers, along with a host of small sucking remoras."

"So where's the resistance coming from?"

Pedey drank more Scotch and looked in the mirror as if trying to decide how much to tell me. We listened to the music for a few seconds—Joe Pass doing "I Got it Bad and That Ain't Good"—and then he shrugged. He might have thought being five-foot-four and three-quarters bald made him look like Dustin Pedroia, but the real Pedey wasn't that soft.

"Oh, just the little people," he cracked. "All those poor bastards who have to drive to work on the Southeast Expressway while the Mittens Romney crowd is looking for the swimming and diving venue." He set the glass down delicately. "None of it's going to make any difference, though."

"Why's that?"

His look questioned my tether to reality.

"You remember *Chinatown*? The movie? Well, it's Boston, Jake."

I reached for the Johnny Walker bottle, but he surprised me by holding up his hand and tossing a twenty on the bar.

"Nah. I think I'm depressed enough. You seem pretty chipper, though. They must have made you an offer."

"Who? What offer?"

"For the bar." He looked momentarily cheerful, that he knew something I didn't.

"You're right on the corner of that velodrome parcel," he said. "The developers are already buying up properties."

He smiled at the shock on my face and headed for the stairs. He'd spread enough sunshine for one day.

"Shit," I said.

It hadn't occurred to me the Esposito might become a casualty of the pro-Olympic movement, but as soon as I thought about it, I knew Pedey was right. None of the small and local business in this neighborhood—the bodegas, the newsstand, Mr. Giaccobi's coffee shop—were likely to survive a determined redevelopment effort. For the first time in weeks, I considered taking a drink.

13

Burton sat in a booth at Albert's Greek Pizza in Cleary Square, wondering why a mother wouldn't have told her own son his father had been murdered. To save his feelings? Kenny would have found out eventually, no matter how hard she tried to protect him. Something was tickling his funk-meter, and like all the clichés in his business, the one that said the best suspects in a murder were family members was often true.

He shook some red pepper flakes onto the last slice and folded the thin triangle to bite off the end. A son shooting his father between the eyes, though? That was a special brand of cold, and most of the family killings Burton saw were hot and messy. Kenny did not come across as anything like a cool type, nor did his mom.

Cool. Elder was cool—as much of a friend as Burton had—but his connection to Kathleen Crawford was not. He'd thought it was a good thing that she disappeared before he had to do anything more than send a copy of her rap sheet to Elder. Her history was only a dozen years deep and all the open burglary warrants made her someone no law-abiding bar owner ought to be hanging around with. And he wouldn't have been surprised to learn that she knew about Elder's inheritance from his father. A few million dollars would have given her an added incentive to hang around.

No, she was a shiny thing the world had dragged across Elder's path when he'd been vulnerable, still stuck on Susan Voisine. Burton wasn't going to wreck their friendship over it, but having her back in the mix was worrying. He hadn't met a criminal yet who didn't have an agenda.

He wiped the grease from his fingers with a bunch of paper napkins, proud of himself for not having a beer with his lunch. His phone vibrated across the Formica table. This was the call back he'd been waiting for.

"Dan Burton."

"Dipali Adams, Detective Burton. Returning your call. From the Boston Olympic Family Foundation."

He understood immediately why she didn't refer to the group by its acronym. The tunnel vision of bureaucrats never failed to amuse him.

"Thanks for calling back. I'd like to come and interview your boss. Today, if possible."

"Hmm. Haw. I don't know. As you can imagine, Mr. Wilder is a very busy man these days. I'm not sure…"

"Ms. Adams. Maybe I wasn't clear? I'm from the Homicide Division of the Boston Police Department. This is in relation to a murder investigation I'm conducting."

"OK. Hmmm. Let me see, then."

Sound of flipping pages. It must not be too modern an outfit if they were using paper calendars.

"Haw. Yes. We have an open slot from 2:20 to 2:50. Would that suit?"

"Yes. Where are you located? I only have the box number."

"Oh." She tittered. "You mean Mr. Wilder's location."

"You don't all work in the same place?"

"Hmmm, no. We're not collocated. All the organization's administrative functions must be outsourced. Per the SEC."

"Understood." Though it sounded like bullshit to him. When did powerful people pay attention to the rules? "Is Mr. Wilder's office in the financial district?"

She tittered again. He was starting to like hearing that sound.

"Oh, no. He works out of his residence. In Milton. It's on Chickatawbut Road."

Her mouth seemed to revel on the street name.

"Thank you, Dipali. You will let him know I'm coming?"

"Of course." Her voice cooled, maybe because he'd used her first name. "Good day."

He crumpled his paper plate and napkins and stuffed them in the overflowing trash can. All he needed from Wilder was some background on the two sides of the Olympic bid. He doubted Connie Boustaloudis had been killed over his civic engagement, but he needed to verify that.

He refilled his coffee and sat down with the iPad. He had an hour to kill and he needed to look into Kenny Boustaloudis's background a little more.

* * *

For a guy whom Google reported as worth several hundred millions of dollars, John T. Wilder (and every news article made sure to emphasize the T., as if there might be more than one John Wilder with that kind of money) lived in a very modest house by Milton standards, an eighties Cape sheathed in white vinyl siding with a waist-high raw wood fence around the untended front lawn.

Burton parked in the driveway that led to a detached garage, behind a twenty-year-old Mercedes wagon with rusted-out wheel wells. The first sign you were dealing with old money in New England was often the beat-to-shit vehicles the owners drove. Not having to be at work on time every morning, they could afford to keep around the very vehicle in which they'd impregnated Muffy, for nostalgia's sake if nothing else. It was also his experience that the very rich were fanatically cheap and rarely embraced much in the way of change.

He slammed the door of the Jeep loudly enough to let someone know he'd arrived, followed a path of poorly-laid pavers from Home Depot through a gate in the fence and up a short staircase to the enclosed porch. The yard out back was as wild-looking as the front, without any signs of human life like a barbecue grill or a swing set.

On the top step, Burton shaded his eyes and looked inside, but the porch was entirely in shadow. He thought he saw someone in a light-colored shirt in the dimness at the far end and rapped on the storm door. The person started and raised a hand and Burton heard an unintelligible noise he assumed was permission to enter.

"Mr. Wilder?" Burton pulled the door outward and stepped in onto the porch. "Dan Burton, BPD."

"You're late. Take off your shoes."

The figure did not turn in his chair. Burton rested his hand on his weapon and checked his watch. 2:22. He toed off his loafers.

"Not by too much."

His small joke fell with a thud.

"Any lateness is too much, Detective. I deal in nanoseconds, if you know what those are." He sounded like he doubted it, then swiveled the chair so they were face to face. "Find a seat, please. My neck hurts if I have to look up while I speak."

Wilder was in a wheel chair, an odd hybrid of a lightweight racing chair and a desk chair with arms and a high back. He held a yellow pad and pen, ready to take notes, so Burton assumed he had some function above the waist.

Burton took a dusty wicker chair that squeaked as his weight settled in.

"Tell me about Constantine Boustaloudis."

Normally, he would have warmed up an interview subject with a few softball questions, but Wilder's prickliness had irritated him.

"Who?"

Wilder wore a starched white shirt with the sleeves folded back twice over tanned and muscled forearms. Burton noticed the wheel chair wasn't powered. The man's eyes bulged, pale as egg white, and the bright tiny capillaries in his nose and across his cheeks made him wonder how much the man drank. A blanket lay across his lap.

"One of the anti-Olympic people."

"They don't have a prayer." Wilder tossed the pen and paper on the table, props abandoned. He wouldn't meet Burton's eyes and Burton wondered if he were what a psychologist might call "on the spectrum."

"A small unfunded group of everyday citizens with an ox to gore. Strictly NIMBY. If they weren't fighting this, it would be puppy mills. Or cannabis dispensaries." He took a breath and launched into what was obviously a canned speech. "The Olympics will bring this city into contention as a world-class destination. The infrastructure investment alone is going to address issues the city has been unwilling to face for decades: the state of the T, the traffic, the number of hotel rooms. And the jobs it's going to provide? The exposure on the world stage? The prestige? We should forgo all this because a high school football team will have to find a new place to practice?"

Burton didn't think it would advance the conversation to ask about the requirement that the taxpayers cover all the cost overruns. The pain of the Big Dig was too fresh.

"I'm not here to debate the politics, Mr. Wilder. Boustaloudis?"

Wilder twisted his neck to the left as if to alleviate a cramp and pouched his lips.

"A pest, a gnat stirring people up against a *fait accompli*. And something that will redound to everyone's benefit, even the masses. And wasted effort in the face of the project's inevitability."

Burton mistrusted boosterism. It was all the classes underneath the one percent who paid the price.

"Would everyone in your organization feel the same way? That Mr. Boustaloudis didn't represent much of a threat?"

"I'm the carrier of the vision here. I'm not very knowledgeable about the rank and file."

They were part of the masses, Burton assumed. He wondered how much trouble he'd get into for slapping a man in a wheel chair.

"You must have to interact with them occasionally. As difficult as that might be."

Wilder sailed past the sarcasm.

"Well. There is one fellow."

He paused. Burton noticed the narrowness of the man's emotional range, which made it clear he was about to deliver someone up as a person of interest. Deliberately? Avenging an old insult? Or some deeper machination?

"Name?"

Wilder seemed to have drifted off.

"I don't want to get anyone in trouble."

Hell you don't, Burton thought.

"We have some board members who are, shall I say, more

emotionally involved in this effort than I am. Let me talk to my board before I give you their names."

Burton left the topic for the moment.

"You yourself don't care that much about the project?" he said. "Is it the sports part you're excited about? Because beyond the money, it's going to be an enormous pain in the ass for the people who live here."

Boston sports fans came in many guises. Wilder hunched his shoulders, as if Burton had attacked him.

"My interest in this is strictly as a boon to the city I live in. Passion for athletics?" He looked down at his body in the chair. "That doesn't seem very likely, does it?"

"So you didn't consider Mr. Boustaloudis a threat to your effort, but others in your group might have. Can you give me a name?"

"I can put you in touch with our Director of Security, Mr. O'Hanian."

A Director of Security for a nonprofit? Burton was about to ask him why they needed one, but Wilder was distracted by the chime of an incoming email.

"I'm sorry, Detective. I must get back to work. Nanoseconds, you know."

He scrawled a name and number on a pink sticky note and handed it over.

"I find it unlikely in the extreme you will find any connection in my organization to Mr. Bousty—the gentleman in question—and his death. But Sanford can give you all the information we've had about threats and the like."

Threats. Burton had no more questions, though he did have the sense Wilder was throwing his security director under the bus.

"Thanks. So. Is there anything I haven't asked you that I should have? About the bid or anything else?"

Wilder had already dismissed Burton and was staring at a multicolored spreadsheet on his wide-screen monitor. He replied without looking up.

"Only that the Olympics are most certainly coming to Boston, Detective. There are too many people with too much at stake for it not to happen."

Burton let himself out the sun porch door. Wilder sounded a touch desperate, as if he'd invested something in the bid he couldn't afford to lose.

It was close enough to the cocktail hour to head for the Esposito and see if Elder had heard anything more from Kathleen. He needed to find out what, if anything, she knew about the Boustaloudis death. And maybe Elder would start taking seriously the threat that the Olympic bid meant to the Esposito.

He doubted that, though. Ever since he'd come into his father's money, Elder's interest in the bar business seemed to be waning.

14

I was rolling in a rare mood of smug satisfaction. Lunchtime in the Esposito had been at capacity. As people finished up, the sound system was driving a nice mellow playlist of guitar and piano instrumentals, not loud enough to disturb the conversation. Marina's fancy pasta special had sold out. Fewer and fewer of my regulars from a year, two years, ago, were showing up any more. There was more eating than drinking going on these days, but wasn't that what I'd been after from the beginning? That, and a civilized place to listen to jazz on the weekends. If this business stayed steady, I was going to have to hire a wait person.

My back was to the bar and I was reaching into the cooler for a bottle of beer when Burton's voice sawed through the music.

"Christ on a goddamned crutch. Wasn't it you who was bitching about wallpaper for the ears the last time I was in here? I almost had to wrestle one of those transgendered hair stylists for the stool. Is this still a bar or you promoting another of those hipster eateries?"

I uncapped the beer and slid it across the bar, not offering him a glass.

"Any news?"

"Not about your girlfriend, no. Though I did manage to achieve an even deeper insight into the ways in which the rich are very different from you and me. Excuse me. From *me*."

Burton had been giving me the needle about my father's money lately, though he'd known it was coming to me for two years.

"How's that?"

"They live in little cracker boxes on Chickatawbut Road and work on their sun porches."

He slugged some beer. I didn't have a clue what he was talking about, but I wasn't going to encourage him by asking.

"I take it you still haven't found Kathleen," I said.

I walked down the bar to collect some dirty dishes. The safest thing for her to do, I realized, was talk to Burton. He disliked her so much he'd bend over backwards to be fair. I planned to tell her that, if she ever contacted me again.

He pressed the heel of his hand against his forehead, as if he had a migraine. He wore one of his better suits today, a navy pinstripe. He didn't have any corpse visits planned.

"Low priority on my list, I'm sorry to say. Basically the party line is that she escaped from a program designed to integrate minor offenders back into the community. No one's expending much energy looking for her at this point."

Except maybe Randolph Coyne.

"Including you?" I didn't like to push him, but he was the only card I had to play. I cared enough about Kathleen to want her safe, even if I didn't want her in my life.

"Not my circus, not my monkey. Sorry." He finished off the beer and tapped the bottom of the bottle on the bar. "Different topic."

I wasn't ready to give up yet.

"What about wanting to talk to her? About the body?"

"That was not the murder scene. Pure coincidence she was there."

I frowned. If he'd dismissed her as a connection to the murder, why was he even here? Usually when he was deep into a murder investigation, I wouldn't see him at all. He was focused then, drank less, and only showed up in the Esposito once in a while for a meal and a breather.

"Then why are you here?"

He flinched microscopically—I must have sounded snappish. It was easy to forget how tender he could be, outside of his work. All of us brothers and sisters of the bottle had open wounds, soft injuries we were working to anesthetize. Because he and I were friends, sometimes I forgot to be kind.

I busied myself with a glass and the soda gun, to hide my

embarrassment, and took back the empty beer bottle.

"Don't underestimate the food in this place," he said. "I understand it's pretty good." He grinned. "I came by for a little perspective."

While I considered that, Marina carried out a large bowl of soup, a plate of bread, and a rolled-up napkin with silverware inside. As she arranged it in front of Burton, she checked the glass I'd just put in front of him, nodded when she saw it was club soda, and retreated to the kitchen without a word.

Burton turned his head to one side, watching her go as if she'd been a ghost.

"I already had lunch," he said.

"Ignore it at your peril."

He unrolled the napkin and picked out the spoon.

"You seen that Rasmussen character around?"

Marina's temporary love interest, from a year ago.

"You know I don't interfere in my employees' lives. Perspective on what?"

"Rich people. What else?"

I groaned.

"Jesus, Burton. I am not your local anthropologist."

He loved playing the dumb blue-collar kid from Charlestown who'd barely skinned through the Police Academy, but I knew better. Both his parents had been high school teachers and he'd earned a degree in American history from Middlebury, and most of a PhD at UNH before something pushed him off track. All of that happened before I knew him, and we did not have the kind of friendship that allowed me to ask questions about it.

My family had Mayflower roots and a banking business that went back to the Massachusetts Bay Colony, though the last of the wealth from that, greatly diminished, had come to me two years ago when my father died. He'd been the last of the family to run the bank as a bank before a New York hedge fund turned the Board of Directors' head and bought it out, kicking Thomas to the curb. He hadn't died of a broken heart, but being the generation who lost the product of a couple centuries of family effort had hurt. And his medical bills had eaten money, too.

"They are not, contrary to your favorite author, Burton, different."

He tasted the soup, added salt and pepper, buttered a slice of bread.

"You can say that because you're one of them, pal."

I shook my head.

"That money isn't mine—I just haven't figured out what to do with it yet. If I were that kind of rich, I'd be someplace warm."

"Attitude, then? Upbringing? Assumptions. You all have this thing."

"That's fairly precise."

He pointed the soup spoon at me.

"That's exactly what I'm talking about. Right there. Smartass, know-it-all, I'm-better-than-you-are shit."

He and I had variations of this conversation constantly. Burton was firm in his belief that people with large sums of money were not susceptible to the same pressures, moods, pains, and wounds as everyone else. I don't know why I kept thinking I could change his mind.

"Which rich guy are we shitting on today?"

"John T. Wilder."

The name was familiar, but I couldn't place it. Burton put down the spoon and picked up the bowl to drink.

"Head of the Boston Olympic Family Foundation," he said. "Which acronymizes very poorly."

"Is that a word?"

"Boff?"

"Never mind. He runs the committee?"

"Started it his own self, I believe. And also owns a boatload of bucks. Works from home, a financial type. From a wheelchair."

The chair made the connection for me.

"Oh. John Wilder."

"John T. Wilder."

"I didn't know he'd gotten rich, but I know how he wound up in a wheelchair. He was two years ahead of me at Exeter. He was working as a lifeguard summers at Carson Beach. They were towing in a boat and the rope snapped. Wrapped itself around his chest."

Burton winced.

"Owie."

"Gets worse. He was an All-NEPSAC quarterback with a full ride to Clemson that fall."

"And now he's rich."

"Some flavor of quantitative analysis," I said. "Hedging grain futures or something like that."

"See what I mean? Right there, you've got four or five words us poor shmucks don't know the meaning of."

"Fuck you. So, he's rich. His group connects to your murder?"

"I don't see how he could have killed Boustaloudis himself, but he was pretty intense about the bid. His organization's a place to start anyway."

"You always assume the rich guy's the one with the nefarious motive?"

Burton toyed with his butter knife.

"Maybe because ninety-five per cent of the time when a murder isn't scumbag on scumbag, it's about greed. A quality I've noticed in abundance in our native wealthy."

I couldn't tell if he was directing his disdain for the rich at me now, but we'd argued about money and morals too often for me to take it personally.

"Best guess? Assuming the opinion of someone with money in the bank is still valid?"

He waved his hand at me to go on.

"Wilder is rich enough and prominent enough that the politicians behind the bid think his name's going to draw in other rich people. The pols sure as shit aren't spending their own money. And there's always a certain amount of weenie-wagging going on among the wealthy, especially the men. Competing for attention. Just entering a bid is going to cost a bundle."

"You think he might order someone killed if they got in his way?"

I lifted my shoulders, made sure the sleeve of my shirt didn't rise to expose where Randolph had carved me.

"Anything's possible, but it seems unlikely. If he were that much of a hardass, you would have heard more about him. The press loves stories about nasty businessmen—feeds the populist narrative."

Burton looked at me like I was waving a protest sign, then stood up.

"Good soup. Thank Marina for me."

And he headed for the stairs, having extracted what he needed from me, apparently.

"Asshole," I muttered. "No manners at all."

15

There were two reasons why I didn't say anything to Burton about Randolph Coyne returning: I didn't want to divert his attention while he was working on a murder, and I didn't want to strain our friendship any more over the fact of Kathleen and the fact that she'd been the one to draw Coyne and Donald Maldonado into my orbit. My forearm throbbed, as if agreeing.

Marina was cleaning up the kitchen after the lunch rush and she must have been in reasonably good spirits because I heard a minimum of clashing pots. The salsa music did leak out enough to compete with Stan Getz.

The Esposito rested in that pleasant anticipatory time between busy hours and I was content, for once. The coolers were full, the bits and pieces of bar service all prepared, the glasses clean and dry.

I'd tamed the Rancilio into producing an acceptable cappuccino, and I was chasing the last peaks of milk foam around the inside of the cup and reading about Red Sox spring training when the upstairs door rattled open. Every time I'd been alone here the last week, something strange or dangerous had happened. I heard myself channeling Dorothy Parker.

"'What fresh hell can this be?'"

The street door swung shut again, blotting out the sun, and only then did I realize the light bulb at the top of the stairs had burned out. But the cadence of the first footsteps down those noisy metal stairs told me who was there and my chest swelled, joy and fear.

Susan hop-skipped the rest of the way down the stairs, emerging from the shadows about a third of the way. Her round face looked tentative, like she was walking into a party where there was no one she knew.

"How's the food in this joint?" Her whiskey-rough voice—though I'd never seen her drink anything but vodka—cut through the Getz solo.

Her eyes, the pale blue green of ocean, focused on me, watching for my reaction. I felt nothing but pleasure, the click in my chest signifying her return, a reconnection, an opportunity. Her boot heels rapped on the linoleum as she walked across the floor and as always, I couldn't believe such a small person could generate such a presence.

"Susan Voisine. As I live and breathe."

My pleasure overflowed—she was back where I could see her, talk to her, touch. Only now did I accept that I'd believed I would never see her again, that she'd gone back to Oregon for good.

She looked around.

"Place looks good."

"Just paint and wallpaper."

She could barely see over the top of the bar, slinging her pale leather bag onto the top and hoisting herself up on a stool. Her purple plaid shirt was open at the neck, and I found myself staring at the pale freckled skin there. I was relieved she hadn't come right around the bar for a hug—she would have seen my knees shaking.

"Still," she said. "Looks nicer than I remember. A Cape Codder, maybe?"

It gave me something to do with my hands. As usual when I got into an emotional situation, I fumbled for something to say. But God, I was glad she was back.

I assembled her cocktail and slid it in front of her, waved off the bills.

"Welcome back. You here for a while?" I didn't say 'home,' thinking that might be pushing things, but I wondered why I always blurted out the one question I dreaded the answer to.

"Henri." She picked up the drink and slugged half of it in a swallow. Her stress was evident. Because she was small, alcohol crept up on her quickly.

The music moved into some Charlie Parker and I was not in a bebop mood. I shut it down.

"He's OK?"

Her father had been a tenant in my apartment building until he started showing signs of dementia. Susan moved into the apartment for a while, after she got Henri into an assisted living place in Roslindale, then ran away to Oregon a month after that. I still wasn't sure what I'd done.

"Tests." Her voice gasped at the end of the word. "They're thinking it might be pancreatic cancer."

"Ah, shit." I held out my hands and she clasped them, but only for a moment. "I'm sorry."

Her looks had changed since the last time I saw her. The ash-blonde hair was shorn to maybe half an inch all around, and her skin had developed a softer, almost translucent cast, maybe a product of the always-humid Pacific coast climate. She dressed more quietly, too, earth tones and looser fits, but her eyes were still the same Mediterranean shade. And, of course, she was still only four feet tall.

"So," she said.

She was as uncomfortable as I was, though my unease was tinged with mild guilt over the interlude with Kathleen, silly as that sounds.

"Not hearing from you was hard," I said. "I'm going to have to take this a little slow—I'm not sure what you want me to say."

She twiddled the little straw in her drink, remixing the juice and vodka.

"I know I can't say I'm sorry and have you believe it. But I am. There's no question I was running away."

I unpacked my memories of the eight weeks or so two years ago, when Burton and I were engaged with the death of Alison Somers, before Susan escaped to the West Coast. It had been an emotional, tempestuous time, and though I believed eventually we would have settled into a manageable way of being together, she'd taken off before we could try.

"No question." I thought about making myself another coffee, but I didn't want to strain the thin connection we'd made. "You're staying at Henri's?"

I maintained the polite fiction the apartment belonged to her father, though she'd been paying the rent on it for the past two years. The fact that she'd kept the place was the one reason I hadn't given up on her altogether.

She nodded.

"It wasn't all fear, you know. Not mine, anyway."

I let that pass.

"I could walk downstairs and cook you breakfast some morning."

She shook her head.

"I'm here but I'm not here, Elder. You know?" Her hand, cool from the glass, crept across the bar to touch mine. "I don't have the capacity at the moment."

That should have been a relief, but all it did was tighten the knot in my gut.

"That's fine. But in the interest of full disclosure…"

She held up a tiny hand.

"Even if something comes out of this, Elder? Let's leave the past out of it. We don't even really have a present right now."

For some reason, all I could think of was who she might have been with in Oregon.

"Fine. You know where I am when you're ready. Days and nights."

She finished the drink and looked at me.

"You're pissed off. I get it. I would be, too."

She hitched herself down off the stool and slung the leather bag over her shoulder. As she started for the stairs, she looked back over her shoulder and grinned when she caught me admiring her rear.

"I'm hopeful," I said.

"I'm glad to know that. But I didn't come back to Boston on your account."

16

Sanford O'Hanian, the Boston Olympics Family Foundation's security director, had an office in their headquarters in Roslindale Square. Burton thought the brick building on Washington Street with the soaped windows and the drainpipe dripping rust down the brick storefront didn't promote much of an image, but it was probably some kind of proletariat feint by the organizers, trying to make the group look more grassroots than it was. Or maybe the organizers were too cheap to set up offices downtown.

He pulled open the door and felt a blast of air conditioning. In March. In Boston.

"It takes the humidity out of the air." The elegant woman of seventy or so behind the front desk must have caught his skeptical look. Her long gray hair was swirled and pinned into a tight chignon, and she wore a shift dress that was too simple not to be expensive. Her forehead bore a crescent-shaped bindi with a small black dot beside it. She was too rich-looking and pulled together to be anything but a volunteer.

"But it's a dry heat, right?" he said. "Would you be Dipali Adams?"

She gave him a dry uncomprehending look, as if she might be one of those rare Bostonians who didn't care for sarcasm. The room had the crisp odor of ozone.

"I'm Mrs. Adams, yes."

"I'm here to see Mr. O'Hanian."

She picked up a paper calendar—Dipali not being a child of the digital revolution, apparently—and pretended to find something in the empty time blocks for today.

91

"Did you have an appointment?"

He groaned inwardly.

"Mr. Wilder assured me he would call. I wouldn't presume on anyone's valuable time otherwise."

If Wilder hadn't announced him as a cop, he wouldn't do so either. The surprise sometimes made people careless. Dipali's look was skeptical, but it was a toss-up whether she didn't believe him or she needed O'Hanian to have something to do.

"Let me see if he's available."

She picked up the phone, looked at the multi-button panel, and hung it up again, stood and walked through the door behind her desk. The dress was tight enough to show her bones.

A deep voice rumbled, counterpoint to Dipali's lighter alto. Burton stepped into the doorway after her.

"Mr. O'Hanian?" he said.

Dipali sniffed and slipped sideways around Burton, back to her post. He smelled cinnamon.

"Who the fuck are you?"

Sanford O'Hanian half-stood to look over the top of a beige fabric-covered cubicle wall. His head, bald as a shaved coconut, barely cleared the top edge.

"Dan Burton." He stepped around the end of the panel with his hand out.

But before he could identify himself as police, O'Hanian stepped forward, pushing his chest into Burton's space. He was built like an offensive lineman only shorter, maybe five-eight, and must have weighed a solid three-twenty, that hard rubbery fat you could bounce punches off all day long without doing much damage. He wore a vintage Patriots jersey and long nylon shorts tight enough to chafe his thighs. He had a dark two-day stubble and red eyes.

Burton didn't carry a baton any more, but he did move his hand toward his weapon. O'Hanian looked more like a hoodlum than any security professional Burton had ever met.

"You're the security director?"

Burton's skepticism irked O'Hanian, who raised his hands as if he was going to come around and chop block Burton. Burton decided it was time to identify himself. He raised his shield.

"I'm with the Boston Police, Sanford. Homicide."

O'Hanian reached for the badge but Burton had seen that move before. He held it up at eye level for a couple seconds, then put it away.

"I didn't kill anyone," O'Hanian said.

Burton noticed he didn't ask the usual question: who got killed? More perplexing, though, was why an upper crust Brahmin like Wilder would have hired this knucklehead for anything more complicated than taking out the trash.

"Good to know. Mr. Wilder said you might be able to help me out with a few questions. An investigation I'm working on."

"J. T.? Nice dude, for a crip." O'Hanian receded into his cubicle, the sole decoration a calendar from the Boston Symphony, and sat down. "What can I tell you?"

Burton settled gingerly into a scummy plastic bucket chair. This was his last pair of clean suit pants and he needed to get one more day out of them at least.

"I know this Olympic thing has been a hot button for a lot of people in the city." He opened a notebook and balanced it on his knee. "Can I assume that, as security director, you have a sense of which of your opponents might be a little over the top? Anyone with violent tendencies or a little too loosely wrapped about what's going on?"

While he spoke, he parsed O'Hanian's appearance and realized he reminded him of the younger gangsters and wannabes he saw around town: reflexively aggressive, poorly dressed, without much in the way of manners. At least most of the old goombahs, the Patriarcas and the Angiullos, were polite in public and dressed well.

He shook himself out of the nostalgic thoughts as O'Hanian reached into his desk drawer. The deliberate way he did it and the attention he paid to Burton's reaction confirmed he'd had some experience with the police.

"J. T. called me, actually." He slid out a piece of lined paper with seven names written out in an elegant cursive. Someone in the office—Dipali?—had gone to Catholic school.

"The first four on the list are people in that anti-group." O'Hanian poked a hot dog sized finger at them. "The other ones are members of BOFF who might be a touch overcommitted to the cause."

His grin tried to ingratiate him.

"Now tell me which ones have the stones to kill someone," Burton said.

"Besides me, you mean?" O'Hanian laughed like it was a joke. "That kind of depends on who got killed, doesn't it?"

"Constantine Boustaloudis." Burton was watching for a reaction and thought he saw a dark flicker in O'Hanian's eyes. "Owned a drug store in Hyde Park."

O'Hanian picked up a pen and scratched a line through one of the names on the list.

"You won't need to talk to him, then."

Burton didn't like the casual way he took the news.

"Do I know you, Sanford? You look familiar."

O'Hanian's dark brown eyes flickered again, fast as a bird's wing passing. He was afraid of something. He shook his head.

"I don't think so, Detective."

"You grow up here?"

"In Boston, you mean?"

Burton gave him the quit-fucking-with-me look.

"Nossir. New Orleans area, thereabouts. It's a lot warmer down there."

His smile turned obsequious, less arrogant, but it didn't scratch Burton's itch. New Orleans didn't square with a Babe Parilli vintage jersey.

"So how did you come to be here in our fair city, then?"

O'Hanian was struggling with either temper or nerves, fingers knitted so tight the knuckles paled, shoulders hunched.

"What difference does that make? I thought you were here to talk about a murder."

"I am, Sanford. I am. So, please answer the question."

"I have a second cousin in Charlestown I grew up with. He helped me get this job."

Recognition dropped into Burton's brain like a pack of cigarettes falling out of a vending machine.

"You're Mickey Barksdale's cousin? You guys share some, uh, facial features."

He'd been about to say they had the same ugly mug.

"So. You like Boston?" Burton now had a connection between BOFF and organized crime in Boston, for whatever that was.

Mickey Barksdale was nominally the leader of the Thompson Square Boyz, a minor offshoot from the dregs of the Winter Hill Gang, most of whom had been hosed off various sidewalks well before Whitey Bulger was recaptured. In the truest criminal spirit of the Town, Mickey was both greedy and vicious, if completely loyal to the people in his neighborhood. There was also a version of history in which Burton owed Mickey his life, which he didn't like to think about.

The big question was what Mickey might do with a link to BOFF and its politics, none of which seemed likely to benefit his organization in any way. Burton was also certain J. T. Wilder had no idea of the connection and probably had never even met Sanford O'Hanian.

Who was currently having a hard time sitting still, his normal physical responses to threat stymied by Burton's status as a cop and the fact he was trapped by the desk.

"I like it fine." His voice pulled a slight semi-quaver. "Except for the cold. Are we done here? Because I have a meeting I have to attend."

Burton reached across the desk and wiped his forefinger over Sanford's naked pate, flicked the sweat away.

"Better dry off before you do, chum. A lot of people interpret sweating as a sign of guilt. You're not guilty of anything, are you?"

O'Hanian shut down then, nothing left to say.

Burton took the list, folded and pocketed it, hearing the "Fuck you" that struggled to escape from O'Hanian's mouth. Out in the foyer, Dipali sat erect as a queen, working on a big book of crossword puzzles. She looked up as he passed and spoke out of the side of her mouth.

"The man is a pluperfect asshole."

He paused at her desk.

"You noticed," he said, giving her his best smile as he walked out the door.

17

I was getting the gnawing feeling something important might be happening outside my little world and the fact that I was on the same old schedule and stuck in the same old place every day meant it was passing me by. Marina didn't confide in me as much as she had, now that she and Burton were getting along again, and I was feeling a little isolated.

I hoped she wasn't planning to quit on me, now that some of my father's money had gotten to her. If she did, I might be screwed. I had no illusions the current success of the Esposito had anything to do with the cocktails I mixed.

It was a quiet Friday morning and she'd brought me a bowl of soup and bread before we opened at eleven-thirty. I was enjoying the quiet, partly because the weekend nights had gotten busy and I knew what was coming. I'd hired a guitar player named Marcus Roeham to play tonight, and though he wouldn't draw the size crowd a bigger band would, business would be brisk.

Charlie Haden was working the bridge to "Body and Soul" when the street door squeaked.

"Open in half an hour," I called up to rectangle of light. "Come back and have lunch."

Steps continued down the stairs. I sighed and shook my head. The Esposito still attracted a dedicated day drinker from time to time, someone who liked to celebrate the morning with a pop or two. I walked over to meet him at the bottom of the stairs.

"Mr. Darrow?"

The voice was high and hesitant, product of a weedy man about thirty years old. He looked like Bill Gates before all that money rounded him out and sanded down his rough edges: rumpled cotton wash pants, a short-sleeved plaid shirt, round-toed black shoes and white socks. I expected to see a plastic protector peeking out of his pocket.

Which meant I was unprepared for the moment when he pulled a long-barreled revolver out of the back of his pants and pointed it at me.

"Let's sit down and have a chat, shall we?"

I glanced back at the kitchen. Pots rattled, the refrigerator opened and closed, Marina's salsa played from her tiny radio.

"There's nothing in the till except what I start the day with," I said. "Fifty bucks in change."

I was having trouble breathing past the clutch in my chest, caused by the gun. He gave me a pitying look.

"I'm not here to take your money, Elder. But let's try and keep this civilized. I don't want to make any noises that would alarm your cook."

I had little trouble imagining what kind of noise he was talking about. I pointed to a four-top to the left of the stairs and against the wall, as far from the bar as we could get. He was correct that I didn't want Marina involved in this at all.

We sat, me with my back to the wall, the gunfighter's position. He rested the pistol on the table, the barrel pointed safely in another direction. Then he smiled, a goofy gap-toothed grin that reminded me of that red-headed kid on the Andy Griffith Show.

"You are Elder Darrow?"

"Guilty. But you didn't have to point a gun at me to find that out."

He spun the big revolver around on the tabletop so I could see the empty cylinder. My chest loosened. Unless he was stupid enough to carry a round under the hammer, the pistol was safe.

"And you, I suppose, would be Donny Maldonado."

"Donald. Please."

He pushed his black-framed spectacles back up his nose.

"I wanted to meet someone unhinged enough to deny my friend Randolph Coyne something he'd asked for politely."

Rage started to bubble in my chest. At the same time, my forearm started itching and my ribs ached.

"Politely? I don't think so."

Maldonado was giving me the weakest eye-fuck I'd ever received. The freckles and teeth made it laughable.

"I'm afraid that's about as polite as Randolph gets."

My conscious mind told me I should be taking this more seriously, but down deep, I was trying not to laugh. An unloaded gun, a hoodlum who looked like a New Hampshire farm boy? All I had to offer him was what I'd told Randolph while he was beating on me.

"As I told your henchman, Donny, I have had no contact with Kathleen Crawford since she disappeared on me, months ago. Other than the fact, of which I informed Randolph, that she showed up here a couple days ago, borrowed the keys to my apartment, took a shower, stole some clothes and cash, and left for parts unknown."

"Do you enjoy running your own establishment, Mr. Darrow?" Maldonado's tone turned pissy and hectoring. "Because I'm getting the sense that more personal means of motivation might be effective."

The threat froze me, but I tried to laugh it off.

"We're underground here, Donny. In a concrete basement under a brick warehouse. Pretty hard to set us on fire or blow us up."

Actually, I had no idea what was possible in that line, but I'd learned over and over, dealing with shifty contractors, dishonest building inspectors, even hoodlums while I was renovating the place: you couldn't roll over for anyone. Everyone thought they were owed a piece of what you'd done.

Maldonado buttoned up his mouth and I saw where Randolph had developed the prissy face.

"Much too crude," he said. "I was thinking more along the lines of what a pain safety inspections could be: fire, health department, egress, and so on. And I have to assume you have a mortgage on the place?"

As the son of a banker and an entrepreneur myself, I understood how effective a quasi-official harassment could be. It interested me that Donny—excuse me, *Donald*—was a much more sophisticated criminal than his cousin Ricky had been.

"How is Ricky, by the way?"

Donald's eyes went almost black and showed me the first glimpse of the dark nature behind the goofy façade. Without hearing another word, I could tell Icky Ricky was getting no love from that quarter.

"As healthy as can be expected, given his lifestyle. He's living in South Beach."

I pictured egg-shaped Ricky on the front porch of one of those grand old crumbling hotels, rocking in a chair alongside all the blue-haired ladies, ogling the skimpily dressed women walking by.

"Elder. I need your help and you need mine. Your paramour—former or not—stole some material from me that is absolutely critical to a business venture I'm involved in here in Boston." He patted the pistol absentmindedly. "It is important that I establish myself here. If you can't deliver either Ms. Crawford or the stolen material, I'm afraid things are going to get ugly, as my grandad used to say. You have me at my wits' end here."

Funny, but his words sounded more desperate than his attitude.

Something shiny and heavy cleaved the air by my ear and stuck in the wall next to Maldonado's head. Both of us levitated. An eight-inch boning knife quivered in the wall board.

I looked over my shoulder and saw Marina standing a dozen feet away with her arms crossed, short hair in spikes, her look fierce as fire. Maldonado reached for his pistol but I got there first.

"I think that's your cue to leave, Donny."

He held out his hand for the gun. I shook my head.

"Another time," I said. "I'd leave while you can."

He headed for the stairs, not before trying his pathetic stare-down again. I ignored it and dropped the pistol's cylinder out. There had been one cartridge ready to feed in under the hammer.

"Thank you," I said to Marina, as the street door sighed shut.

She burst into tears.

18

Burton climbed into his Jeep and sat for a minute. Aside from the list of pro- and anti- fanatics O'Hanian had given him—which had been suspiciously close to hand when Burton asked for them—the only new information he had was the connection between the BOFF and the upper tier of organized crime in the city.

They probably should have called it *dis*organized crime, at least since the days of the Boys on the Hill, when Raymond Patriarca ran the New England Mafia out of Federal Hill in Providence. The criminal enterprise nowadays showed little cohesion, a general zeitgeist of every man for himself. And it was every man, still a male-dominated world. But roles were fluid and power transferred back and forth as easily as the swing of a baseball bat or the pull of a trigger.

And the last person Burton wanted anything to do with was Mickey Barksdale. Despite how he'd saved Burton's life on the ballfield near the old Navy Yard, all the neighborhood ties dissolved when you were on different sides of the law, despite, or maybe because of, what a couple FBI agents had done while working with Whitey Bulger. Though he didn't spend too much time in Charlestown these days, Burton knew memories ran long. You could still start an argument in a bar by mentioning bussing.

He turned on the ignition. The single gunshot to Boustaloudis's head implied an execution rather than a hot-blooded murder. And maybe this had nothing to do with Mickey—cold wasn't his normal operating temperature.

Burton's stomach rumbled. He hadn't eaten since this morning.

Any meet with Mickey would have to wait until he ate. There was nothing in the apartment's refrigerator except beer, hot sauce, coffee, and some leftover Pad Kee Maow. And he wanted to see Marina, remind her that he was still around. He pointed the car up Washington Street and headed into the city.

He parked in the alley behind the building, next to Elder's Cougar, and tried the Esposito's back door. It wasn't locked and he walked inside, down the short corridor past Elder's office into the steamy kitchen, seeing Marina working the grill and plating meals as if she had four hands. He admired the economy of motion and, secondarily, her ass, then stepped up to where she'd see him in her peripheral vision.

Her face was mottled and tear-stained, her eyes pink.

"Marina. What?"

She shook her head and kept moving between the sandwich bar and the grill.

Elder's back was to the kitchen door. He was hanging clean wine glasses in an overhead rack, water drops sparkling in the lights. Up on the tiny stage, a guitar player was plugging in his amp. Half a dozen tables were full, seven or eight people along the bar.

He stepped out and pushed Elder's shoulder.

"The fuck is going on?"

Elder turned with his fists clenched. Burton tended to forget his friend could fight. He'd faced down some tough people in the early days. He relaxed when he saw Burton.

"What?"

"What happened to Marina?"

He knew Elder wouldn't have hurt her, but the frustration of the day was boiling up, pushing at his temper. Elder would forgive him for acting like an asshole, though. What good was a friend you couldn't piss off once in a while?

Elder exhaled and turned to rack the rest of the glasses, raising a palm to a wide-shouldered young guy at the bar who looked ready to jump in. He shoved the empty dishwasher rack underneath the machine.

"You want a beer? Or coffee?"

Burton read something off in Elder's reaction, too, and wondered what had happened.

"It is after working hours."

Elder checked first to see that everyone at the bar was adequately provisioned, then pulled two Heinekens out of the cooler and popped the caps. First weird thing: Elder was going to drink with him? And second—while he was working? He rarely did that.

Burton pointed at the bottles.

"Don't go down that road on my account."

Elder tucked the bottles' necks between his fingers and led Burton to an open table away from the stage, where the guitar player noodled some chords. Elder sat down and pushed one of the beers at Burton.

"I need to clear you up on a couple things. Including about Kathleen."

Burton felt his mouth tighten. He hadn't liked the woman when Elder first met her and liked her even less when she disappeared on him. He'd been assuming her being present when Boustaloudis's body was found had been a fluke, but maybe not.

Elder looked at his face, sipped the beer, winced at it.

"I know you don't have any use for her. Just listen to me."

He unfolded the whole story, the first visit from Randolph Coyne, Kathleen's borrowing the apartment key, then disappearing with his money. Randolph's second visit, the beating and the knife work, then Donald Maldonado showing up to threaten him.

"She threw a knife at him?"

Burton felt proud—he'd witnessed her temper, but he'd never been frightened by it. Maybe he should be.

"God knows where she learned to do it," Elder said. "But she probably saved my ass. And she's been crying about it ever since."

"Shock. Emotional backlash. What's with all the gangster interest in you all of a sudden?"

"That would be in Kathleen, through me." Disgusted, Elder left the beer on the table. "They think I'm hiding her. And whatever she stole from Maldonado."

"And you have no idea where she is? Or what it is she stole?"

"No on both counts. The night you came over to look at the bloodstain? I haven't seen her since then."

Burton nodded.

"The other thing." Elder shoved the bottle away. "Maldonado and Coyne made it sound like they're trying to establish themselves here, take over what Ricky had."

Burton took a long pull of the bitter beer.

"Really. Don't you think Mickey Barksdale might have something unpleasant to say about that?"

"That's your sandbox. Not mine. Though Donny seems marginally more competent than Ricky was."

Burton hmm-ed.

"Man still caused a lot of damage."

"Well, Donny's threats to the bar were more white-collar, like he could fuck me up with the bank, maybe the city. Does he have that kind of juice?"

Burton chased a flash of insight but couldn't catch up to it.

"No idea. I suppose if he does get himself connected locally, he might. Any idea what it is he lost to Kathleen?"

Elder shook his head.

"Unless it had something to do with what Ricky was doing before. Otherwise, there's no there there."

The guitar player's tunings squealed feedback through the sound system and both of them shuddered. Silence dropped on the room like a hatchet, then the conversations restarted.

"I love it when you go all literary on me," Burton said. "You of all people know how unbelievably small-time Ricky was. And not connected at all to the rest of OC in the state."

In fact, Ricky had almost been a casualty of that group of hoods when he ripped off the wrong van full of pot.

"This Maldonado," Elder said. "He comes across as a nerd, but he's got a nasty core. Projects like a doofus and waves guns around. I think he uses Randolph for everything that involves hands-on."

Elder hadn't given him any details of his encounter with Coyne, but Burton noticed he was moving stiffly. Maybe Randolph had been by to do a little talking with his hands.

"Kathleen seems to be the key, though," he said.

Elder stiffened.

"I know you don't like her, but she's been all right with me. Except for the stealing the money part. And if she does have what Maldonado's after, she's in jeopardy. You find her, you might also find out what's so important about what it is."

"She is a fugitive," Burton said.

"I'm not lying to you. I do not know where she is."

A bell rang out in the kitchen and Elder stood up and headed out back.

"Touchy, touchy. I believe you, ace. I was just thinking out loud. What I meant was, if I can find her, I have a reason to hold her. Legally. Whether she wants the protection or not."

Though he was still seventy-thirty in favor of Elder knowing where she was.

Elder emerged from the kitchen with plates stacked up both arms and dealt them out to people waiting for food. He refreshed drinks, then came back to the table, though he didn't sit.

"What about the Olympic thing?" he said. "You getting anywhere with that?"

Burton shrugged. "You care about that?"

"They're talking about razing the entire block. Including this building."

"The velodrome thing?"

Elder nodded. "I'm trying to decide how worried I should get. Sometimes these plans are all talk."

Burton finished his beer. "Can't help you there. You do know the money guys in this town usually get what they want."

"Well. It's got to be a couple years out, right?"

Burton stood up, the beer singing protest songs in his empty stomach. He decided he needed to go somewhere else to eat. "I'll let you know if I hear anything. But I'm really only working the murder."

Elder picked up the empty, nodded. "If I hear a word from Kathleen, I'll let you know."

"You'd better." Burton headed for the kitchen. "You think she's calmed down yet?"

"Your guess is as good as mine."

Burton headed out of the Esposito through the fluorescent brightness of the kitchen, wondering if anything he could say would help. She'd grown up in a tough neighborhood, too, not far from here, but that could have made her more sensitive to the violence than hardening her to it. She was a big part of the Esposito's success, and Elder was good about letting her know. Working here had helped her build the confidence to move out of her mother's house, something she and Burton both wanted before he screwed up the whole thing a few months ago. And then again last week.

If he'd been going to fall for someone after divorcing the vicious Sharon, he wouldn't have thought it would be a short sallow stringy woman with muscled-up forearms and big hands. What attracted him finally was her practical outlook on the world, a relentless work ethic and, her mother aside, the independence of a cat.

"Marina."

He pitched his voice into a gap in the salsa playing on the radio. She was wiping down counters with her back to him, but her shoulders rose, so he knew she heard him.

"I'm sorry," he said. "I was acting pretty shitty. It was thoughtless."

She turned and glared at him, not crying any more. Her cheeks were splotchy.

"What you were was drunk on your ass. After you promised."

He held up his hands.

"No excuses. I don't know if it makes any difference now. But I was wrong not to apologize. I do now."

She inspected him, as if testing his sincerity. She nodded, once.

"And you did a good thing today," he said. "For Elder."

She flushed.

"You're hungry, aren't you?" she said.

Relief flowed through him like a warm wind. Nothing was fixed, but it could be getting better.

19

Kathleen wasn't too proud of how she'd done it, but she'd winkled enough cash out of Ted's wallet to buy herself a ticket to New Orleans. She walked off the plane at Louis Armstrong Airport, up the humid jetway into the gate area, past clots of people with multicolored beads strung around their sunburned necks and holding plastic glasses with the dregs of neon blue and green drinks. Inside the terminal itself, the air conditioning was down to polar levels. Outside in the heat, she stopped long enough to stuff the fleece she'd worn on the plane into the cheap nylon duffel she'd bought at Logan.

The airport shuttle was pulling away as she reached the stop, but she slapped the tail of the van hard enough for the driver to stop. He got out, limped around to the end of the vehicle, and stowed her duffle as carefully as if it were a Louis Vuitton suitcase.

"Which hotel, miss?"

She loved that everyone she ran into down here seemed easy and kind, and rarely in a hurry. Unlike up North.

"Marriott on Canal Street." She passed him a ten dollar bill and he thanked her and handed her up into the van.

The lobby of the hotel was chaos, but she'd chosen it because it was one of the largest convention venues in the city. A month past Mardi Gras, the crowds were somewhat smaller, but no less subdued. Parades were scheduled for St. Patrick's Day, not that anyone in this town needed an excuse to party. The back of the seat in the van held a poster advertising the Saturn Club with the post-Katrina mantra: "Rebuilding New Orleans one party at a time."

She checked in using a card she'd slipped out of Ted at the Mobil

106

station's wallet, rode the elevator to the seventeenth floor, and tossed her bag on the bed. She had some minimal toiletries and fresh underwear, and she could buy a cheap T-shirt in one of the tourist shops for her flight home in the morning. She wouldn't be carrying anything back the TSA would get riled up about.

Slipping the room key in her pocket, she put the Do Not Disturb sign on the door knob and descended. The din in the high-ceilinged atrium was deafening, and she hustled out the Canal Street door to escape it, turned left, then left again down Decatur.

The thickness of the air after eight or ten months up north almost overwhelmed her and it was hard to believe she'd ever been comfortable here. There were good reasons why everyone walked and talked slow and no one got too excited about anything. Which was what made it a good home base for her, that, and the fact that a certain acceptance of lawlessness prevailed, even among the churchgoers. She wondered if Elder had ever been here and, if so, whether he'd liked it. Probably not—the man was not long on ease or spontaneity.

She walked past the station house for the New Orleans Fire Department's Second District and turned into an alley a block and half beyond. Like so many of the niches and nooks off the main drags in the Quarter, the alley smelled like old piss, fresh vomit, and spilled booze. She couldn't help herself. She smiled.

Forty feet in, another smaller alley cut off at a right angle. The buildings didn't quite brush her shoulders, but they seemed to lean in. She reached a row of low padlocked garages, more like storage units. You couldn't get a vehicle bigger than a motor scooter around those corners.

Once she recovered the item she'd stolen from Donny Maldonado, she could decide whether returning it to him would get him off her back, or if she could hold it against future concessions. She'd be much safer with it in her hot little hand, regardless.

She reached number 19, which had a brass reinforcing plate around the hasp, and opened the padlock with the key she'd managed to keep on her person the entire time she was in jail. She pulled the green wooden door sideways with a squeal of the tracks and stepped inside. A cotton string brushed her face and she pulled on it, lighting a single bulb on a wire.

Her throat closed and she gasped. The unit was empty. All of the antiques she'd hoarded from her jobs, all the clothes, books, and tools she'd stored before leaving the city were gone, including the chiffonier where she used to store Maldonado's object of desire. The place was as empty as a whorehouse on Easter morning, all the way out to its water-stained walls.

* * *

She stood there loose-jawed on the damp concrete floor, the green flashes of a migraine flickering out at the edges of her vision. This could not have happened. She'd rented the space under a false name, not the one she'd been jailed in, paid two years in cash in advance, and whenever she visited—as seldom as possible and always at odd hours—she always watched for anyone following. The whole time she'd been on the run from Donald Maldonado, especially in jail, she'd comforted herself with the thought of her stash, this fifteen years' worth of the curated proceeds of a life of burglary. Losing it left an abyss inside her she didn't know what to do with—the idea of starting over from zero made her want to throw up.

A white envelope thumbtacked to the inside of the door bore her full name, her birth name, across the front in nun-approved cursive. If the thieves knew her real name, she already knew who was responsible for this.

She ripped down the envelope and tore it open.

Dearest Kathleen—You have driven me to wits' end. No doubt this terrible surprise will convince you that I know you hold what belongs to me. I'm uninterested in these baubles and furbelows you've stolen from other people, but knowing they're important to you means I take delight in destroying them. Signed with an elaborate *D*.

She snorted, stung. If she'd known then what she knew now, she wouldn't have gone near the little red A-frame in the woods near Stannard, Vermont, last winter. From the outside, it had looked like another blue-collar ski chalet—they weren't too far from Craftsbury—

poorly insulated, cheaply built, abandoned for half the year. She'd been waitressing at the little bakery in town, hiding out and resting up from a busy summer of burglaries down South. Considering Hanover, New Hampshire, as a place to investigate.

The two-Escalade caravan had caught her attention as it pulled past the front window of the bake shop and stopped at the corner for the town's one stoplight. Both vehicles had Florida plates and their suspensions rode low, the tires slightly flattened by the weight of the cargo. They parked outside the hardware store, which also sold guns, and she glimpsed three of the riders: long black topcoats, low shoes, no hats or gloves. City boys, held together by hair gel and attitude.

Kathleen's rest period in Vermont was partly self-inflicted. She'd had a bit of bad luck in southern Louisiana, and an old woman who was supposed to be out of town had instead been in bed with a cold when Kathleen and her crew were backing up the truck. Kathleen had rabbit-punched the dowager to shut her up, but the woman was a distant cousin of the mayor, and say what you wanted about the Crescent City and its environs, blood does run thicker than the Mississippi. Since Katrina and the terrible flooding around Baton Rouge, people down there seemed more united than before. Kathleen had escaped on a quick flight to Atlanta with a fake ID. The woman's jewelry had been real, however.

The Escalade boys drove back past the coffee shop the next morning, minus the loads. Three days passed after she saw them head for the 89 interchange and the route back to the city. She drove past the A-frame at random hours of the day and night to check for lights or smoke from the chimney. By the time she convinced herself it was safe, a cold front had moved in, and on the night of the new moon when she went out to reconnoiter, the temperature was ten above zero, the air dry as a desert.

She left the borrowed Subaru in a layby about a quarter mile up the road and worked her way toward the cottage through the thin strip of woods separating the houses on the road from the golf course behind. Her steps crunched quietly and she flashed the taped-up lens of the tactical penlight occasionally to check her path. Drunken voices carried from the golf course—cross-country skiers out at night.

Kathleen never carried burglar tools, and up there, half the people don't lock their doors. If she needed an implement to help her break in, there was almost always a tool shed or a hatchet stuck in a stump by the back door.

Shivering, exhaling down inside her parka so her breath wouldn't show, she watched the house for fifteen minutes by her watch before stepping up onto the back porch and pulling open the warped wooden screen door.

The steel-clad inner door was ajar, maybe two inches. She reached to push it open when an alarm sounded deep in the lizard part of her brain. This was too easy.

She stepped down off the porch, breathing harder, and swathed her flash. A ragged broom stood propped against the railing and she picked it up with the bristle end toward her. Putting her back to the cedar clapboards on the right side of the door, she extended the broom handle and pushed the door in.

The explosion shredded the end of the broomstick, sending splinters twenty feet out onto the thin layer of snow. Her ears rang and her heart tried to jump up into her throat. Out on the golf course, a drunken skier yelled in reply.

"Woo-hoo!"

"Idiot," she said.

She stood where she was until she felt her pulse slow down. Anyone who heard the sound would have assumed fireworks or someone shooting a gun into the air in celebration. Happened a lot up here in the boonies.

She pushed the door the rest of the way open and peeked around the doorjamb, her flashlight shining on a stumpy shotgun C-clamped to a table with a pulley and wire attached to the door. Simple, effective, and brutal.

Kathleen thought hard about leaving then and there. Her entire success as a burglar rested on what she called the Gandhi approach: peace first and always. She was not one of those lunatic cat burglars who liked to listen to their victims snore while they looted the dresser drawers. And she never planned for violence in her jobs. If the need arose, she only used enough to keep herself free.

But—and she knew this would undo her some day—she possessed a deep undifferentiated curiosity and a mania to satisfy it, almost no matter what it took. Hoodlums in black topcoats in a little Vermont town pushed her buttons hard.

She stepped inside on the balls of her feet, aware that there might be more booby traps. The other reason she didn't quit was that she understood fear—if she gave up now, fear would win. And thus the hoods would win. And she wouldn't have that. If there was anything worth stealing in the place, it was leaving with her.

The kitchen was empty except for the shotgun-enabled table and a half dozen chairs, but when she eased into the front room, the view out the windows was blocked. She risked the penlight again, sluiced the beam around, and gasped. Ah, yes. There was plenty worth stealing here. And she wasn't going to touch a bit of it.

Wooden crates, a couple dozen in all, were stacked against the front wall. Stenciled black lettering on the olive green crates made her knees watery: U. S. Army Ordnance, followed by a string of letters and numbers in white that would make sense only to the Army.

She was disappointed. Her most desired objects as a thief were portable wealth: cash, jewelry, art, and antiques. Even when she did a truckload cleanout of someone's home, she left behind anything two people couldn't carry. But if she could have lifted the crates, she wouldn't have bothered. Getting caught with any of this would get her branded a terrorist, Guantanamo-bound for sure.

Though she did know a guy in South Boston, Con Malley, who sold arms into the jungle of small-time criminals up and down the East Coast. Maybe she could touch him for a finder's fee, assuming he could get some guys up here fast enough to clean the place out.

By the front door, she illuminated another burglar alarm, a Remington 870 pump shotgun with the barrel sawn off down to the fore stock, bungee-corded to a recliner and pointed at the front door. These were primitive people, she thought. Nasty.

Carefully easing the safety back into place, she snipped the string to the trigger with the scissors on her Swiss Army Knife, then froze at a scratching sound at the back door, a sound like boots tracking grit across a linoleum floor.

A beautiful light brown leather briefcase—Coach, and she could get a few bucks for that—hung from the coat rack by the ladder to the loft. She unhooked it and wound the strap around her left hand. It had enough heft to startle someone, give her a few seconds to run out the door.

Her breath caught as the scratching sound came closer, long sliding steps across the floor. She stripped the tape off the lens of her flashlight, a high-intensity LED that was strong enough to blind, and stepped around the door jamb.

Just as she flicked the light on, a loud raucous screech sounded down by her feet, then a black and white streak—house cat, but a big one, with an ear missing—shot out the back door like a thunderbolt of fur. She laughed at herself, shakily looped the briefcase over her shoulder and slipped out the back door herself, wondering if she still had Con's number in her phone.

* * *

The humid musty smell of her alleyway garage made her sneeze. She stepped back into the farthest corner of the space, hoping whoever Donny had hired to do the work—this was much too physical for him to take on himself—hadn't been too thorough.

She smiled when she saw the big eyebolt sticking out of the brick wall. Though it looked as if it had been mortared in place a hundred years ago, it turned easily and a four by four section of bricks pulled out of the wall. She breathed a good deal easier, though she wasn't going to forgive the loss of all her worldly goods.

Removing a plastic-wrapped parcel that held a hundred hundred-dollar bills and three sets of false ID, among other useful things, she nodded at her foresight.

"Fuck you, Donald Maldonado, and the horse you rode in on. And take that fucking Randolph with you."

20

Burton seemed less concerned with my problems than with Marina. He might have been worried about blowback from her throwing the knife at Donny. I knew he was still tentative around her, after her fling with Rasmussen Carter.

My major worry, too, was how Donny was going to react. All the contact I'd had with the criminal class, both in cleaning up the Esposito and brushing up against Icky Ricky, taught me that other than a naked bottomless greed, pride was a prime driver of most criminal activity, both the illegal and the immoral. The only difference between the two tended to be how well-dressed the perpetrators were.

All of which was on my mind when I got home from closing up and found a message on my answering machine to call Daniel Markham, my father's attorney, and also the one who'd handled all the legal work for my purchase of the bar. It was too late at night to call even an avowed workaholic, and since I didn't have the easy experience in legal and financial affairs my father had had, I was awake most of the night with my brain spinning about what couldn't be good news.

At 7:30 the next morning, I gave up and made myself a pot of strong coffee with chicory one of my customers had brought me from New Orleans, then called Markham.

"Attorney Markham, please," I said to the automated voice, then cussed myself for trying to be polite to a machine.

"Five. Seven. Nine. One," the voice replied. Then a long buzz.

"Markham." He was inordinately proud of his deep bass voice, which he exercised with the Boston Chorale every year when it sang the Messiah. Markham loved to reverberate.

"Elder Darrow. Got your message."

"Elder. How nice to hear from you." Insincere pleasantry? I never expected good news from a lawyer. "Can you come down to the office today?"

The last thing I wanted to do before a long Saturday at the bar was schlep down to the financial district to Markham's office.

"Is there a problem?" I said. "One of the licenses up for renewal and someone wants a bribe? An inspection? What is it?"

My entire family on both sides, at least four generations back, had been registered Republicans. In a Democrat-controlled city that meant we were second-class citizens, tolerated only for our contributions to the tax base. One of my great uncles had been a temporary building inspector for the city, temporary for thirty-one years because of his incorrect political affiliation. It was always reasonable to assume a political problem.

"No, no. Nothing untoward at all. More of an opportunity for you, in fact. The principals have asked me to present their offer to you in person."

My neck stiffened up. I'd spent enough time around the perpetually positive to be suspicious of someone telling me something was "an opportunity" for me, but I tried to listen with an open mind. Unfortunately, Donny Maldonado's visit, Katherine's disappearance, and Burton's distant attitude had conspired to make me feel as if I were standing in the ocean while the tide dug the sand out from under my feet.

"Opportunity."

"Yes. I don't know if you've given any thought to your exit strategy down there."

The South End being "down there," as far away from the city's seat of power as the Dudley Street MBTA station. As for an exit strategy, I hadn't been in the Esposito so long I was worried about leaving it. The bar's function had been to get and keep me sober, not make me millions. Markham was making it sound like I'd gone into the venture as if it were a tech startup.

"Not exactly, no. How do you mean?"

"I've had a buyout offer for the Esposito and the building.

114

Unsolicited, I assumed."

I'd leased the bar space first, then bought the building from the owner last year, the only thing I'd done with the money from my father. My heart thumped.

"Of course. I haven't been shopping the place. From whom?"

"Well. I don't know, precisely."

Just the kind of lawyer bullshit that drove me crazy.

"You're my attorney, Daniel. Aren't you supposed to know these kinds of things?"

Long silence at the other end of the phone. Markham didn't like my nontrusting nature any more than my father had. But letting people walk all over you only led to more of the same.

"It's what's known as a shell corporation, Elder. Designed to hide who the principals are. And the name is generic: Lakeview Partners."

My first thought was this might be Maldonado's initial foray into making my life miserable, though I didn't see how it would help him find Kathleen. It was possible he thought owning a bar would give him a base of operations for his other activities. Possible, if a little convoluted.

"Does this have something to do with the Olympic bid? I know you're in a position to hear things like that."

Markham was the epitome of the well-connected private side mover in Boston, having worked in the Middlesex DA's office for a while before trying out the criminal defense side. Eventually, my father told me, Markham got more interested in how a sharp lawyer could work with the halls of power to accumulate some capital, and gave up courtroom work altogether. In a sense, he'd been a gift from my father, but I usually assumed that if he was taking a side, it was probably his own.

"That might be a good call." He sighed, as if I'd missed something important. "You do realize your building is right in the center of the Velodrome Parcel."

The minute people started naming projects, you knew the insiders were massing to scheme. And Markham was nothing if not an insider.

"This is actually going to happen, then? We're going to build all this infrastructure and bring in seven or eight million tourists to a city this size over two weeks?"

"I don't see it not happening," he said, after an elegantly condescending pause. "There's too much momentum behind it."

"You're advising me to sell, then."

"I'm your attorney, Elder, not your investment advisor. All I can do is present what I'm given and advocate for your interests."

"What's the offer?"

"I can't get you to come down to the office?"

"Not today."

"Two point seven million. For the building and the business."

"They'd keep the bar? Or it's going to be a teardown?"

"That's all the information I have, Elder. If you decided to pursue it, there are obviously questions to ask. We could probably negotiate the price upward, test how serious the buyers are. I'm sure you want to consider it for a bit, though."

"I will have to think about it. You know how much time and money I've put into the place."

"I also know how much you paid for it in the first place," Markham said sharply. "This represents a substantial profit."

That price would net me two million, more or less, after I paid off the mortgage, so in that sense it was a good offer. Too good to snap at like a trout on a fly. And with my inheritance out in the market making me money, I didn't have any financial pressure to act.

"You can tell them I'm considering it. I'll have an answer in a week."

"There's a three-day expiration on the offer, Elder."

I wondered uncharitably if Attorney Markham was getting a fee out of this, beyond his legal services. No one ever went broke underestimating the integrity of a fixer in the face of a payoff.

"As soon as I can. This would be a big change of direction."

"Very good." Message delivered, Markham's tone crisped. "I'll wait for your call, then. Good day."

I sank back into the kitchen chair and felt a weird peace come over me, as if I'd accomplished something intelligent and worthwhile. It's always tempting to disregard the function of luck sprinkling gold dust on your head.

But as satisfied as the offer made me feel, I had no illusion that the money was coming to me because of my brains or even my entrepreneurial spirit. On the other hand, this money would be money I earned, unlike the inheritance, and I wondered what different kind of life I might build for myself with it, what more interesting things than running a bar I could manage. The only anchor on the decision was whether giving up the Esposito would make it harder for me to stay sober. It occurred to me that it might be time to take a risk.

21

All she'd really lost was the key, she kept reassuring herself as she walked back up Canal Street and into the branch of the Home Bank. She walked over to the open desk of the customer service representative, wishing she'd left the key to the safety deposit box in the hidey-hole instead of in the drawer of a chiffonier Donny Maldonado had taken along with everything else. Knowing him, he'd burned everything.

She didn't expect any trouble getting into the box, though, or reclaiming Donny's stolen papers.

"Is Mr. Giroux available?" she asked the young woman in the crisp khaki shirtdress. "I'd like to say hello."

Dark as black coffee, her dreads tipped blonde, the woman frowned at Kathleen's T-shirt and jeans, then picked up the phone.

Alphie Giroux had been an assistant vice president the last time they'd been together, eating turtle soup at Antoine's, but she had no doubt he'd climbed higher on the ladder by now. Today, she was going to need a favor from a friend in high places. She no longer had the ID she'd opened the box with, but Alphie knew her, well, personally.

"Kathleen!" He beamed as he rushed from behind the glass door leading to the bank's back office. He grasped both her hands and almost dragged her to a couch by the window. "Darling, how have you been?"

His blue seersucker suit, a little ahead of the season, was appropriately rumpled, his white shirtfront stiff and blinding. A Kelly green bow tie snugged up under his pointed chin. He'd given up and started shaving his head, though it didn't hide the dark boundaries of his pattern baldness. She wondered why men couldn't accept their genetic inheritances any better than women.

* * *

He shook his head so hard, the bare skin sent out flashes of light.

"It's a completely different world since 2008," he said. "Even in a gentleman's bank like ours. We have a million forms. Procedures. Oversight. Without the ID? There is literally nothing I can do."

She regarded him with the fond look that always seemed to sway him before, a mix of exasperation and the promise of sex. She didn't want to tangle herself up with him again, but she was desperate.

"But you know who I am, Alph." She placed her hand on his knee, let him feel how warm it was. "It's not like I'm asking for access to something I don't own. And have been paying rent on for dog's years."

The African queen at the front desk was showing a lot of interest in their conversation, leaning in their direction without realizing it.

"Let's take this back to my office," he said.

That was the moment when she knew he was going to do it, even if he didn't know it yet.

"Of course."

She flashed the queen a look designed to confuse and confound her, as Giroux conducted Kathleen in through the security doors.

"I'm a little disappointed," she said, following him down the plushly carpeted hall.

"How so?"

The one thing he couldn't abide was someone questioning his value to the bank, his importance.

"These aren't really offices, are they? Just kind of upgraded cubicles."

Shoulder-high partitions, glass common walls, no doors, though the furniture was a small cut above what was out in the lobby.

At the end of the hall stood an actual solid wood door.

"How about this, then?" He couldn't hide his pride.

"Very impressive Alphonse. Walls and everything."

He gave her a wounded look. She'd better quit indulging her snark if she wanted his help.

"Just teasing, hon. You've done very well for yourself."

She didn't need to remind him he'd done well for himself partly because of a couple semi-legal side roads she'd directed him down. That might not be so important inside the bank, but an outward appearance of probity had to be crucial.

He locked the door behind her and her stomach cramped. Was he expecting her to get down on her knees literally as well as figuratively? Sex hadn't been that big a part of their relationship before. She decided not to encourage the idea.

"Have a seat," he said. "We haven't had a chance to just visit in some time. How have you been and why haven't I been seeing you around town?"

The stilted conversation felt like a foreplay gambit. She picked up a silver-framed photo from his desk.

"Lovely girls," she said. "Six and eight now? And this must be your wife. My, she is attractive."

That was the beauty of dealing with someone you knew. Even if the pressure points weren't obvious, they were easy to locate.

"I. Uh."

"Alph. I am not the person I was four years ago, I'm sorry to report. But if you get me into my safe deposit box..." She leaned over the desk and stared him in the eyes. Even then, the eyes dropped to her chest. "You will never have to see me again. You know all I want is what belongs to me. If I can't get it today, I don't know what I'd do."

Giroux's forehead shone and his cheeks got pink. Anger warred with fear, but she knew which one would win.

"I had no intention of..." he sputtered. "You don't know."

Time to put her boot down. She had a flight to catch.

"Could we please just go down to the vault?"

He reached into his desk and pulled out a jingling key ring, then slammed the drawer shut.

"Of course, Ms. Crawford. Come with me."

120

* * *

She breathed easier once he extracted the box from the wall for her and left her alone. Lifting the metal cover, she felt her breathing hitch, but everything was as she'd left it. The light brown leather briefcase she'd picked up in Vermont lay on top of everything, a greenish foxing of mildew on the brass clasps. Ridiculous that Maldonado was so hot to retrieve this and she didn't even understand what was inside, other than the fact it was papers. She'd have to look at it closely, but not here and not today. Alphie might not stay frightened of her for long, and he knew enough of her extralegal life to make a believable phone call to the police. He was far better connected in this city than she'd ever be.

She opened the soft-sided bag and made space inside for the carry version of the Sig Sauer P320 she liked. She'd never fired it except at the range, but up until six months ago, she'd shot at the range every week. She wasn't sure how she could get it back to Boston—maybe FedEx.

Hesitating over the stacks of currency, she crammed them in, too. She wasn't coming back. Her relationship with Alphie was her last one in this city, and she'd just snapped that off at the roots.

Burdened by the weight of the bag, she felt lightened by being solvent, which meant safer. She stalked out through the bank's lobby, noticing Alphie and the African queen in intense conversation. She waved a languid Mardi Gras princess wave at them—elbow, elbow, wrist, wrist—then walked out into the humid sunshine.

22

Burton drew his knees up under the sheets. Marina groaned in her sleep and ground her teeth, one of the night sounds he'd missed, though it woke him up three or four times a night. He ran his hand over her smooth bare back, feeling the pleasant physical depletion of their lovemaking. He'd known the same feeling when he was younger, running cross-country races and giving everything he had, win or lose.

He eased out from under the quilt, pulled on a pair of flannel pajama bottoms and a red University of Denver sweatshirt from the precinct lost and found. Singing at 5 AM wasn't his thing, nor was praying, but he felt grateful and full as he walked across the cold wooden floor barefoot.

Shielding the coffee grinder with his torso so the buzzing wouldn't wake her, he thought about the Boustaloudis case. There had to be ways he could make progress without dealing with Mickey Barksdale. He'd worked so hard to pull himself out of that swamp, to lose the ignorant us-against-everyone view of the world, he wondered if his reluctance might not be fear he would fall back into it. Or maybe it was that he hadn't been face to face with Mickey since the gangster saved his life.

He shook his head as he pulled the omelet makings out of the avocado green refrigerator. He was still a prisoner of that stereotype of Charlestown, in a way—most of the people who lived on that little peninsula of the city were god-fearing and relatively innocent, the town's reputation stained by history, a few criminal neighbors, and a human need to belong. The gangsters always got the press.

"Bacon," Marina said as she shuffled into the kitchen in an old flannel shirt of his and gray sweat socks. Her hair stuck up in spikes. The last time she'd been in his apartment, months ago, she'd lectured him about his eating habits.

""Don't stock it any more," he said.

She aimed a kiss at his ear that he dodged.

"Way back in the freezer," she said. "I hid it the last time I was here."

"That long ago?"

He dug into the frost encrustation, unreasonably happy and without the usual anticipation of what might go wrong. A little joy in his life was allowed.

She came back from the bathroom, smelling of Ivory soap and mint. He handed her a mug of coffee and she swished a mouthful around and spat it into the sink.

"Toothpaste taste," she said.

"That was a pretty ballsy move, throwing a knife at him like that. You spend some time in the circus?"

He laid strips of bacon in the old cast iron fry pan, turned up the heat until it started to sizzle. She ducked her head, blushing.

"More like stupid. He was carrying a gun."

"Still. Could you hear what they were arguing about?"

Burton had heard Elder's side of the story, but he understood people and memory too well to believe it was complete. She shook her head and sat down at the table, took a drink of coffee. She giggled.

"I can't believe it stuck in the wall."

"Marina."

"He's my boss—I can't break a confidence."

He poked at the bacon with a fork.

"Even in the presence of a sworn law enforcement professional?" he asked.

Her mug banged on the table, his first hint she was irritated.

"OK," he said. "I get it."

"What if I told him some of the things you and I have talked about? That wouldn't be right, would it?"

"I said I get it. You want eggs?"

123

She shook her head.

"Just toast. And bacon."

"Look. I worry. Especially with all the gangsters coming in and out of the bar. And Kathleen Crawford."

"That one—she's not doing Elder any good. I thought it might be a good thing for him at first, after that Susan ran away."

"You think he knows where she is?"

She glared in a way that sent him back to the bacon.

"Same answer as before." Her spoon clanked as she added sugar to her coffee. "How's your case going?"

"Which one? The Greek? Very slowly. Everyone loves the idea of the Olympics in Boston, except the ones that don't. Constantine Boustaloudis was an upstanding family man, except when he wasn't. There might be a connection between the bid and organized crime, or as organized as it gets around here. Or there might not be. I'm stymied, but I have things I can do."

"Sounds like I should be worrying about you," she said.

She passed him to pull a bag of wheat bread out of the freezer and lined up four slices in the toaster. On the way back to her chair, she rubbed the back of his neck, then leaned over his shoulder.

"You'll figure it out. You always do."

She reached down into the open fly of his pajama bottoms.

"How committed are you to that bacon?" he said, setting the fork down.

"Not that much. But turn off the burner, all right?"

* * *

The loose light feeling buoyed him through a shave and a shower and a second cup of coffee.

"Your mother's not going to fuss that you were out all night?" he asked as they left the apartment.

Carmen was an over-protective Italian Catholic widow who'd always assumed Marina was not attractive enough to find a decent man. Burton didn't know if she considered him decent, and he had no idea what she'd thought of Rasmussen Carter.

Marina picked up the newspaper from the mat and handed it to him.

"That's one of the few benefits of the dementia," she said. "She doesn't always remember if I've been home. She also doesn't remember I moved out."

Burton pushed down a jolt of jealousy. She'd probably been able to stay out all night with Carter, too.

"The other day, she thought I was Teresa. Her older sister."

Burton winced.

"Is there a family resemblance, at least?"

"Teresa's dead twenty-two years now."

"Ah." He squeezed her hand. "I'm sorry."

She straightened her shoulders.

"I'll have to do something about her soon." She grinned. "But at least I can stay out nights."

23

Burton dropped Marina on Mercy Street, right outside the Esposito. The door was propped open, though the sky threatened sleet, and he worried momentarily. Elder's establishment was attracting violence again and he felt vaguely as if he were sending Marina into danger.

He drove across Mass. Ave. to Commonwealth and up into the block where Icky Ricky's luncheonette used to be. After Ricky retired to Florida, the place had been shuttered for a long time, but Burton had found out yesterday Ricky had left the building to his two long-time enforcers, Tesar and Donnie Spengler. He was slightly ashamed he was using them to avoid Mickey Barksdale, but one or the other might be able to tell him what he needed to know.

A rusty blue Dempster Dumpster occupied three or four parking spaces in front of the plate glass windows of Ricky's former haunt. In its own sweet way, the luncheonette had been as much of a shithole as the Esposito was when Elder took it over. Ricky's shtick had been to insult anyone foolish enough to walk inside and order, a combination of pre-renovation Durgin Park and the Soup Nazi.

The windows were soaped so he couldn't see in, but the front door was open. A table saw whined through lumber and eighties rock and roll competed with the clash.

"Closed," someone yelled as he stepped inside.

Burton turned.

"Spengler! You don't remember me?"

Donnie Spengler always dressed to play up his resemblance to a young Gene Kelly: blade-sharp creases in his cuffed khaki pants, plain white T-shirt, black belt and shoes, though those looked like custom-built New Balance, not loafers. His feet looked flat and misshapen, in fact, spread out in the soft sneakers. Not so much dancing now, then.

His eyes were a muddy gray and though his upper body was taut, it was unhealthily thin. Burton tried to remember if Spengler was the one with the amphetamine habit.

"Detective Burton." Spengler spoke coolly, but couldn't control a faint tic in the corner of his left eye. "How have you been, sir?"

Burton looked around. The old luncheonette had been gutted to the brick, which had then been power-washed and sealed. A chest-high wall with a pass-through counter marked off the kitchen and a man in an olive-green coverall was cutting and gluing random-length strips of wood to the face of it. Twined cast-iron light fixtures hung from a ceiling so high it disappeared into shadow. The flooring, stacked in boxes to the side, was ipé, an expensive South American hardwood.

"Jesus, Spengs. We need another bistro in town?"

Spengler loosed a faint smile of pride.

"A little upscale from what it used to be, yes? Come on back out of the line of fire."

Burton hoped he meant that figuratively, as he avoided two brutes carrying in a stainless steel sink.

The kitchen was fitted out and ready to go, a massive copper hood over the eight-burner stove. Refrigerator, freezer, countertops—everything was new and unmarked.

"Must be costing you a bundle," Burton said. Elder would have loved a setup like this.

"Always nice to see you, Detective. More so, now that we're a legitimate business. On the same side, so to speak. Did you come in to check out the menu? Or was there a professional reason for your visit?"

Someone had been polishing Spengler's act, or maybe it had always been this smooth, just buried under Ricky's outsized personality.

"Have you met Ricky's cousin yet?" Burton said. "I understand he moved to Boston to pick up where Ricky left off."

There. He'd seen that flicker before, a slight shoulder hitch that said he'd touched a raw spot. Spengler's face froze.

"We're pretty busy here," he said. "Soft opening next weekend."

"That isn't a no," Burton pointed out.

The guys with the sink were trying to jockey it into a tight alcove in the far corner of the kitchen. Spengler watched them for a minute, then smiled.

"You know, then."

It wasn't too hard to play dumb, since he had no idea what Spengler was talking about.

"In general. Why don't you give me your version and we'll see how they match up."

Burton loved these hoodlums who thought they were masterminds. Spengler unfolded a couple of chairs and invited Burton to sit down.

"Mr. Maldonado—Donald Maldonado—is funding our renovation." Spengler looked almost misty with gratitude. "Ricky gave me and Tesar the building, you understand. Like a severance package. But we couldn't make no money out of ham and eggs."

"And why would Mr. Maldonado do that?"

Spengler rested his hands on his knees and leaned forward, a parody of man-to-man conversation.

"He said he wanted to create a legacy for his cousin. We're going to name it for him."

"What? You're going to call it Ricky's?" Burton couldn't hide his amusement.

Spengler nodded.

"Rick's, actually. I guess the two of them were close when they were kids."

"Hmmph." Burton couldn't imagine anyone being close to Ricky. It sounded like bullshit.

"And of course, when the Olympics come to town, we expect to do a very thriving business."

"You're sure they're coming?"

"Mr. Maldonado is, and that's good enough for me. It's part of the reason he's bankrolling us. You know how many individual tickets get sold in the sixteen days? That's a lot of cannelloni, my friend."

"So you're cooking Italian?"

Maldonado might have killed Connie Boustaloudis over his anti-

Olympic efforts, but that wasn't ringing Burton's bell.

Spengler's capped teeth gleamed.

"All my Nonna's recipes."

Though Spengler had perpetrated violence on behalf of Icky Ricky—maybe he was doing the same for Donald.

"Good to hear, Spengs. So have you met any of Donald's partners? I know they're all in there pushing for the games."

Spengler flushed, probably irked by the fact that no savvy business person, straight or criminal, wanted to be seen with such an obvious lowlife as himself, even if he was running a legitimate business.

"Silent partner, eh?" Burton said.

Spengler looked at the floor.

"I don't get involved in the politics," he said. "That's Mr. Maldonado's bailiwick."

"Where's Tesar in all this? Doesn't he have a piece?"

Spengler donned a sad face.

"Rehab. We're trying to get him straightened out again. There'll always be a job for him here, though."

Burton remembered now—Tesar was the one with need for speed. The last time he'd seen him, the man was skinnier than an abused greyhound, consuming anything that kept his engine running. Ricky had sponsored him in rehab twice, once when police suspected Tesar of a street killing. He was mean enough to have shot Boustaloudis, but Burton couldn't imagine anyone trusting Tesar with the job.

"Loyalty, Spengs. Am I right?" He gave the would-be restaurateur his evilest smile. "Let's hope it runs in both directions for you."

He stood up, patted Spengler on the shoulder, and walked out.

A cloud of pot smoke hung in the air in the dining room and the guy who'd been running the table saw hid the joint down at his side as Burton walked through.

He shook his head—evolution in action.

"Carry on." He stepped out onto the sidewalk.

Spengler believed Donald Maldonado that the Olympics were definitely coming to town, but Ricky's cousin hadn't been anywhere near the city of Boston until recently. Or had he?

Owning a restaurant was a prime way of laundering cash and

co-opting Spengler and Tesar by bankrolling the bistro—Rick's? Really?—meant they'd be loyal, or at least as loyal as they could be.

So Maldonado was trying to dig himself into the city, another jot of information, if not actual progress in finding Boustaloudis's killer. This murder was turning out to be a stone whodunnit—even the ballistics report hadn't been useful.

He keyed the ignition and sat for a moment. Nothing else left but to go see Mickey Barksdale.

24

I hadn't been able to sleep, so around five in the morning, I gave up and drove down to the bar, thinking I'd catch up on some of the paperwork I kept trying to ignore. The idea someone would pay me a big whack of money for something I hadn't done with an eye to profit was disorienting. But I couldn't ignore the feeling that this, unlike my inheritance, meant a little more because I'd earned it. It would be my money, not my father's.

To add to my confused state, as I came out of the alley where I parked the Cougar, Kathleen stepped out of a brick doorway.

I'd been hoping, I realized in that instant, she was gone from my life. If there was any relationship I hoped had a future, it was the one with Susan Voisine, not the one with a sociopathic house burglar on the run.

"Where the hell did you get to?" I said.

I looked around to see if there was anyone else on the street: Randolph Coyne, Maldonado, Burton. Any one of them would be a problem.

I hurried the lock open and pushed her inside. Sometimes I left the street door open to air the place out, but not this morning.

"Burton isn't looking for you any more, if that's what you're worried about." We walked down the stairs. "Though I think he still wants to talk to you."

She watched me flick on the espresso machine.

"Good," she said. "I need coffee."

"It takes twenty minutes to heat the boiler. What are you doing here?"

She gave me a mock-insulted look, but I read sadness in it, too, as if she understood now that anything we'd had was all we were going to have.

"Can I get a glass of water, at least?" She slung a soft tan leather bag up on the bar and sat on a stool.

I turned on every light in the place, performed my morning routine in the kitchen by turning on the grill and the fryer. Back out front, I looked at her closely.

Her eyes were red and tired-looking, but she was otherwise turned out impeccably: fresh haircut, light makeup, black slacks, white boat neck sweater, and a thin gold chain around her neck. It was a great contrast to what she'd looked like the last time I saw her and I couldn't help a light hit of desire.

She drank from the glass I handed her, then laid her hand on top of the leather bag.

"Did Donny give you a way to get a hold of him?"

"Sure." I rolled up the sleeve of my dress shirt—I'd been wearing long sleeves to avoid questions. I stripped off the grimy bandage and peeled away the gauze.

"Oh shit." She touched my hand. "That was Randolph, wasn't it? I'm so sorry you got involved."

I let her take a good look at the thinly scabbed numbers. She seemed genuinely disturbed, but not so much that she couldn't pull a piece of paper out of her bag and write down the number.

Then she looked at me with those luminous eyes I knew I would never trust again.

"I am sorry," she said again. "I was sure I'd cut that trail."

"Nice verb choice. What are you going to do now?"

She patted the leather bag.

"This is what all the fuss was about. The item Mr. Maldonado lost track of."

"That you stole from him, you mean."

She moved the empty glass back and forth between her hands and stared at the photo of a young Miles Davis up on the wall. Then she squared her shoulders and looked me in the eye.

"I'm a thief, Elder. Been one all the way back to shoplifting from

Target when I was in middle school. No strong arm stuff, no violence, no desire to do anything but live a quiet life."

"And steal. What, for the thrills?"

She shrugged.

"I'm not going to tell you I didn't like it." She looked down at her hands. "But if you don't have something in your life that gives you a charge…I can't explain it. In my defense, though? I never stole from anyone who couldn't afford it. And I never hurt anyone when I stole." She slapped the bag. "I wouldn't have touched this thing if I'd known it was going to cause this much grief."

"That I don't doubt. But your grief more than anyone else's, am I right?"

"Take all the shots at me you want," she said. "But don't forget you and I had some pretty good times that had nothing to do with my stealing. You could have convinced me…"

"To give it up? Don't even try that. I've had all the experience I need with people telling me that chicken shit is chicken salad."

"Believe it or don't. There was something else there, and you know it."

"And we're not going to find out what it was now, are we?"

My words tasted bitter, but I'd let go of her much sooner than now, sooner than my conscious mind realized.

"I need one last thing from you," she said.

"You have one fuck of a nerve."

She shook her head.

"There's a benefit to you—it will get Randolph off your back." She pushed the briefcase across the bar. "I need you to hold onto this for me. You still have a safe out back?"

I started to shake my head. She grabbed onto my wrist.

"You might think you hate me, Elder. But I don't think you want to see me dead, do you? If I take this to a meeting with him, Donny will kill me on the spot. If I can convince him not to, maybe I can trade it for my life. You see where I'm going?"

"You're going to be your own hostage. Clever."

"More or less. I won't tell him you have it, just that I told you where to find it."

"You have any doubt this will keep Randolph off my back?"

"I'm way short of time, Elder. And I need to get free of this. I'm betting he won't bother me if he gets his bag back, and I can slip away."

"What's in it?"

"No idea. And you don't want to know either. In case he asks."

I took a breath, and a chance.

"Two conditions. One, I'm not going to tell you where I hide it."

She nodded. "Perfect. So I won't be able to tell him."

I tucked the bag on the shelf under the bar.

"And when you leave today, I don't have to see you again. Ever."

Her face didn't move. She nodded again and stood up.

"Done and done. You probably don't want it, but consider yourself kissed. Thank you."

She tucked the paper with Randolph's phone number into the pocket of her slacks and started for the stairs. I watched her go and shook my head at my own gullibility, trying my best to think of it as a favor for a friend and not as a final act of love.

25

The offer to buy the Esposito nagged at my brain enough that I wanted to get some perspective. I called Burton and asked him to drop by this morning and then I called Marina to come in early. Both of them understood the anchor the bar had been for me, keeping me from drifting off on a sea of boozy days and nights as I had before I bought it. They were the only people whose opinion on the topic I cared about.

I no longer believed I would die without the daily discipline of running the place, opening the doors in the morning, serving my customers. I'd progressed out of the direst level of my alcoholism reasonably quickly, though like any human, I was probably more sure of myself than was warranted. If I did sell the place, I would still have my sobriety and I would also have capital, which meant freedom. Or at least a different kind of responsibility. The question was whether the sobriety would survive the freedom.

Marina walked in and closed the door at the top of the stairs behind her, her winter boots thumping as she came down the stairs.

"It must be thirty out there this morning," she said. "I shut the door. You don't need to be heating the outdoors."

"You know I like to leave it open. Air the place out."

She sat down at one of the four-tops, slinging the cloth bag with her work sneakers and everything else she deemed necessary to have here onto the chair beside her.

"Elder." Her voice was sad and gentle as she unbuttoned her black wool coat and unwound the scarf. "The place doesn't stink any more. You don't have to do that."

Habits. That was what it would come down to, I guess—keeping or losing habits. If I wanted portents, what she'd said just then might mean my work here was through.

I made her a cappuccino, frothing the milk a little longer because I knew she liked it extra hot. I'd pretty much tamed the Rancilio monster and could turn out decent coffee drinks, but I refused to serve from it until after the lunch rush. The Esposito wasn't going to turn into a breakfast joint and the last thing I wanted was people coming in here in the mornings to buy to-go coffee on the way to work.

"You like working here, don't you?" I said.

Her face shadowed, the old insecurity surfacing in her worried look.

"Are you firing me?"

"Whoa, whoa. Of course not."

"What, then?" She fumbled in her bag, drew out a pack of American Spirits, and lit one.

I frowned at it.

"Burton and I are back together," she said. "Is that the problem?"

"I don't have a problem. But it sounds like you do. What?"

"Carmen. I have to find a place for her. She punched out a window last night."

Carmen was about five feet nothing and weighed a solid ninety-five pounds.

"She went out to pick up the mail and locked herself out. Or thought she did."

"She didn't?"

Marina drew in cigarette smoke.

"They were right there in the pocket of her housedress."

I didn't know what to say to her. It's not that I was grateful that my mother and father had both left the earth, but at least in neither case was it prolonged or painful. I stepped behind the bar and queued up some music, a playlist of instrumental piano that didn't require too much attention.

"How's the beer in this joint?" Burton yelled from the top of the stairs.

136

He trotted down. I sensed ebullience—something in the case must have broken.

He walked behind the bar, helped himself to a green bottle of beer, and walked over to the table. He squeezed Marina's shoulder and sat.

"I hope this isn't going to take too long." He smiled at Marina with the closest thing to honest pleasure I'd seen in him in quite a while. "I thought I might promote a lunch date."

"You're in a good mood." I drank the cold dregs of my coffee.

He pulled at the beer.

"Let's just say your phone call came at an opportune time. Kept me from having to do something I wasn't looking forward to."

I frowned. Let him go all secret and cryptic, if that's what he needed.

"So what's this very important issue, Mr. Darrow? Deciding whether to go with the chardonnay or the sauvignon blanc? You know how I feel about white wine. Also, you look like shit. I hope you haven't been on a bender."

Marina hissed at him. He was only half-joking—he knew as well as I did the perils of the grape and the grain. Maybe better, since he hadn't ever quit completely.

"Nope. But I needed some advice from my brain trust."

"Let's not get all sloppy here, pal."

Completely expected that he'd push back on anything remotely sentimental.

"I've had an offer to buy the Esposito. Out of the blue. I wasn't shopping it."

That seemed important to me, that they knew I hadn't been looking to sell.

Marina hunched her shoulders, wrapped both hands around the white china mug, and stared down into it. Burton, on the other hand, lit up.

"Excellent! Tough call, maybe, after you put so much into it. But it gives you options, right?"

I noticed he didn't say anything about Marina's help in making the place work.

"Marina?"

She raised her head, as bleak as if I'd told her I was dying. Or Burton was.

"I don't know," she said. "It's your place, right? I can't help you decide. But good, if that's what you want to do."

Burton was giving me a sharp-eyed look over the rim of his bottle.

"But Elder's not sure what he wants to do. Am I right?"

I rolled my shoulders.

"It's a decent offer. Generous, even. The money's not the problem."

"Don't worry about me." Marina straightened up. "It's a good job, but it's a job, if you know what I mean."

That stung a little, but I could see she was trying to make it easy for me.

"Do it," Burton said. "Hasn't this place done everything for you that you asked it to?"

He did have a talent for pressing his thumb on the sore spot.

"The whole idea was that you'd stay sober if you hung around the booze all the time," he said. "Am I right?"

Not the whole idea—there was the music—but close enough.

"And you've done that. Licked the problem."

I pinched my lips together.

"Supposedly, you don't ever lick it."

"But it actually puts more pressure on you not to drink here?"

That was my worry, that losing the pressure might make it easier to fall.

"I don't know. Maybe that would take away the wall that's holding me up." I rapped my knuckles on the table. "Then boom. Down I go again."

Burton shook his head. I appreciated his confidence in me, but I was the one who had to believe. Not him.

"Marina?" I said. "What do you think? Really."

She rubbed at her eyes, dredged up a smile. "I'm happy for you. You do whatever your stomach tells you is right. You always pretend you're going to do the rational thing, but the truth is you always go with your gut."

Burton looked at her as if she were a stranger.

"Then afterwards, you build this elaborate explanation for why you did what you did and pretend that's how you decided."

I didn't think I'd asked to be profiled this morning, though I recognized some of what she'd said.

"So you think I should do what I want because I'll do what I want?"

She showed a faint smile. "Truth hurts, doesn't it?"

Burton laughed.

"Either way, Elder." He knocked the bottom of his beer bottle on the table top. "Everyone will be fine. It's your bar to sell."

"Of course." Marina lapsed into her inner thoughts.

"Well, this has been extremely unhelpful." I was irritated with myself for expecting a clear answer either way.

Burton stood up and walked behind the bar to slot his empty in the case.

"What are friends for?" he said, slapping my shoulder. "Friend."

26

Kathleen exited the T at Park Street and followed the rest of the afternoon crowd up the stairs onto the plaza at the corner of Tremont Street and breathed in the city air, half late-winter humidity, half exhaust. She was going to be done with this today, and while she doubted Elder appreciated her manipulating him one more time, she still had a hope she might convince him to see her again. He was someone who floated along, reacting to people and events more than driving them—he didn't follow his own path so much as take the open one.

At least she'd be free if she could pull this off. She grinned up at the pale blue sky, at the bright energy she felt, at her peace with who she was and what she'd done. If nothing else, she drove her own life. No one else had a say.

She looked up at the spire of the Park Street Church, one of the stops on the Freedom Trail, then circled around behind the stone building at the subway entrance and started up Park Street in the direction of the State House. Checking behind to make sure no one followed, she cut down Beacon Street and back onto the Common, following the wide path to the Frog Pond.

A warm spell had ended the ice-skating season and the cobbled bottom was slick with wet leaves and blown trash, moss showing dark green in the shady corners. She walked on until she saw the small hip-roofed building where they rented skates—closed for the year—and parked herself on a bench outside.

She took several long deep breaths, trying to relieve the tension in her chest. Donald had barely balked when she told him she would only meet to discuss a safe way to return what he wanted. And she knew it wasn't because he'd learned to be calm—she was pretty sure he'd try and kill her eventually.

Sitting here exposed her, but at least it was public. She'd been as careful as she could be, taking the long way around so anyone following her could see she wasn't carrying the bag. She wouldn't put it past Donny or Randolph to try a smash and grab.

She waited ten minutes past the time they'd agreed on, knowing Donny would try to make her nervous. But the bag was all he wanted—he hadn't lost the guns in Vermont. When her friend Con Malley from Southie got to the red A-frame, they'd been gone. And he hadn't been happy with her. Join the crowd, she'd told him.

A woman, far too young to be the mother of the four-year-old twins she had with her, led them, bundled, red-nosed, and squealing, down the brick path on the far side of the pond. Kathleen thought about what she'd do with the rest of her life once she was out of this. Elder wasn't daddy material, but maybe she could find someone as steady as he was to spend time with. No rug rats, though.

A metal rod poked into the back of her head. Kathleen set her hands flat on her lap and didn't move. Whoever Donny had sent—the little weasel wouldn't dirty his own paws—would have instructions to terrorize her, maybe even slap her around a little bit before having the conversation. She didn't care, at this point. A little pain would be worth it if she could reclaim her future.

"Look." She did not try to turn or otherwise move. "Tell Donald I haven't looked inside the bag. I have no idea why the papers are so important to him. If it isn't cash or jewels, I'm not interested in it. It was a mistake, pure and simple."

No answer, no sound, heavy breathing. Somehow familiar. Fear dug at her. Maybe Donny would cut off his nose to spite his face. Maybe the papers were meaningless and he only wanted vengeance for her stealing from him. Or maybe he was worried about the fact she'd seen the guns. He might have been misdirecting her all along.

Her breath clutched at her throat.

"Look, I've apologized to you a dozen times." She started to lay her arm along the back of the bench, but the gun barrel poked her hard behind the ear. "Sorry. I wasn't trying to turn around—I don't need to see you." She held up her hands. "Just tell me what Donald needs to make this right."

"Donald? Who's Donald?"

Kathleen locked up as she recognized the voice.

"You? But why?"

A sound like a coke addict's sniffle, but no answer.

"At least come around here and look me in the face," Kathleen said. "If you're going to kill me? Have that much courage."

More deadly silence, as if deep thinking were going on. Kathleen knew better.

"Seriously," she said.

The thought went no further than that. There came the snapping sound of a brittle stick and then the impact, then blackness.

A hundred yards away, the au pair with the toddlers looked up as if she'd heard something, then picked up her pace with the children, almost dragging them along.

Kathleen slumped forward, her arms on her thighs.

The killer walked around to the front, now that they could not look each other in the eyes and checked Kathleen's pockets. Burner cell phone, a bundle of hundred dollar bills. This was how the thief of everything important was going to be remembered.

27

Nothing on the Boston Common depressed Burton more than the Frog Pond when it was drained and dry. When he was small, the pond was only open for skating sporadically, nothing like the organized and city-sponsored ice rink and warming shed with cocoa dispensary that operated there now, in season at least. There'd been better-maintained rinks in his neighborhood for pickup hockey, no pads or helmets. On the shoulder season, the Pond was drained and ready to be scrubbed by city workers before refilling for the summer splashers. Right now, it was a desert of slimy and icy concrete.

And the corpse only made it more depressing. He knew if he ever lost the deep anger he felt every time he came to a murder scene, it would be time for him to retire, go work at Wonderland as a beer vendor or sell programs at Fenway. But what angered him more than usual about this particular body was that news of its state was going to hit one of his few good friends very hard.

Kathleen Crawford's body slumped against the back of the bench as if she were napping. The tail of her long coat caught in the slats and kept her from sliding onto the ground, an inadvertent kindness.

He approached from the rear and saw the char on the wood, just below where her head would have been if she were sitting upright. Point-blank, from behind. Unlikely it was a mugging gone bad.

A patrolman stood at negligent attention, keeping a small clot of lookie-loos at bay. Burton saw Jasmine Altay, the one forensic investigator he would have called if he were allowed to choose. His breathing eased a bit, as if he realized now he didn't have to solve this alone.

"Jazz."

She looked up at him from her crouch, her smooth chestnut-colored skin making him wonder, as always, at the people in this city who could not see the beauty in people who weren't Italian, Irish, or otherwise white.

"Danny-boy."

"Don't sing," he begged. "What are you seeing?"

"Well, it wasn't a robbery."

She pulled open one of Kathleen's coat pockets and showed him the pack of hundred dollar bills.

"And nothing sexual. Or at least her clothes weren't fiddled with."

"Too cold for outdoor sex anyway," Burton said.

"As if you'd know. Random, you think?"

The psychological thrillers of TV and the movies notwithstanding, the motiveless killer was a trope Burton didn't put stock in. He understood how it made a story more frightening, but his long experience said most murders stemmed from a depressingly small set of causes: greed, sexual conflict, or an inability to control one's self. Maybe if his job were more like the cop shows, he'd be having a better time.

"You know how I feel about random anything," he said.

Jazz rose, her knee joints cracking. She was as tall as he was, wearing tight black stretch jeans and a fleece-lined windbreaker. Her skin smelled like cinnamon and coconut and he had an instant of wishing he were away on a beach somewhere. Not with her, necessarily. Though if the opportunity arose…

"Maintain composure, Daniel." She laughed as if she were reading his mind. "There is some scene-related detritus: trash, cigarette butts. We might find something useful, but it's doubtful."

"DNA?" he said hopefully.

"If you can wait a year or so. You need to stop watching television; it rots your mind. You know how it goes."

He was avoiding Kathleen, because he knew he would see hair and blood and brain and shattered bone in an amalgamated mess congealed by the cold. There was no Kathleen here now, and though he'd been angry about the way she'd treated Elder and intrigued by the mystery of her identity, he knew none of that would minimize his commitment to the case.

"You know her," Jazz said.

"Not closely," he said. "She was a friend of a friend. I'm just wondering if it's connected to something else."

"The Rinker Island thing? That was weird."

He'd absorbed as much information as he could from the scene. He turned to face Jazz.

"Very. The weirdest thing is how they got the extra coffin onto the island. No, check that. The weirdest thing is why the coffin got sent out to the island to be buried. The guy was anti-Olympics, but if that had anything to do with it..."

"Why hide it?"

"Yep." He grinned at her. "Ever consider the detective branch?"

"Too many people like you." She grinned back and set to work, setting up a grid around the bench and laying out a search. A troop of police cadets was on its way to help with the grunt work.

Burton sat down at the far end of the bench and let his mind ramble a little, something he liked to do at the beginning of a case. Sometimes his subconscious picked up something he didn't realize until later.

The only connection between Kathleen and the Boustaloudis murder was that they'd been on Rinker Island as the same time. Not much of a linkage—whoever had put the body on the truck couldn't have known Kathleen would be on the burial detail. She hadn't even been in the system under her real name, assuming it was Kathleen Crawford.

The wind cut through the unlined topcoat, starting to make him shiver. He was not looking forward to informing Elder, even though his friend had been uncoupling himself from his obsession with the thief. Burton had seen many times how a murder left family and friends hanging, trying to convince themselves a relationship with the deceased had been more important than it was. Elder was also prone to depression, and in his case, that might mean another duel-to-the-death with a bottle.

"Let me know what you come up with," he called to Jazz, who

knelt in the frozen grass at the edge of the concrete pond. "I'm on the cell."

She raised a hand, intent on whatever she'd found.

He pulled the coat tighter around him and headed upslope toward Beacon Street. There was a Peet's on Charles where he could get a decent cup of coffee and consider the best way to break the news to Elder.

Of course, with the way his cop mind worked, he had to consider whether Elder had wanted her dead. Sometimes he hated his job, for the thoughts he had to have, but this road had to be walked. Kathleen had screwed Elder over in significant ways: cutting off the relationship without a word, dragging him into whatever she was doing with Donald Maldonado.

It was more than likely she'd been killed for a reason connected to her life as a thief. But he had to consider all the possibilities, accumulate the facts and build from them, not indulge in supposition or reaction. Just because a man poured him free drinks or because he considered him a brother didn't exempt him from the process. Still. Though Elder was capable of violence, it was unlikely in the extreme he could be this cold-blooded.

The cold wind slapped Burton in the face as he turned uphill on Charles Street. Coffee first. Then the Esposito.

28

Burton felt guilty when he heard the voice mail from Mrs. Boustaloudis, though less so when she said she wasn't checking up on progress into her husband's murder but that she had something else to talk to him about. He put off going to the Esposito and drove straight out to Hyde Park, parked up the street from the drug store. It was about two in the afternoon, but he could see the red *Closed* sign in the window.

He peeled the paper off another stick of gum and chewed it into the wad he was working, locked the car and headed up the sidewalk, wondering what Elder was going to do with himself if he did sell the Esposito. Burton couldn't imagine him in an office or a desk job, though maybe he would make enough from the sale that he didn't have to work for a while. That was a legitimate point about his drinking, though—with nothing to do, it could easily take him over again.

Peeking into the drug store past the green-tinted window shades, he felt worry grab at his stomach. He'd heard from her no more than an hour ago—where was she?

He rapped his college ring on the glass three or four times, then saw movement in the dimness at the back of the store. The black curtain rippled, then Mrs. Boustaloudis swam into view like the reverse of a movie fadeout, and took a key out of the pocket of her pants.

She unlocked the door, let him step inside, then relocked it.

"Thank you, thank you for coming," she said.

"Why isn't the store open?"

She peered out through the windows as if expecting an armed

147

assault. Her deep purple velour track suit, gold-trimmed, had been tailored to minimize her bulk, and the medium heels were not the right kind of footwear for a day behind the counter. The kid—Kevin? Kenny?—must have been scheduled to work today.

"My boy." Dorris spoke in a hushed rap, as if the hot water bottles and cough syrup were eavesdropping. "He was supposed to open up this morning." She held up an iPhone with a jeweled leather cover. "He doesn't answer and I don't know where he could be."

Burton shook his head. He understood the small business mind better than that—dressed up or not, she wouldn't have failed to open the store if there was money to be made. There was more to the story and more to her nervousness.

"What really happened?" he said.

She fiddled with a display of gum and mints by the register, adjusting the alignment of the packages, stacking and unstacking the small boxes. He didn't like the fact that she wouldn't look at him.

"Who's been bothering you, Dorris?"

He was assuming thugs or at least people thuggish enough to frighten a middle-aged female store owner who'd probably been robbed at least once before.

She glared as if he'd insulted her.

"Bums," she said. "Baby hoodlums. But not from here."

Of course she'd know the local hoods.

"Was this about the Olympics business? And Connie? What your husband was doing?"

She set her jaw and shook her head.

"They said they wanted to 'talk' to Kenny." She held up pudgy ringed hands. "I know what that means."

"They frightened you."

Her voice wavered. He heard her pain behind the tough mother façade.

"I think Kenny might be involved," she said. "In the drugs?"

"What makes you say that?"

She gave him another version of the you-think-I'm-a-dummy look.

"What did they look like?" he said.

"Like you. Fair, pale. Irish. One of them almost albino, with the red hair."

"And what did they say that upset you?"

"'Where's Kenny, when does he get here, why isn't he here running the store?'"

She straightened up to her full four-foot-eleven.

"I told them, they get the answers, let me know. I don't know where he is."

"No one tried to put a hand on you?"

She shook her forearm and a click announced the appearance of a five-inch stiletto blade from her sleeve.

"They wouldn't have." She refolded the knife. "One of them, he said something was supposed to scare me, but I didn't understand it."

Burton raised his eyebrows, still fighting the surge of adrenaline from her pulling the knife.

"He says to me: 'You can talk to us or you can talk to the dog.' What's that supposed to mean?"

Burton shut his eyes. Before Mickey Barksdale cleaned up his public act, back when he only ruled Charlestown, he'd been known as The Dog. Burton didn't know where it had come from—top dog, bad dog—but he purely hated hearing about this connection.

"I don't know, Mrs. Boustaloudis. I really don't know." He put his pen and notebook away. "I can't do anything official unless he's missing longer than a day or two. But I will ask some questions."

Especially of Mickey Barksdale, he thought morosely.

Unsatisfied and deflated, Mrs. Boustaloudis shook her head at him as he left her behind in the drug store. He couldn't put this off any longer, and because of that, he wasn't sure which of them felt worse.

29

After my unmomentous talk with Burton and Marina, I hadn't slept very well and I felt the dragon need for alcohol stirring down in my core like a distant warning. Kathleen coming back into my life after I thought she was gone, all the trouble she brought, actually bothered me less than having Susan Voisine one floor down in my apartment building and not talking to her. I was thinking about manufacturing some questions about Henri's condition so I could walk down and knock on the door some morning. She and I had unresolved business and I didn't want her to go back to Oregon without us trying to address it.

All the same, it was ridiculous for me to be in the Esposito at such an ungodly hour. Even in the worst of its bucket of blood days, the bar hadn't been serving at five a.m. But sitting in the dim light with Keith Jarrett in Stockholm playing low through the speakers, I could at least look around and feel some pleasure in what I'd accomplished, the refinished wood floors, the fresh paint, the black and white photos of jazz greats along the walls. I wondered if I could say goodbye to it.

I'd built the place for all the wrong reasons, entrepreneurially speaking at least, not because I was looking to build a business or make a fat living or because I enjoyed playing the publican that much. Not for any other reason, in fact, than that I thought it might save me from drinking myself to death. I'd accomplished that much, which made the decision harder. Was my success at that dependent on the Esposito? And did I want to find out?

On a memo pad, I divided the page into pluses and minuses. The minus column was easy: losing a place to work, a structure to my day, the daily conscious reminder I had to fight my addiction. Without the bar, I'd have to recreate myself, remake my life in a way that would support what the Esposito did for me now. The only item in the plus column was the two million dollars, which represented the means to do all that.

A garbage truck passed out on Mercy Street, its intermittent roar punctuated by the crash and clank of the masher. Everyone was working the early shift today.

Marina and Burton had been no help in my making a decision, but not because they didn't care. They understood I had to decide for myself. The neighborhood had supported me, but the gentrification would have happened regardless.

If I didn't sell, there might not be an Esposito in one or two years anyway. The money would help me buy a new location if I wanted, hire better musicians, though I wondered if I had the energy to start all over again.

A loud hissing, followed by something heavy and metallic bouncing off the stairs, yanked me out of my reverie. For once, Marina had been right about not leaving the door open.

An all-encompassing flash lit up the bar's interior like last call, and an explosion knocked me out of my chair, flinging the coffee carafe and the mug to a far corner and slamming me back against the bar. Something in my rib cage cracked loudly. I shook my head trying to focus.

It took the longest five seconds of my life for my vision to clear and even then, the tables, the stairway, the small fire burning in a stack of wooden chairs under the stairs, showed up in reverse, like a photographic negative. I was deaf, and as I struggled around the bar, wobbly. I leaned on the wall as I stumbled into the kitchen for the fire extinguisher.

My balance righted itself. I ran out front, still locked in that silent after-land, pulled the pin on the extinguisher, and sprayed down the flames that were charring the chairs. The fire kept returning until I kicked the stack apart and sprayed each chair individually. The burnt smell was more chemical than wood, and I sneezed hard several times. I dropped the exhausted canister and slumped on the edge of the stage.

As my hearing returned, a siren whined up on the street. The landline under the bar rang and rang. I tried to ignore it but eventually limped over and answered it.

"Mr. Darrow."

A voice I'd encountered only once, but knew as well as my own.

"Donald. You fucking psychopath. What if someone had been in here?"

"Words, Elder. You said something to me about not responding well to threats. I thought I'd remind you I'm not only about the threats. If you understand."

The smoke from the stun grenade flowed up the stairs and out the open door, a marker for the fire department, if they were coming. There was nothing they could do that I hadn't taken care of.

"Not your smartest move, Donald. What makes you think this will make any difference to me?"

"Because next time, my friend, it will be eight o'clock on a Saturday night. In the middle of a show. You have heard of IEDs?"

I cringed. The frightening part of those was they could appear as anything innocent: a purse, a briefcase, a bag of groceries.

"Look. I'm sorry if my cook's knife skills frightened you. But that's no reason to take it out on the bar. Especially since I'm getting closer to finding Kathleen."

A long silence on the other end of the phone. A firefighter in a yellow turnout coat appeared in the doorway, carrying a larger version of the fire extinguisher I'd used. I waved him inside.

"Elder. You keep promising to deliver and I don't see a thing. How do you expect me to believe you?"

I weighed the bar's safety, my patrons', against Kathleen's and made a decision.

"Maybe because I actually have my hands on what you're after. It would be pretty stupid for you to burn it up."

He laughed.

"I suspect you of *ex post facto* yanking my chain. But I suppose I can't afford to take the chance. Kathleen told me she'd hidden it. You'll meet me?"

"Not in person."

The firefighter doused the smoldering ruins of the chair and made a motion that he wanted to talk to me.

"Gotta go, Donald. We'll chat, though. Yes?" And I hung up.

"Should be OK now, sir." The fireman turned for the stairs. "But the arson investigator will be down in a minute."

I rolled my eyes. Someone thought I'd torch my own bar while I was sitting in it?

"Send him down," I said. "I've got to clean up so I can open."

I walked out back to the utility closet and picked out a snow shovel, grabbed a metal trash barrel, and headed back out front. But before I could start picking up the debris, a tall man in a khaki jumpsuit and hardhat stomped down the stairs.

"Tim Hunt. You the owner? Don't move anything yet, please."

Arson investigator. I hoped he wouldn't waste a lot of time investigating. The damage was minor and my injuries temporary. But I knew how the bureaucrats must be served.

"Yes." I stood with the shovel at port arms, feeling impatient.

Hunt leaned over, looking at the circular cutouts on the pipe-shaped cartridge of the stun grenade.

"Yup," he said. "Stun grenade. You been looked at? Ears and so forth?"

My vision was clear of the afterimages, and though I still heard a faint ringing in my ears, it was fading.

"I'm fine," I said. "Just need to get the mess cleared up."

He straightened, rubbing his lower back.

"I doubt you did this yourself," he said. "You might want to call in a police detective. Could be a hate crime."

Against a middle-aged white bartender? It was all I could do not to laugh out loud.

"I know some folks at the precinct," I said. "I'll call it in."

"Nothing too exciting here," he said, with a hint of disappointment. "But I'd keep that street door closed when you're not open for business. It would have been an easy toss from a car window down your stairs." He smirked. "Make it hard on them, at least."

He clanged his way up the stairs.

The burned chairs I broke into pieces as if they were matches, which showed how much adrenaline I had going. The rest of the debris I shoveled into the can, dragged it out into the alley, and doused it with water in case all the embers weren't out.

I didn't owe Kathleen anything more. I would give Donald what he wanted, though I supposed that would be no guarantee he wouldn't try and bomb me. He and Ricky shared a scorched-earth mentality toward revenge.

I flipped on the espresso machine. Out in the kitchen, I fired up the grill and the fryer so everything would be hot by the time Marina came in. Then I headed down the corridor to my office and opened the safe, took out the briefcase Kathleen had entrusted to me, and laid it on the desk.

I sat down and undid the straps. It was about time I figured out what I was risking my life for.

30

All the myths around Whitey Bulger had polluted the annals of criminal wrongdoing in the city of Boston and the rest of the state. Bulger had grown up from a baby hoodlum to show a remarkable ability to steal, fight, kill, and otherwise wreak havoc among his peer group, at the same time building the legend that he cared for his straight neighbors and brought them turkeys at Christmas.

It was typical Robin Hood bullshit, Burton thought as he drove up Medford Street past the high school and took a right onto Terminal, following it out to the boat ramp. Mickey never made it easy to talk to him, but Burton appreciated his discretion. Growing up in Charlestown and becoming a Boston cop was the closest thing most of the Town's residents could think of to giving up your American citizenship to join ISIS.

The March wind was brutal coming off the water, straight into his face and cold as iron. A rusted chain swung between two posts across the boat ramp, which was slicked with old ice and lime-green algae. One other car, an orange Dodge Charger from the sixties, sat in the farthest corner of the lot, belching exhaust out of its twin tailpipes.

Burton felt the balding tires on the unmarked car try and slide out from under as he drove across the asphalt toward the Charger. It had been easy enough to contact Mickey—they had any number of bartenders in the Town in common—but he was never certain Mickey himself would show up to meet with a cop, even one from the neighborhood. Though this dismal, windswept, godforsaken plain implied he might have.

He stopped with his open front window aligned with the driver's side of the Charger, a meticulously restored example of muscle car, its sleek paint as pristine as if it had come here directly from the car wash. Burton contemplated the knot in his stomach—nothing torqued his nuts like dealing with his past.

The Charger's tinted window didn't budge. Burton rolled his eyes, but the weenie-wagging also eased his worry. Mickey and he had been in fifth grade together—some old habits never died. He took the big cardboard Dunkin's cup out of the holder and drank some of the coffee while it was still hot, turned the defroster down a notch, and waited.

After what Mickey deemed an appropriate interval to send his message, the window rolled down, sending a blast of foreign cigarette smoke—dark and spicy—across to Burton. Mickey's head materialized like a magic trick as the wind whipped the smoke away: round, freckled, pink, and mottled high on the left cheek where a cherry bomb had nearly taken an eye when he was a boy.

"Michael," Burton said. He looked past Mickey into the Charger's interior, which was empty.

"No partners today, Mick? No one to watch your back?"

Mickey's thin lips parted in a doggish smile, exposing one dark incisor.

"I need protection from you? Way I remember, it was the other way around."

Burton wasn't supposed to know Mickey had killed Viktoriya Lin to save Burton's life. Elder had told him.

"Don't know what you mean," Burton said.

"I shouldn't need protection when I'm meeting with the police anyway, should I? And there are people in my organization who might question my commitment if they viewed us together."

"True enough. Especially Seamus."

Mickey had only one tell Burton knew, a twitch of the nostrils when he heard something he didn't like. As in now.

"Funny you should mention the wild one," he said. "I was just with the young feller yesterday."

"Shouldn't send him out to shake people down, Mickey. A red-headed albino? Much too easy to tell who owns him."

Mickey sighed, as if Burton had caught him at something.

"The Boustaloudis kid? That's what this is about?"

"What about him?"

"Owes me money."

Burton considered the most politic way to ask the next question.

"You're the only one in that business sector these days?"

Mickey shrugged and lipped a cigarette, shorter and thicker than an American one, out of a blue-gray package. He pushed in the lighter on the dash.

"This is the '68 Charger, you know. Like the one in the movie?"

Burton had no idea what he was talking about.

"So what?"

"*Bullitt*? Man. You never saw it? The stunt drivers in the chase scene had to back off the gas so they wouldn't run right up the ass of that Mustang."

The lighter popped. He charred the end of his smoke.

"Kenny Boustaloudis," Burton said.

"You know, I owe you nothing." Mickey slitted his eyes against the smoke. "But I'll give you this. He was our guy in Cleary Square. Something happened to his bank, we thought he'd gone walkabout. We're still looking for him."

"Don't hassle the mother," Burton said. "It'll be bad for business."

Mickey waved the cigarette, as if the nicotine had amped him up.

"That's it? You dragged my Irish ass out here to threaten me?"

"The Olympics."

"Got nothing to do with that shit." But his expression closed up and he looked down at his feet. Burton loved all the faces that could not tell a lie.

"One of your guys is doing security for the organizers."

"Is he."

"Jesus, Mickey. You going to make me pull teeth? Sanford O'Hanian."

"Oh yeah. Sandy. How's he doing for them?"

"Mick."

Mickey flicked the butt out into the parking lot.

"OK. The Olympics. Are you paying attention to who the players are?"

Burton waited. The fact that he'd linked O'Hanian to Mickey answered that question.

"I'm only telling you all this because I'm not involved, Burton. And because you're from the neighborhood. You know that."

Burton knew enough to be wary when anyone talked about old neighborhood ties.

"And you know all I care about is catching killers."

"Killing is very poor for the business climate," Mickey agreed. "Which Whitey and his boys found out eventually. Shit always catches up with you."

"O'Hanian."

"An acquaintance of mine, he's involved in that whole Olympics bid thing. Major investor, major player. The outfit that's behind the bid…"

"BOFF."

"Right. Someone wasn't thinking too far ahead, were they?"

"Your friend."

Burton was wondering how Mickey knew J. T. Wilder.

"There were protests, threats, some other bullshit. He asked me if I knew someone to handle security for them. Someone who wasn't local."

"So O'Hanian's not from around here."

For some reason, the question irked Mickey. He fiddled with the lighter.

"You know, I'm only talking to you because that killing—Boustaloudis?—it wasn't me. I don't give a rat's ass about the fucking Olympics."

Burton doubted that. Mickey was connected to the unions and to the longshoremen, who'd see plenty of new work if the bid went through.

"Who's your friend, Mickey? And where's he from?"

"Come north from New Orleans. But he's got local ties."

Mickey said Orleans like the town on the Cape.

"Such as? Besides you, I mean."

"You remember Ricky Maldonado? Fat little guy, used to run some street level dealers over by the Fens and Back Bay?"

Burton felt that electric sizzle that came when things started to fall into place. He played the dunce, though—it was never a good idea to let a hoodlum know what you knew and didn't know.

"Your guy knows Icky Ricky? I thought he retired."

Mickey spit a fleck of tobacco out the window. If not for the wind, it would have landed on Burton's coat. He controlled his irritation. If Mickey was nervous about this, that was information, too.

"Not Ricky. He's down in South Beach, working on his tan."

The mental image of egg-shaped Ricky lying on a beach basting in suntan oil made Burton wince.

"Who, then?"

"He has a cousin. Donald. Moved up north a couple months ago to get into this whole Olympic shindig."

The only reason Mickey would give up a fellow hood was if he were some kind of threat.

"Why would he do that? Big project like that, won't it all go to the local guys? Outsiders go begging, usually."

Mickey was elaborately casual.

"Beats me. But he's here and people seem to listen to him. He must have some kind of leverage. I heard he might own property the games might need."

"Is he the kind of gangster who kills people who get in his way?"

"You thinking about the Boustaloudis kid's father?"

Burton wasn't surprised Mickey knew about Connie Boustaloudis. The man's sources were deep and various.

"He's no killer, but he's got muscle."

"Randolph Coyne."

Now Mickey looked surprised. "That's the one. It wouldn't be Sandy—he's trying to get away from the violent side of things. That's why he's in an office."

Burton was learning more than he'd hoped, which begged the question of how much to believe.

"You're being awful accommodating here, Mick. Where's your horse in the race?"

159

Mickey shrugged.

"Where it always was. The money. We're into the construction unions now, electrical, pipefitters. I'm moving us out of the heavier stuff. There's plenty of money to make without all that extra risk."

He assumed Mickey was talking about the cheating and the violence and the possibility of jail inherent in Mickey's usual activities. There was enough truth in what he said to believe him, for now.

Burton started to roll up his window.

"Leave the kid's mother alone."

"Fuck you." Mickey flicked his finger at him. "I don't even get a thank you?"

He popped the clutch and threw the Charger forward toward the exit, spraying grit against the side of Burton's car. Barely missing the curb, he took the hard left and screamed away up Terminal Street.

Burton waited for him to disappear. Information, he had plenty of, but no knowledge. At least Mickey hadn't made too much of a point of the fact that he'd saved Burton's life.

31

I stared at the leather bag as if it might be full of snakes, but if getting rid of it would get Donald Maldonado out of my hair, I'd chance getting bitten. I turned the brass clasps and opened the flap.

The case was stuffed with papers, manila folders full of what looked like real estate contracts, deeds, and a net worth statement for someone whose name I didn't recognize. The smell of ancient paper made my nose itch. At the bottom of the stack was a dark green folder, faded and stained. I put that one aside.

The real estate papers were for properties with addresses in Jamaica Plain. I went and grabbed Marina's iPad from over the sink and called up a map of the city. All of the paper-clipped sets of contracts were for properties along the western boundary of Franklin Park. They weren't deeds, but legal descriptions of the properties and signed options for future purchase, all dated in the last year. I guessed Donald had been doing some real estate speculation, anticipating the Olympic bid.

That didn't seem enough to want to kill Kathleen over, though, unless it was Donald's ego feeling the insult.

I opened the old green folder, releasing more of that old-paper mustiness. What would happen to the records of history when everything was digital, I wondered? What other medium had the longevity and the acceptance of paper? I'd seen 8-track tapes, cassettes, floppy disks all come and go. What else would get lost because you couldn't get access to a medium any more?

I unclipped the pages and spread them out on the desk. The top three were a narrative summary of a plan, and as I read, I understood why the papers would be invaluable to someone who wanted to make a killing off a successful Olympic bid, especially someone without local connections or reputation.

Footsteps sounded out in the kitchen. I scooped everything into the briefcase. No sense involving anyone else in this clusterfuck.

I walked out into the kitchen, where Marina was humming. Life around here was a lot lighter now that she and Burton were getting along again. She grimaced at the briefcase.

"You going back to work at the bank?"

"Why? You planning an early retirement?"

My father had left her and Carmen a chunk of money, too, but she was being very close-mouthed about what they were planning to do with it.

She blew me a raspberry and took off her coat.

"It was a joke," she said. "What happened out front?"

"Little mess."

Out in the bar, I called Donald back.

"How resourceful of you to find me, Darrow." The call seemed to discomfit him.

"You never heard of star sixty-nine?"

"You have what I want, I take it."

"I have something here. I don't know if it's what you want."

"Bring it to me."

I shook my head before remembering he couldn't see me. Marina turned on the radio in the kitchen and salsa music leaked into the bar through the doorway. I put a finger in my open ear.

"I'm running a business here, Donald. I can't just jump up and run out the door every time someone wants me to. Why don't you haul your ass back down here and pick it up?"

"I'll send Randolph."

He sounded unsure, as if Marina's knife skills demonstration had had a lasting effect.

"You do and I'll burn your folders in the trash barrel out in my alley. And keep the briefcase for myself. It is a nice one."

I thought that might convince him I was holding what he wanted. His voice turned smooth, as if it were his idea to compromise. He'd reached the moment where he couldn't pretend I was bluffing.

"You really want me to come to your establishment again?"

"And I would like you to bring money."

Silence buzzed at the other end of the line.

"You would," he said. "Then you understand how valuable these papers are."

I was bluffing my ass off, hoping I might get Kathleen a little consideration.

"Token payment would be fine, Donald. Let's call it ten thousand dollars and be done with it."

"Agreed."

The fact that he didn't hesitate probably meant I should have asked for more. Or that he didn't intend to pay me a cent. But the other part of the plan was to get Burton here and have Donald talk about his crimes out loud, whatever they happened to be. If Burton could arrest him, it would put the cherry in the Manhattan.

"Thursday morning," I said. "Eight a.m. Here. I know you're out of bed that early if you're throwing stun grenades down my stairwell. And I am serious about your Rottweiler. If I see Randolph, I'll shoot him, and then I'll burn your papers. Understood?"

I ran my fingers across the scabs on my forearm. Donald allowed himself what he probably thought was a sophisticated chuckle. It sounded like he was spitting up.

"Randolph will be gratified to know he made such an impression."

"Thursday," I said. "If you don't show up alone, everything goes into the burn barrel."

32

I closed the bar early Tuesday night, not something I allowed myself very often, but it was only early by half an hour and only because the place had been empty before that. I'd been listening to a bootleg of the Duke Ellington opera *Black, Brown, and Beige*, a live recording of a full performance at Symphony Hall in 1943, one of only three times he'd presented it entirely. The music temporarily pushed my worries to the back of my mind.

But as I unlocked the downstairs door to my apartment building, it all crashed over me like a rogue wave: Kathleen and her using me, her dishonesty, the conflicts with Randolph Coyne and Donald Maldonado, my decision whether to sell the Esposito, and if I did, what I might owe to Marina. But none of those things was as important as what I found on the stairs as I stepped inside and pulled the balky door shut.

Henri Voisin's apartment was on the second floor, mine on the third. When he'd been in residence, before he went off to memory care, he would often hear me come in after a night in the bar and, being a night person himself, open his door to offer me a game of backgammon and a glass of port. No matter how often I told him, he routinely forgot that I didn't drink. I only took up the backgammon offer once in a while, but the breadth and depth of the old man's conversation astounded me. Somehow that made his collapse into dementia a much farther fall.

Susan Voisine sat on the top step of the landing in front of Henri's doorway. Even though she paid the rent now, I couldn't think of it as her apartment. Her back leaned against the wall next to the door, one

164

knee bent, her legs sheathed in peacock-blue leather pants. She wore a black waffle-weave undershirt on top with three buttons down from the neck and her feet were bare, her toenails a matte gray. An old blister on the side of one foot looked raw.

"Henri?" I said.

Her eyes were webbed with red capillaries, map lines to her emotions. Her hair was a mess and I had to fight a familiar desire to pick her up and hold her. She crossed her arms and dropped her head.

"It's gotten pretty far along," she said.

I reached down to help her up, maybe make her a cup of tea, but the touch of her warm hand sent a shock through my limbic system, direct to my libido. At that moment, I wanted her so badly I would have chanced the carpet. Then I felt like an utter ass.

She used my grip to haul herself to her feet. For an instant, I hoped she might hug me, but she turned away and opened the door.

"Can you come in and sit for a bit? You know him. And I need to talk to someone. I won't keep you long."

"Of course."

She hadn't changed a thing in Henri's one-bedroom. The living room walls were still lined with cases full of the volumes he'd read, as well as editions he'd repaired or rescued over the years. Fresh flowers sat in a Chinese vase on the iron and glass coffee table, and the musty old-book and pipe tobacco odor mixed with fresh air from an open window. And a subtle charge of Susan's perfume—I'd never learned the name of it.

"You don't want coffee, at this hour?" she said.

I shook my head and sat on one end of a vined and flowered chintz love seat, furniture from a century before.

"No, I don't need anything. But I am pretty whipped."

It wasn't that I wanted to hurry her, but I was uncomfortable being alone with her, feeling as I did and not knowing if I dared say or do anything about it. I felt as if she were holding me off with both hands, figuratively.

Then she came and sat on the love seat beside me, close enough I could feel the heat of her thigh.

"There's not a lot to say about it." Her voice was low and sad.

"It's just that's he's going to die sooner rather than later. I knew it in my head, but here?" She thumped her chest. "No way. How did you cope?"

I thought about how Thomas, my father, had died two and a half years ago. We'd had an uneasy relationship—his rigidity and expectations, my drinking—but we'd managed a rapprochement before he died. It would be harder for her to do that with Henri in dementia, though I didn't think their relationship had been all that fraught, either.

"I don't know that I did anything," I said. "You don't stop thinking about it, even afterward. I didn't understand the effects until later."

I'd been sober for quite a while when he died, but I ran myself into a relapse soon after. Work and my friends had eventually dragged me out of it, as had finding out what happened to Alison Somers.

"What's the timeline?" I said.

"I'm blaming him, you know. For having to come back here."

The non sequitur whipsawed me for a second.

"You weren't planning to?"

"I don't know what I was planning." She turned her face up to look at me and it was all I could do not to try and kiss her. "You were so locked into what happened to Alison. Being with you didn't seem like a very safe bet."

"That's probably fair," I said. "I wish we could have talked about it."

"And now you're all tied up with someone else, aren't you? If there was a window, I missed it."

Irritation swelled to a boil.

"Someone's been talking to you about me?"

"Marina."

"You'd talk to her, but not to me?"

"It was easier that way. I didn't want to start anything if you were attached."

"I'm not attached to anyone," I said. "If you want details, I'll explain it to you. Whatever it was, it's been over for a while."

She sighed.

"My life in Oregon is very complicated right now. I don't know how much I can promise you."

I looked down into her eyes.

"No promises, then. Whatever works for today? Tonight?"

"If we can do that."

And she offered up her mouth like a hope.

* * *

Naked, she was as lovely as I remembered, strong and generous in her lovemaking. I touched the ends of her nipples, remembering, and sent a shudder through her body, kissed her behind the right ear in the one place I knew that reached her center.

"Cold." She slid under the duvet, holding up the edge until I slipped in beside her.

"Slowly," she said then. "It's been a while."

I ran my hands down her flanks, so hungry for her I barely breathed. When I kissed her again, it felt almost chaste. As our bodies warmed the air under the cover, her mouth loosened and we kissed as if we could take each other in that way alone.

The pleasure of touching her was almost too much to give up, but when I opened her with my fingers, she reached for me and ran her fingernails lightly up and down, only hardening me.

"Please." I shifted my weight to one side.

She turned over on her back and I brought myself up over her, marveling again at how small she was, and placed myself between her legs, prolonging that sweet moment of entry as long as we could endure it. Finally, she reached down and placed me inside and the molten world took me over.

"All right." She shifted her hips and I felt all my problems and worries escape me, until all there was was the two of us joined and moving together like the sea.

* * *

The doorbell rang not half an hour later. I was half-asleep, tracing circles on the skin of her back with my fingertips and pondering the old saw about absence and a fond heart. Susan was sleeping, her tiny

167

snore like messages from the depths of her unconscious. She twitched and sat up straight.

"Did the doorbell ring?" Her voice was muzzy.

I kissed her and climbed off the bed to look for my pants.

"It did," I said. "I'll handle it."

"It might be Mrs. Rinaldi," she said. "I told her to knock if anything was wrong."

My first floor tenant had had a mild heart attack not too long ago.

Susan threw on a robe and started for the front door.

"Stay here," she said. "I told her I didn't have any boyfriends."

I shrugged and started to dress, not wanting to assume Susan would have me stay all night. I didn't want to add extra weight to where we were right now. Buttoning my shirt, I only stepped out into the living room when I recognized the voice at the door.

Susan slipped the chain off the apartment door and let the caller in.

"There you are," Burton said. "I've been looking all over the place for you."

He walked inside as if he had a right to be here. I didn't like the manic energy rolling off of him, nor did I like the worry that showed on Susan's face.

"Doesn't look like you're bringing me good news," I said. "Maybe we ought to take this upstairs."

He looked at Susan, nodded. She would wonder how Burton knew to find me here, but it had to be intuition. And important enough to intrude. I had the idea what he wanted to tell me was something I didn't want her to know about. Yet.

"Coffee in the morning?" I said to her. "This is probably just something to do with the bar."

She didn't appear to believe me, but was willing to let it go.

"I'm up by seven," she said.

But when I bent over to kiss her, she backed away and patted my hand.

Feeling confused, I followed Burton out the door and up the stairs to my apartment.

33

"You closed the joint up early tonight," Burton said as they climbed the stairs to Elder's floor. "Any particular reason?"

"Other than the fact the place was empty?"

He sounded cranky, and Burton assumed it had something to do with his catching Elder with Susan Voisine. They hadn't been playing cribbage before he arrived.

"There's no easy way to say this."

They were stopped in the landing outside Elder's door while he fiddled with his keys.

"Kathleen," Elder said. "Is she dead?"

Burton had wanted to tell him out here, gauge his reaction before Elder could get comfortable in his own space. They were friends, but Elder was a person of interest. If he'd done it, though, Burton would have bet on a heat of passion thing. Not a cold-blooded execution. The likelihood he'd killed Kathleen evaporated when Burton saw the pain in Elder's eyes.

"No question it was her?" he said.

"I'm sorry, bud. Remember. I knew her, too."

Elder frowned.

"If not exactly the same way."

He locked the apartment door behind him, a long-time city dweller's habit. They went into the kitchen and Elder sank into a kitchen chair, put his hands over his mouth.

"How did it happen? Was it Maldonado?"

Burton started to make coffee. He would have preferred a stiff drink, but Elder didn't keep any in the house.

"She was shot in the head. From behind. Maybe a foot away."

"Coward's way," Elder said.

It was an odd comment, but Burton had heard stranger reactions. He watched Elder from the corner of his eyes as the water dripped through the coffee maker. Elder had always been stronger than he appeared to the world, but the sudden transformation, from grief to anger, was still startling.

"If you know something about this I don't," Burton said. "Now would be the time to tell me."

He would never get used to people who thought they were smarter than the police, withholding information, attempting to control the narrative. He was doubly irked because Elder knew better, he'd thought.

His friend's eyes were spit-gray, cold, and dry.

"I do," he said.

Burton tamped down his anticipation. It might be bullshit.

"This Maldonado thing. I think there might be a connection to the Olympic bid."

Burton poured them both coffee and sat down across the table, arranging his expression into the attitude of a disinterested listener. He knew Elder well enough to understand that once he started a story, he had to tell the whole thing, including his surmises. Burton's role was to listen and identify any facts that might support a theory of the crime.

"I told you about Icky Ricky's cousin and his henchman, right?" Elder said.

"Refresh me."

"Donald Maldonado comes to Boston to take over what was Ricky's 'enterprise,' except Ricky's enterprise turns out to be shit."

"The street dealers all push for someone else now, and Tesar and Spengler are busy trying to run the old luncheonette. You don't think Donald knew that?" Burton said.

"Probably not." Elder looked surprised. "I didn't know about the luncheonette."

"Think a meth head's version of a fern bar. So, Maldonado comes to Boston."

"Right. His factotum, Randolph Coyne, comes into the bar to tell me Maldonado is looking for Kathleen, that she stole something of his. At this point, I have no idea where Kathleen is. Obviously."

Burton had wondered idly if Kathleen had told Elder she was going to hide in the prison system. Apparently not.

"Then Kathleen shows up in the Esposito, after her daring jailbreak from Rinker Island."

Burton reached for his cigarettes, then decided not to break Elder's rhythm.

"At which point, unknowing, I stupidly let her use my apartment to shower and change clothes. I think she'll tell me what's going on but she bolts before I get home. Stealing clothes and some cash."

Burton knew most of this, but it helped to hear it whole.

"Somehow Randolph Coyne discovers she's back in Boston and returns to, uh, interrogate me about her whereabouts.' Elder rolled back his sleeve and showed the white scar lines on his forearm.

"Is that a phone number?"

"Yes." He shrugged it off, but Burton could tell the memory bothered him. "So Kathleen shows up at the bar one last time and says she's going to settle with Maldonado once and for all. She leaves me a briefcase full of papers and tells me she's going off to set up a meeting with him."

"So, at the very least," Burton said. "Maldonado could have been the last guy to see her alive."

"He has to be the one who killed her. Or maybe Randolph, who's the muscle. Have you met Maldonado?"

Burton shook his head.

"Wouldn't have had a reason to, if you hadn't told me all this."

Elder did like to keep things close. And he didn't ask for help.

"I don't know what would have kept her alive if he decided to kill her. But that's neither here nor there. I have the briefcase he was after."

"And what's inside?"

"Papers. Real estate options that allow the bearer to buy a bunch of properties around Franklin Park."

"For the Olympic thing?"

Elder hadn't touched his coffee, but he wrapped his hands around the mug as if he were cold.

"I suppose. I was going to call you after the stun grenade incident."

Burton shut his eyes and shook his head. "I don't even want to know."

"I set up a meeting with Maldonado. Tomorrow. I'll hand him his documents and he'll get off my back. I hope."

"You think he might send you this Coyne character instead?"

"I told him I'd shoot the fucker on sight if he did. Donald I can handle—the other guy's too scary to deal with."

"Unless Donald's carrying grenades?"

Elder blew out a sigh.

"Just want it done. I had a thing for that woman and it caused me nothing but grief." His face creased. "Does it make me an asshole that I'm relieved she's gone?"

"Not really. I never thought that much of her. As you know."

"But you treat the dead ones all alike. Tomorrow at the bar." Elder looked up at the clock. "This morning now, I guess. Did Maldonado kill her, you think? Once he found out I had what he wanted?"

Burton felt like Elder was shopping for guilt to take on.

"No way to know yet. We better get some rest."

"We?"

"I'm OK on the couch."

He wanted to keep an eye on Elder—he didn't think the news about Kathleen made him a danger to himself, but he worried.

"Whatever. You know where everything is."

Elder shuffled toward the bedroom like an old man.

"Hey," Burton said. "Nice to see you and Susan back together."

"Yeah. I guess it was."

34

Burton leaned over from his side of the bar, leafing through the papers from Maldonado's briefcase.

"I don't know that these are legally enforceable," he said. "But each set is an option to buy the property at a certain price. Like twenty-five or so houses. You looked up where they are on a map?"

"All around Franklin Park. Maybe he is going to use them as rentals, if the Olympics come through?"

Burton shoved the papers back into a pile, matched their edges, and slipped them back into the folder. His eyes burned as he stared into the bar mirror.

"Normally this kind of shit is way above my pay grade. But you notice every one of those offer sheets was signed by Dorris Boustaloudis? Assigning them to Maldonado?"

"That the Rinker Island body?"

"His wife. And you know how much I believe in co-inky-dink."

"You said you didn't have the evidence to arrest him for Kathleen's murder. What about this Bousti-whatsis?"

"I can use these to put pressure on him. Maybe. Especially if I have these documents in custody."

"Be my guest. They've got no value for me. Will you be able to arrest him?"

"Take him in for questioning, at least."

The street door squeaked. Though I'd been meaning to spray the hinges with WD-40, I was glad I'd forgotten.

Burton slipped off the stool and padded across the floor to sit in the dark at the edge of the stage. I hadn't turned on any lights except the

173

ones behind the bar because I wanted Donald focused on his footing coming down the stairs.

"Darrow?"

His thin and reedy voice echoed in the empty room.

"Over here. At the bar."

He reached the bottom of the stairs and paused.

"You didn't pay your electric bill?"

"Come on over here and get what you came for. And convince me I'm not going to have to look at you or Randolph Coyne ever again."

He turned to me and when he saw the briefcase, he strode over, reaching for it. I slapped my hand down on top of it.

"Talk to me, Donald. There's always the burn barrel."

"What do you want to know?"

He shucked his ragged navy parka as if he were hot. Under it, he sported a white Celtics sweatshirt, baggy khaki pants. It occurred to me again how hard it was to take the man seriously and what a mistake it had been not to.

"I want to know that you and I will be strangers. Henceforth and always."

His interest was entirely on the briefcase.

"Whatever you say, Darrow. Beyond that..." He pointed. "I have no interest in you. Though I still owe Kathleen a few words when I find her."

Which implied he hadn't been the one to kill her. Who, then? Randolph? I kept talking to cover the sound of Burton crossing the floor.

"They're all there," I said. "Though how would I know. Right?"

Maldonado pulled the folder out and flipped it open. He counted the number of clipped sets of papers.

"Good enough," he said, stepping back. "I guess our..."

The street door squeaked again, that tiny noise followed by the loud snap of a shot. Maldonado spun until he faced the stairway and a dark red blossom spread on the back of his white sweatshirt. I thought Burton had shot him, at first, and couldn't fathom why.

I froze long enough for the gunman to trigger another round, which splintered the top of Maldonado's head and sprayed blood and tissue all over the bar. I gathered enough sense to duck down, but no more shots were fired.

Steps banged up the stairs toward the street, Burton going after the shooter. The door opened and a screech of tires ripped through the outside air. I collapsed on the duck boards behind the bar, and considered whether I could still drink a whole bottle of Scotch.

* * *

I'd been through this process once before, back when Timmy McGuire's body got dumped in the Esposito, and nothing much about the process had changed. The crime scene people used chairs to block off a space around Donald's body, crumpled at the base of his bar stool, and the investigators who weren't looking at the body themselves were on hands and knees performing an intensive search of the floor. The medical examiner's attendant stood by, waiting for approval to bag the body and transport it to the morgue, though I didn't see what an autopsy would tell them that wasn't obvious: death by gunshot. Multiple.

Burton was the main difference from the last time. When he'd first come into the Esposito to investigate Timmy McGuire's murder, he'd been his most professional self: aloof, composed, collecting the facts. This morning, he was white-hot angry, I assumed because someone had performed an execution in front of him, the one person in the room who would take it most personally.

"Had to be a rifle," he said.

We stood at the far end of the bar, away from the mess and the activity, though the bar owner in me wanted badly to wipe up the top of the bar before the mess dried out. I also wanted to put on some music, but the lead investigator—not Burton, for obvious reasons, but a thick-necked specimen named Cooper—denied my request. Something about the integrity of the crime scene. Aural?

"Or a very good pistol shot. Dim light, a downward angle."

"But why?" Burton said.

"Don't' ask me. I thought this would be the end of it. Donald would take his fucking papers and get out of my life."

175

My legs were shaking and the outrage sharpened my voice. Burton stared at the Jameson bottle like he wanted to give it a good long kiss.

"If this was only about the papers," he said. "Whoever it was could have waited and taken them away from him when he left."

"If whoever it was knew they were valuable."

"Are they?" Burton shivered his shoulders. "Jesus, I need a drink."

"Stand up," I said.

He looked at me strangely, but obeyed. With his body screening me from the investigators, I reached down for the Irish bottle, set up a couple rocks glasses under the bar, poured a couple fingers into each one.

Burton cupped the glass so it wasn't visible unless you were sitting right next to him.

"You sure you want that?" he said to me.

I was not, but I wasn't in a philosophizing mood, either. I turned my back on the activity at the other end and downed the shot like a vaccine. The heat flowed through me like summer sunlight and the alcohol started to massage my damaged nerves. My neck muscles loosened and I blinked.

"Don't ask me any more questions," I said. "All right?"

Burton sipped, making sure none of the CSIs were watching. I didn't know what kind of short leash he was on with his boss this month, but I doubted drinking on the job would help. I poured myself another, if only to join him in trouble.

"What don't we know?" he said. "Is there anything else you haven't told me?"

"You know what I know. My best guess is that the shooter was Randolph. He's the mean side of that partnership—the two of them could have gotten crosswise with each other."

"But he was muscle, right? If it was him, he obviously didn't care about the papers."

"Nasty muscle, but yeah. Pure intimidator. I don't see him giving a shit about the Olympics or real estate or any of that."

Burton tilted his glass up as Cooper glanced at us, then hustled down the bar.

"I need you sober," he said to Burton.

Burton put the glass down gently. I thought he might snap, but his reply was mild.

"Whatever you need, Coop."

"No more today. Got it?"

And he returned to where the investigators were meeting around a table.

"Asshole," Burton muttered. "What about Ricky, strange as that would be? Could he be mounting a comeback?"

"From the land of the thong bikini? The lotus-eaters? That's about as unlikely as I could imagine. Even if he was out of money, he wasn't healthy enough."

"The lotus-eaters is LA." Burton's joke was half-hearted, his mood damped down from the initial rage, but still smoldering. "There must be a connection to the BOFF here, somewhere."

"The dead guy on the island connects to Donald through the documents, right? But he was against the bid and Donald must have been in favor? But why kill any of these people?"

Burton shoved the glass at me as if he wanted another, but I slipped it under the counter.

"Donald had no reason to kill Boustaloudis. The options already belonged to him. And you think Donald killed Kathleen."

"It didn't sound like he had," I said. "But who else cared?"

He tossed his hands in the air.

"If I knew that, I'd go home and take a nap. This was all making a kind of half-assed sense an hour ago."

"Burton." Cooper called from the far end of the bar. "Let's talk."

"Delightful," Burton mumbled. "Interrogated by the third stomach of a cow."

"Is that the omasum? Or the reticulum?"

Burton looked stunned. I carried all kinds of useless information in my head.

"Any way you look at it," he said. "What comes out is shit."

* * *

Marina showed up later, around eleven-thirty. I'd cleaned up the bar and the floor around where Donald's body had been, but in my imagination, the mess remained. My legs were still shaky and my head felt light. I told her what had happened, sent her home after Cooper spoke to her, and locked the street door.

It was Kathleen's death that finally hit me hardest. I wondered if I were like that character in the old comic strip who dragged a storm cloud around over his head everywhere he went. Only in my case, it was a death cloud.

I walked back behind the bar, my purpose singular. I hadn't put the Jameson bottle away after Burton and I had tapped it, and since there were only four or five inches left in the bottom, I told myself it couldn't hurt too much to finish it off. I scrolled up an instrumental playlist on the iPad, headed by Brad Meldhau, and walked out and sat on a bar stool as if I were my own customer.

I realized, as I let the whiskey soak away my jangle, that I was going to have to sell the bar. As much as it had been a lifeline when I started, its history of violence was steeped in the walls, impervious to the work I'd done cleaning and repainting them. Once a bucket of blood, apparently, always one, and the violence was harsher now, more associated with death than petty crimes.

At least, I hoped it was the place and not me. I couldn't ignore the possibility that I was what attracted the violence, the people I associated with, the situations I kept stumbling into. I'd created something better out of the Esposito, but maybe under all the surface improvements, I hadn't improved myself.

As Brubeck swung into the classic version of "Take Five," I reached across the bar for the phone. As I poured out the last of the Irish, leaving the glass half-empty, I punched in the number for Daniel Markham.

"Attorney Markham's office."

"Markham, please."

"Whom shall I say…"

"Elder Darrow."

The curt cutoff told me what she thought of my telephone manners.

"Elder."

"Take the offer. I'm ready to sell."

"Yes. I was going to call you this afternoon. Which was the deadline?"

Somewhere he'd acquired a younger person's habit of ending his sentences on an interrogatory note, and I wondered if I hadn't found a good working definition of a lawyer, someone who turned everything into a question.

"Yes. I'm accepting the offer. How soon can we close?"

Now that I'd made the decision, I was in a hurry to shed the burden.

"Elder. I was going to call you because the buyer called me."

"He wants to negotiate."

"Ah, well. I understand there was an incident this morning? At the Esposito?"

That was one way to say it, if trivializing. And I wasn't drunk enough not to wonder about his, and the buyer's, sources.

"Why?"

"Because the buyer called and reduced the offer. A half million."

"He dropped the price by half a million? Take it anyway."

Markham coughed politely.

"No. *To* half a million."

"Really."

That ran me up another possibility for a motive for Donald's death. Was a mystery buyer crazy enough to kill someone to drag the value of my bar down?

"Do you still wish me to accept?"

Markham sounded hopeful, as if there might be some benefit to him in the sale. Taking an actual commission would be dishonest, but in his world, rewards also came in intangible ways: access, power, knowledge.

I considered it for all of five seconds. The amount would still pay off the mortgage and leave me a hundred grand or so. I looked down into my empty glass and realized what that would mean.

"No. I'll accept the original offer, even a five per cent haircut. No less. Did you find out who the buyer is?"

Markham hesitated. I knew he thought of himself as part of the city's power structure and not knowing threatened his self-image.

"I have a hunch. But I don't want to say if I'm not sure."

But he definitely sounded disappointed by my decision, which reduced my trust in him further.

"Let me know if anything changes. You know where I'll be."

And I hung up, decision averted for now. I thought about opening another bottle of the Irish, but some shred of self-preservation intervened, and I turned on the espresso machine instead.

As it hissed and gurgled, I realized that Kathleen's hold on me had started to slip away even before she died. I'd thought I was all done with her when she disappeared the first time, but she'd drawn me back in, not because she cared about me, but because she thought I might save her. Was that how I'd looked to her, as someone who gave until it hurt?

I cleared the steam wand on the Rancilio, ground some beans, and charged the gruppa. As I set a cup under the spout, someone tried the upstairs door, then knocked on it, loudly.

I jogged up the stairs. I should have put up a sign. Cooper hadn't told me I had to close up, but I didn't feel like dealing with customers today.

Unlocking the door, I had to push it open against the wind.

"Elder?" she said, surprised. "You're not open?"

"Come on in. I'm having coffee."

Susan did her hip-hop thing down the stairs, then frowned at the empty bottle and the glass sitting on the bar. The music segued into a ballad version of "Love for Sale." Not Miles. The Clifford Brown version.

"You've been drinking," she said.

"Uh, yes."

"I don't mean having a drink. Drinking as if you were serious about it."

"Just today," I said.

"No."

She walked toward the espresso machine, forcing me to follow her to that end of the bar. When I looked down, I saw the whiteness of the scalp in the part of her hair and thought of the bone fragments of Donald Maldonado I'd cleaned off the bar only hours ago.

"Looks like it's been going on for a while." She turned her

disappointed face up to me. "I thought you were done, but I take it you still have the problem."

"I like to think of it as an opportunity."

She winced. Alcohol always made me think I was wittier than I am.

"Very amusing." She climbed up onto a stool. "Is there hot water in that machine? I could use a cup of tea."

I busied myself with maybe the one order I'd be able to fill today. I didn't feel like a bartender at all.

I ran hot water into a small metal pitcher and set it in front of her with a mug and a basket of tea bags, then walked down the bar and retrieved my glass. I tossed the empty Jameson's bottle into the trash with a crash, then racked the glass in the dishwasher. I was unaffected by the drinks, except for a looseness of emotion and, of course, the need for more. Soon.

"I always knew you were an alcoholic." She tore the foil off a packet of raspberry herb tea. "But you seemed to have it under control."

I took in what she said, nodded. There wasn't any percentage in denying the obvious.

"Recovering," I said.

"Or re-recovering. Relapsing?"

The drinks I'd had didn't help me dampen my anger.

"I haven't tried to hide this from anyone."

"You've been sober as long as I've known you, Elder. I don't think I've ever seen you take a drink."

Of course that was true. Susan had come into my orbit after Alison Somers killed herself, while I was busy trying to gentrify the Esposito and working with Burton to find out what had happened. Except for one major slip—and only Marina knew about that one—I'd been sober the whole time.

"I'm sorry you're surprised," I said. "I understand how you might think it's a problem. But it's not."

She dunked the tea bag a half dozen times before squeezing it out with a spoon and setting it on a napkin.

"You know that's not true." She laughed acidly. "Oregon might be the addiction recovery capital of the universe, with all the coaches and therapists and psychologists set up out there. Even if you're not going to be the AA type, you have to know there's no cure that includes still drinking."

"I had a slip," I said. "That's all. It's been a hard road these last few weeks."

Her grimace discarded that rationalization and I had to agree with her. The booze in me was only trying to justify its existence. I pressed the button on the espresso machine. Coffee did make more sense.

"Why didn't you tell me about it, Elder?"

How much did I want to involve her in all this craziness? And what would I have to leave out so as not to hurt her feelings? Or risk that we might not be able to get back together?

She leaned forward.

"All of it," she said. "You're doing that thing again, where you think because I'm small I'm not strong."

The shot finished filling the tiny cup. I carried it around the bar and sat beside her.

"After you left, I was involved with someone." I watched her for a reaction—nothing. "Somewhat seriously. I was pretty sure I wasn't going to see you again. We had a couple of months together, then she disappeared."

Susan put her hand over mine, remembering, I was sure, other women who'd disappeared on me: Alison, of course. Jacquie Robillard. Susan herself.

I sipped the coffee.

"Got around that all right—not by drinking, by the way. Then a couple of weeks ago, she shows up at one of Burton's crime scenes. Rinker Island, the paupers' cemetery? A murder victim found out there."

"Not her," I said quickly as Susan raised a hand to her mouth. "She was a prisoner on the burial detail."

"She was in jail?"

"Put herself there," I said. "Trying to hide from some people who were chasing her."

"Meaning she was a criminal."

"She stole something that belonged to those people."

"And came back to you for help when she got out?"

"She escaped actually. She wasn't released."

Susan shook her head. As I listened, I had to agree that it sounded crazy. I finished my coffee, wanting to finish the story, too.

"She left the stuff she'd stolen with me. The people it belonged to came looking for it. I set up a meeting to return it. Kathleen got herself killed up on the Common, then the man who came to pick up the material got shot in here this morning. Two stools down from where you're sitting."

If I'd thought that was going to shake her up, I was wrong. She sipped her tea, her green eyes steady on me.

"So you can see it's been a little more than a slightly bad day."

I was aware I was still trying to excuse the drinking as much as explain why it had happened, but I wasn't ready for what she said next.

"Well. Whining about it isn't going to help."

She glared at me. The caffeine warred with the booze in my blood and I realized she'd wanted to shock me.

"OK. I'm making excuses. All I can do is start over."

"Did you love her so much?" Susan's voice hitched.

"Good question." Losing Susan would tear me up at a much deeper level than losing Kathleen had. Her leaving for Oregon the first time had felt like having her leave the earth. "I think I loved the idea of her, being an outlaw. And that she made me forget about you for a while."

She winced.

"So what happened to the man who got shot here? Am I in danger sitting here talking to you?"

I shook my head.

"Burton was here. He's on all three of the killings. Somehow it's tied in with this notion of bringing the Olympics to Boston."

"Three. Your old girlfriend, the guy here. Who else?"

"A man who was part of the anti-Olympics movement. Kathleen found his body out on Rinker Island."

She finished her tea and I wondered why she'd come into the bar to see me in the first place. Certainly not for this discussion.

She climbed down, using the rungs of the stool.

"I was on my way to see Henri," she said. "I wanted to let you know they're operating tomorrow morning. I could use some company."

"I'll be there. What time?"

"Scheduled for eight." She hiked her bag up on her shoulder and pulled on a beret over her short bristly hair. "This drinking thing, Elder? I'm not planning to spend my life taking care of anyone."

Enough of the whiskey remained in me to fuel my anger. I just managed not to say anything stupid.

"Understood. We'll talk."

She touched the back of my hand.

"Oh, yeah. We will definitely talk."

* * *

I'd like to say the coffee and serious conversation sobered me up, but I'd be lying. The beautiful consistency of alcohol-love is that the more you drink, the easier it is to drink more. The first drink gives permission for the second and so on, on to the last. I wasn't so much interested in attaining some optimal level of alcoholic functioning that afternoon as I was in hammering myself flat.

A sympathetic onlooker might have labeled Susan the proximate cause, but her disapproval had only reminded me of another woman who could not accept my affair with the grain, the late Alison Somers. I knew too well how that had come out—though her career had dragged her off to New York City, my drinking had made the decision easy for her.

So my current belief, I suppose, was that Susan would use the same reason to leave me here and return to Oregon, once Henri was gone. Still, she wasn't allowing for the stresses I'd been under: Kathleen reappearing, then disappearing; the various episodes of violence; the threats to the Esposito's actual existence. Any one of those things would have launched a thousand drunks.

But, and I knew this, the truth of it all was that my soul hosted a black worm, a sick creature that required occasional oblivion for me to survive.

I kept the volume of the music low—ballads and instrumentals, no bebop or big band—and commenced to drinking my way down a fresh bottle of Jameson's finest. No Kathleen, no Susan, and if I couldn't believe any longer in the Esposito's power to keep me sober, what did I have?

Should have sold it when I had the chance. Still would. Maybe.

In the crepuscular darkness, I drank and listened to the music that used to give me such pleasure and tried to let it crowd out my thinking, fill the vacant spaces in my hollowed-out heart. Halfway through Miles's extended version of "Autumn Leaves," I decided it didn't matter at all if I drank until I passed out, and that it might be the only way I found any peace tonight. I staggered to the coat rack, wrapped myself in a long wool topcoat a customer left behind, and lay down on the floor to die.

35

Burton tried to stay away from his desk at D-4 as much as he could, even when he wasn't out at a crime scene. He was a cop who solved his cases being out on the street, not Googling or interviewing people over the phone, faces he couldn't see, eyes he couldn't look into. Another good reason why he wasn't usually here stood in the opening to his cubicle: Lieutenant Martines.

"Burton. Long time no see."

Martines had the build of a middleweight boxer, his waist gone slack and soft since he'd quit smoking. His gray linen jacket wouldn't button across the front, and crumbs dotted his thick black mustache.

"Still not smoking, Lou? Good for you."

"Fuck that. What do you have for me?"

"The three of them are linked up now. Boustaloudis, the Duck Pond woman, this Maldonado thug."

"Linked how?"

"The Olympic bid."

Martines rolled his eyes, chewing on what looked like a yakitori skewer.

"How good?" The links, he meant.

"OK. Still trying to tighten them up."

Martines spread his arms across the top of the cubicle wall. The armpits of his shirt were dark, though the precinct was perpetually underheated. Nicotine withdrawal, maybe?

"I'm getting pushback from the Olympic Foundation. They want us to say publicly the Boustaloudis thing isn't related to the bid."

Pushback from his bosses is what Martines meant. The BOFF wouldn't bother to talk to any of the actual cops doing police work.

"So is it or isn't it?" Martines said.

Burton's face heated up. Whenever the politician and the bureaucrats—departmental or otherwise—stuck their noses in, important things got glossed, even lost. He remembered something Dorris Boustaloudis had told him—maybe that would help Martines stave off pressure.

"There is a hint some Hyde Park thugs were pressuring Mr. Boustaloudis over something, maybe his store? Maybe the anti-Olympic work. There might be a connection there."

Martines shredded more fibers on his chew stick and pointed it at him.

"Tinker—from the Drug Control Unit?—gave me a heads-up that the Boustaloudis kid is Mickey Barksdale's dealer in Cleary Square. You're looking into that, right?"

Burton hoped his surprise that Martines knew that didn't show.

"It's on the list. Pretty sure it's peripheral, though."

Martines frowned.

"Look. I know you and Mickey go way back. But if Constantine Boustaloudis had a connection to Mickey…you talked to him, right?"

Burton nodded.

"I'm not accusing you of anything, Burton. But the appearances suck."

He latched down his temper—Martines could make his life much worse than it was.

"So I want you to—today—take a six-pack over to the wife and see if she can identify him."

"To what end, Loo?"

He hated being directed to do something in a way he couldn't step around. And Martines knew that, which was why he'd made the request explicit.

"If we can get an ID, even just that he was harassing them, we'll bring Barksdale in and brace him."

Martines walked away, reaching into his shirt pocket as if he still carried cigarettes.

"That shit only works on TV," Burton said, but not loud enough for the lieutenant to hear.

* * *

"Mrs. Boustaloudis. Dorris. Please put the knife away."

Dorris must have been pounding the Red Bull again, because as soon as she saw the picture of Mickey Barksdale, she'd slipped the stiletto out of her sleeve and tried to stab the six-pack.

"That rat-bastard." Saliva sprayed from her lips.

The drug store was all cleaned up, everything back in its place, the windows washed, too. The magazines rested neatly in their serried rows, the *Playboys* and *Penthouses* in clear plastic bags. Burton had the feeling something had changed, but he couldn't tell what.

"So, you do identify him as one of the men who threatened you?"

Burton was going to need a new way to keep from dragging Mickey into this, not because he cared what happened to the man, but whatever he'd been doing with Kenny Boustaloudis had nothing to do with the Olympics or Boustaloudis's murder. He didn't want to get dragged down some side road while he was trying to chase down the real story.

Dorris slipped the knife back up her voluminous sleeve and put on an expression of fear so phony it was all Burton could do not to laugh.

"He frighten me."

Burton cocked an eyebrow. Something smelled wrong.

"He threatened you?"

"What you think?"

All of a sudden, her diction had gone to hell.

"How, Mrs. Boustaloudis. What did he say to you?"

"He say 'I'm going to eff you up.'"

And that didn't sound like Mickey at all—he might talk to another thug that way, but he was unfailingly polite to old women and children, whether he was threatening them or not. Like a lot of Irish-Catholic boys, he still lived with his mother. Burton wondered what Dorris was up to.

He'd stepped away from her when she pulled the knife, back into the nook where the paperbacks were racked, so he was hidden from view when the shadow filled the open door.

"Kenny," Dorris said.

Burton was shocked by how quickly she devolved from fierce defender of the faith to the semi-helpless mother figure who needed her son's support.

Kenny wrapped his arms around her.

"Are you all right? They should stop bothering you now. I took care of everything."

"Took care of what, Kenny?" Burton stepped out into view.

The kid started. Dorris worked the evil eye on Burton.

"What's he doing here, Ma?" Kenny whined.

Excellent question, since Burton had gotten what he came for, an ID of Mickey to satisfy Martines.

"I came by to see if everything was OK."

It sounded lame and he hoped no one asked him for an update on Boustaloudis's murder, since he still only had vague and murky possibilities and weak connections. His instinct was telling him he needed two or three more pieces of information to pull everything into focus, but he had no idea where to find them.

"We're fine," Kenny said. "Maybe you'd be better off finding out who killed my father."

He stood shoulder-to-shoulder with his mother, dressed like a hood from a bad seventies movie: tight black rayon shirt open to the breast bone, pegged sharkskin pants, pointed brown tie shoes. Burton wondered what role he was playing today. An old bruise yellowed up on his left cheekbone.

Burton pointed at it.

"That looks like it hurts. Mickey give you that?"

"Mickey who?" Kenny stepped away from his mom. "Can we talk? Outside?"

This was interesting. Dorris looked put out at being excluded.

He followed Kenny out and around the corner, where they stopped in front of the smoke shop, several doors up. Across the street, two guys the size of offensive linemen loaded a couch into a black pickup.

"I didn't want to say anything in front of Ma."

Burton suspected Ma knew more of what went on in the world than her son did, but he nodded, happy to maintain the fiction as long as Kenny was talking.

"I guess you must know Mickey, then?" Kenny said.

Burton leveled a look at him.

"Yeah. And I know what you're doing for him. Not too smart."

Kenny let the advice sail by, as he probably had with every piece of advice his father had given him.

"We—me and Mickey—had a disagreement. Over money." Kenny touched the mouse on his cheekbone unconsciously. "But it's all cleared up."

"You know I know Mickey. So I can find out if you're lying to me. You stole money from him? Also not smart."

"Not exactly. But we're cool. I hit the number last Tuesday for… well, for enough. We're square now."

When Burton was a boy, the number people bet on was the last four digits of the daily handle at Suffolk Downs. He had no idea if that had changed. Nor did he believe that was where Kenny had gotten the money to pay Mickey back.

"So, then. Mickey came around the store? Maybe leaned on your mom a little bit?"

Kenny looked horrified. "Jesus, no. She would have killed me."

At least he wasn't completely clueless.

"Which is what she's going to do if she finds out you were doing for Mickey what you were doing. Past tense, correct? Because, you get caught, she could lose the store."

Kenny was moving from one foot to the other, what Burton called the dirty-perp shuffle, listening to Burton without absorbing any of it. Certainly not changing any of his plans because of it.

"I know. I'm working something else out. I'm trying to finish school."

Burton grabbed him by the slick shirt.

"Whatever it is, don't do it around the store any more, all right? Because I can get the Hyde Park cops down here to bust your ass any time I say the word."

"What do you care?" Kenny sounded aggrieved. "You're supposed to be catching my father's killer. Not worrying about dope."

"Kenny. I don't give a flying Philadelphia fuck what happens to you. But something happens to your mother, or her livelihood here, you are going to pay the price. And when I put pressure on Mickey, he's going to know why. Which means you won't be working for him much longer."

"Yeah, yeah. Of course." Kenny's lizard brain managed to process that threat quickly enough. He stuck out his chin. "So if you're not spending time busting my balls, maybe you could find out what happened to my father? Me and my mom would sure appreciate it."

Burton stared at him, tempted to slap the little turd.

"You heard what I said, Kenny. Be smart."

* * *

Dorris had to be lying about something. Burton believed Kenny that Mickey hadn't come around, so why would she try and implicate him? And after their conversation at the boat ramp, Burton was pretty sure Mickey wasn't putting any pressure on the Olympic bid effort either way. He had no reason to kill Constantine Boustaloudis, and the one thing Mickey did not do was expend effort for no benefit.

Moreover, there was nothing on Burton's grapevine, either. One of the advantages of roots in a neighborhood that produced a majority of the city's homegrown criminals was that he could monitor, in a highly unofficial way, how various enterprises and personnel operated: who was heading up the ladder, who down, what activities were in the ascendant and which ones were being tabled, temporarily or otherwise. There were no other quivers about the Olympic bid along his web of connection. He was inclined to believe Mickey's wish to move his organization a little closer to the legitimate.

Heading back to D-4, he knew he'd have to finesse Dorris's ID of Mickey in the six-pack. Martines could be as stubborn as Burton when he got an idea in his head, and he wouldn't let Burton slide on something he'd ordered him directly to do. Burton knew he could lie, but that had a way of snapping back on you and he was pretty sure law enforcement hadn't seen the last of the Boustaloudis family.

He pulled into a space on Harrison Street, very rare in the middle of the day, as his cell chimed with an incoming text. He turned off the engine and picked up his phone: Unknown Number.

"Harbor Patrol says Randisi steals from corpses. How bodies get onto the island."

The Harbor cop—hell was his name again?—had tried to make himself part of the case. This must be him again. But how likely was it he had anything useful to share?

On the other hand, it would postpone his confrontation with Martines.

"Where you?" he texted back. "Meet?"

"Rico's"

Dive bar on Columbus Ave. He knew it well. *Too* well.

"Ten minutes."

"K."

36

Except that I didn't die, though when I woke in the forest of chair legs, I wondered what I was doing on the floor. As sometimes happened when I drank beyond my usual limits, I felt exceptionally good: clear-headed, bright, even energized. I also knew I'd be singing a different tune a few hours from now. But at the moment, the only physical complaint I had was a sore neck and back from sleeping on the cold concrete floor.

My second conscious thought was that something had wakened me. I had the dim aural after-impression of a noise out back. I climbed the foot rails of a bar stool until I could support myself, then rotated my head right and left to stretch out the ache. The noise came again, louder, and I walked around the bar and grabbed the Junior Slugger.

My first few steps down the darkened hallway must have looked comical. I needed my hands on both walls to keep from tripping over my feet. My joints loosened with the movement and by the time I reached the office door, I was moving smoothly enough.

A narrow beam of flashlight played over my desk, someone leafing through the paperwork. Looking for those goddamned real estate papers, no doubt. I reached around the jamb and flicked on the light switch.

"Randolph Coyne. I should have guessed I'd see you again."

Cool as a Popsicle, he turned off the flash and stowed it in a pocket of his cargo pants. He wore a black T-shirt, his jacket over the back of my chair.

"Very tactical look," I said.

"Where are they?"

193

He wasn't flustered in the slightest by being caught.

"Where's what, Randolph? Didn't I tell you I was tired of seeing your face?"

Randolph sighed.

"Donald sent me to get the papers. He knows you have them."

"Maybe you should have been here this morning then. You could have gotten them from him. After you shot him."

Randolph never showed much, but there was a glint of surprise.

"Someone shot Donald? Who?"

"If it wasn't you? I have no idea. But his brains were all over my bar. And the papers are gone."

Randolph tipped his head.

"Where?"

"With your boss's corpse. The police confiscated all of it. Big briefcase full of stuff?"

Randolph banged his fist on the desk top, a rare loss of cool.

"Jesus! You'd think these things were a treasure map or something. The way they keep appearing and disappearing."

"You don't know what they are?" I said.

"All I know is they are worth a bundle." He started around the desk. "That's it for me here, then."

I blocked the doorway.

"Excuse me," he said when I didn't move.

"Fuck you, Randolph. Feels like I owe you something."

All my frustration, my guilt, and my shame exploded in one swing of the bat, my rage exacerbated by the belief that he'd probably killed Kathleen. I wasn't channeling Big Papi so much as Robert DeNiro in the *Untouchables*, so I went for his arm and not for his skull.

First strike, direct hit, crunch and a sharp scream. Frightened by the depth of my rage, I stopped there, watched the bruised flesh on his forearm swell up dark, so fast I thought it might split the skin.

After that one scream, Randolph gritted his teeth and used his good arm to push past me, as if he knew I wouldn't swing again. He went through the fire door at a run.

I stood stunned by my capacity for violence. I walked out into the corridor and looped the chain around the fire door handle, padlocked it shut. A certain satisfaction carried me out to the front to turn on the coffee machine. The monster hangover was looming and though caffeine wouldn't solve it, it would keep me awake. Thinking about the way Randolph's forearm had flopped as he ran made me feel immeasurably better.

37

Rico's was the kind of bar the new Boston wanted out of its sight and out of its hair. But there were still plenty of neighborhoods in the city where money and high taste hadn't yet forced the people who'd grown up there to relocate, just as there were still neighborhood taverns where no one but the locals wanted to drink.

Like many of the old-school bars around the city, Rico's had a second door in back with a sign bearing a different name, in Rico's case, The Green Door. This habit, obscured in history, allowed a husband to tell his wife he was at one bar when he was really at another. Since wives tended to live in the same neighborhoods as their husbands, Burton didn't think anyone was fooling anyone else. But he loved knowing things about his city that the incoming yupsters and hipsters would never find out.

He entered through Rico's door, since otherwise he would have had to traverse a narrow alley choked with garbage, urine-anointed bricks, and at least one or two serious derelicts. As his eyes adjusted to the underwater light inside, he thought about how much like this place Elder's Esposito had been a few years ago and how little it was now.

First impression was the worst: smell of sawdust and sour beer, underlain with the sharp acid of vomit and a disgusting cherry-scented disinfectant from the bathroom urinals. At this hour of the afternoon, the bar was crowded with hunch-shouldered men in canvas vests, Levi jackets, a fleece or two. Rico's did not spend a ton of its overhead on heat, relying on the alcohol to generate enough internal warmth to make up for it.

Heads turned as he entered and noted Burton for a cop, but Rico's patrons, even if they were involved in criminal activities, were too passive to worry about him. Too, there was an odd sense of sanctuary about the place—almost no one wanted to interfere in another man's drinking.

The Harbor Patrol cop sat in a booth by the poker machines with a pitcher of beer and a bag of jalapeno potato chips. Burton watched him lick the salt off a chip, slide it back into the bag, then take a sip of beer. Other than not relying on how clean a glass in this place might be, he couldn't guess a reason for the potato chip thing.

He walked across the floor, the boards bouncing underfoot. Good thing the bar wasn't built out over the water. The other cop half-rose when Burton walked over.

"Frank Aschult, Detective."

Burton rested his hand on the high back of the booth, then snatched it back. The varnish, or something else, was sticky.

"Right."

At least the kid had the good sense to be out of uniform, a smart decision in any dive bar, no matter the neighborhood. His open face reminded Burton of how much energy and drive, even love, he'd had for the job when he started.

The pitcher of beer sparkled on the table. Burton slid into the booth, a duct tape patch catching on the seat of his pants, and poured himself a glass.

"Tell me."

Frank looked a little disappointed Burton wasn't a little more collegial, but he swallowed it, picked up his own glass. Probably telling himself all homicide detectives were dicks, in one way or another.

"This Trick Randisi," he said.

"Who's that again?"

"The guy who drove the Corpse Cruiser. The truck with the coffins that came out on the barge?"

Burton glared at him—nothing about dead people was funny to him, even if they hadn't been murdered.

"Is he an employee of the Corrections Department?"

Frank's shoulders stiffened up. He obviously wanted to tell the story his own way. Burton thought he needed to learn a little patience.

"Contractor. Outside vendor. He supervises loading and unloading the coffins, drives the truck. But to deal with the prison system, he had to be bonded, right?"

"OK. And what does all this have to do with Connie Boustaloudis?"

"Look." Frank thumped his glass in frustration. "Can I just tell you what I know and then you can ask me questions?"

Burton took a long swig of beer and almost spit it out again: cat piss. He supposed it would go faster if he gave the kid his head.

"All right. Tell me."

Frank relaxed, sat back.

"Like I said. This Randisi had to be bonded for this job."

Burton was more interested in how prisoners, Kathleen Crawford, for example, got assigned to the detail. He added that to his mental list of questions.

"I'm keeping up all right." He waved his hand. "You can go faster."

"So you know that includes a drug test and a background check, criminal and financial. Right?"

Burton drew in a long breath through his nose and counseled himself to wait.

"So," Frank said. "Randisi's file with the company that provides the trucking service to Rinker?"

"You got ahold of it?" Not bad for a boat cop. "How did that come about?"

Frank went coy.

"Friends," he said. "But the upshot is Randisi is a gambler, degenerate variety. He's on probation with his company because of it. Supposedly, he attends Gamblers Anonymous, but a little bird told me he still bets heavily. College basketball, this time of year."

"This little bird a source we can use in court, if we have to?"

Frank colored.

"Uh. Probably not. He's a runner for Eddie Macalester."

Main bookmaker for the waterfront, one of Mickey's employees.

"What else?"

"Randisi had been betting small before this, but he ramped up about three weeks ago."

"Right after Boustaloudis fell out of the box."

"Who?"

"The body. The victim? You're thinking Trick got paid off for burying Boustaloudis."

"It would have been easy. The route the truck takes to the dock goes through half a dozen back streets. Could have stopped anywhere and tossed on another coffin. And the paperwork's sloppy, too."

"What about the prisoners? They in on it?"

"They wouldn't know how many were supposed to be on the truck. They come out in a van, separately. Get picked up on the dock, then out to the island."

"OK." Burton started to rise. "This is all useful. Send me your boss's name and contact info and I'll write you a goodie."

"One more thing."

Burton cursed the evil TV writer who'd invented Columbo. Frank reached into his olive-drab windbreaker and brought out a plastic bag.

"Randisi gave my cousin—he's a bookie—this as collateral. Until he comes up with the cash."

A gambler who was broke? Startling.

Burton turned the bag over in his hand. It held a flashy, oversized, expensive-looking watch with a gold-link bracelet. An inscription on the back read: CB from DB, 2010.

"Constantine Boustaloudis," he said.

"I thought it might be important."

"OK," Burton said again. "You did good. Though no chain of custody."

He slipped it into his pocket. Frank—he kept wanting to call him Frankie—winced.

"I need to give that back?"

Burton shook his head. That would teach the kid to pretend to be a cop.

"It's part of the case now. In the system."

"Can you keep my cousin out of it?"

"Don't even know his name, Frankie. Do I?"

Which was not to say he couldn't find it out in half an hour. But he'd try and respect the family tie. For now.

"Thanks."

"No, buddy. Thank you. I don't know what it means yet, but it's a lead."

Frankie beamed like he'd just won Megabucks.

"Awesome," he said.

38

I walked back out front, moving like a football player twenty years retired, my neck and shoulders knotted from sleeping on the floor, my pulse starting to drive icy knives through my temples, my tongue the flavor of wet cardboard. And I had to pee.

I limped across the linoleum to the men's room, used the toilet, and ran the water until it was hot enough to raise steam. I scooped handfuls over my face, wet down my hair, then scrubbed myself dry with paper towels. At least my skin was awake now.

It was six-thirty by the clock out front and the Rancilio was finally up to heat. I pulled four shots of espresso and carried the cup over to the bar. As the caffeine percolated into my brain, I realized a couple of things.

Randolph had not known Donald had been killed, which suggested he hadn't been the one pulling the trigger. And he'd still been hunting those goddamned papers in my office. That disappointed me faintly—his meanness and his skills made him a likely assassin and I would have liked a reason not to eliminate him as a suspect.

But if he and Donald hadn't been in contact still, if Randolph hadn't known Donald was coming to the Esposito to pick up the papers, who was he working for now? Himself? Someone else? Which increased the mystery of where the threats would come from next.

The lock on the upstairs door clicked. I flinched, my tender gray matter not yet ready for the world. Marina walked down the stairs carrying two brown paper shopping bags.

"Talking to yourself again?"

I looked up at the clock again—somehow it was almost nine. I'd missed meeting Susan at the hospital and my espresso was cold. Had I fallen asleep? Had some kind of brain dropout? Fear shoved its way into me.

"Yes."

I got up off the stool befuddled. Had the leftover alcohol ganged up on my brain and shut it down? My cheek had a dent on the side, maybe where I'd rested it on the bar. I shook my head.

"You look, uh, sick." She set the bags down in the doorway to the kitchen and removed her coat. "You're not getting the flu, are you?"

I must have moved within sniffing distance then. Her nose wrinkled and she reared her head back.

"You've been drinking."

"Guilty. You want to know why?"

"Not really. But I would like a latté."

She unpacked her supplies in the kitchen while I made her coffee, then carried it in, and told her everything that had happened since the last time I saw her. I knew she wanted to be sympathetic, but she was wary, knowing from dealing with me how every resident of Planet Drunk was long on rationale and short on rationality. In someone who didn't understand alcoholics, my reaction might have seemed reasonable, a slip.

"Sorry if you've had it tough," she said.

She put the last of the big bottles of spice away on a high shelf, turned to face me, and picked up her coffee.

"But we've been here before."

"I know. I have no excuses. I don't guess it's ever not going to be a problem."

"When I came to work here," she said. "I didn't have a lot going on—Carlos, work. Not much at all.

Carlos was the boyfriend who abused her. She'd come to work for me on my father's recommendation, the daughter of the woman who used to cook for my family. The woman who was losing her mind right now.

"I'm a different person now, Elder. I learned a lot about myself. I could go do something else now—could you?"

And that was the crux of it, wasn't it? I was wondering if my original plan had a false core, based on an assumption that hadn't been accurate, that being around the liquor all the time would keep me sober. Somehow I'd thought I could inoculate myself against my own tendencies, and it had only worked partially.

"Interesting question," I said.

"You asked me before what I think about you selling the place? I think you should."

I stood up straight.

"One of the reasons I asked was that you and Burton rely on the place," I said. "You for the work, him for—I don't know what—free drinks? Someone to bitch to?"

She gave me a disappointed look.

"He's your friend, Elder. Don't make it any more complicated than that. And I am, too. But I can go get a job somewhere tomorrow. You know what a shortage of people there is in this business."

She was right about that. A couple months ago, I'd tried to find a bartender to relieve me a few days a week and I'd interviewed the saddest collection of drunks, misfits, and inexperienced kids I could have imagined.

"I don't know what to say," I said.

"You're afraid. Sometimes you need to make the decision you don't want to."

"Pop psychology?" I tried to smile. "I thought you were going to study culinary arts."

"It's a minor. Seriously, Elder. This isn't working for you any more. You can't see that?"

Someone pounded on the door. I looked at the little clock above her work space. Past eleven now, almost opening time.

"Thanks. I think. Discussion to be continued?"

She ducked her head, as if realizing how intimate the talk had gotten.

I jogged up the stairs to open the bar. I didn't usually have customers knocking down the door for their first drink of the day any more, but this was Pedey Thomas, the Metro guy for the Record, and he was often on time for opening.

"You keeping fucking bankers' hours now?" he carped. "Although

I have to say, I'm surprised you're still here."

I got myself behind the bar, poured him his Johnny Walker, and took his money. Checking the clock, he lipped the glass without drinking, as if to savor what was to come. It annoyed me that I knew exactly what he was talking about.

"What do you mean?"

"Heard you were selling out," he said. "That Carton and Feinburg bought the building."

"And where did you hear that?"

He gestured vaguely and sipped.

"Around and about."

"I suppose you know how much they're paying me?"

"Two million to start, I heard." He frowned. "Then the price went down because someone got killed in here. Is that why you were closed yesterday? You had a murder?" He chortled. "Just like the old days, huh?"

39

Burton recognized Martines's hard-on as soon as he saw his boss blocking the way at the top of the stairs into the Homicide offices at D-4.

"You showed her the six-pack, right? What did she say?"

"Yeh." Burton hadn't wanted to lie, but he needed to get around the question, since he had no confidence in Dorris Boustaloudis's identification of Mickey Barksdale. "She wasn't that definite. But look, I've got something else."

Maybe he could distract the man with something shiny and get him to ignore how wishy-washy the answer was.

"Better than Mickey Barksdale's ass on a platter? This better be good."

Burton wondered how Mickey had climbed so far up Martines's shit list. But he knew better than to oversell what he had.

"I know how the body—Boustaloudis, that is—got onto the island. And I've got a witness that people were robbing the graves. Or the corpses, at least."

"Robbing people so poor they needed to be buried in a pauper's grave?"

Martines's mustache twitched like a small animal.

"It isn't just poor people who get buried out there, Loo." Frank, who'd been assigned to that detail for two years, had told him that. "Anyone without a next of kin. Or no identification."

"Still don't see it." Martines grumbled. "How are they going to have anything worth stealing?"

"Wouldn't be much," Burton agreed. "Wedding rings, maybe.

Earrings?" He pulled out the watch and held it up. "But it's my lever to talk to the assholes who do it. If I can find out who sent the body out there, I might be able to figure out who killed the poor bastard."

Martines still wasn't liking it, maybe because it moved the case away from Mickey. Burton wondered what kind of pressure he was getting from people in Schroeder Plaza: Mickey? The Olympic thing?

And Martines would hate anything unpredictable in the way a case he thought he understood rolled out, which was why he was an administrator and not an investigator. His fingers plucked at his shirt pocket, the outline of a pack of cigarettes. Why was Martines torturing himself by carrying around the very thing he was trying to quit?

"Also," Burton said. "These guys have jobs under a state contract. Nothing they're grabbing off an occasional corpse is worth losing that."

Martines jittered at the top of the stairs, but let Burton pass.

"All right," he said. "Just keep me in the fucking loop."

"Jesus, Loo. Go smoke one, will you?"

40

Pedey drank up and left before the lunch rush, but the whole time I was serving soup and sandwiches, I was thinking about what he'd told me. Murray Carton and Harry Feinberg were two of the city's most prominent real estate developers. The projects they'd built, both in the city and out in the exurbs, had made them wealthy men and household names, at least in the Commonwealth. Both of them lived in Brookline, two streets apart, and the legend was that they'd met forty years ago as seventh-graders at Boston Latin and had been friends ever since.

None of which meant squat to me, except that they were very likely to be involved in the Olympic bid and thus in a strong position to know whether properties like my bar were in the path of development for that. Even if the bid was successful, though, the Games would be eight or nine years out, plenty of time to speculate on property. They might not even be planning to build anything themselves, just flip the real estate for its appreciation.

In the lull after the lunch rush, my head started to hurt again. I was surprised the rest of my body hadn't rebelled from being drunk after so long a dry spell, though. I kept on drinking club soda as I filled the dishwasher and prepped the bar for the evening.

The Donald papers, as I'd started to think of them, were on my mind again after Randolph's visit. When the shooting started, I'd shoved the briefcase under the bar, and in the aftermath, I'd failed to mention it to Cooper, the investigator. I couldn't count lying to Randolph Coyne as a sin.

I laid out a couple of the paper-clipped packets on the bar, trying to make sense of them, and only after I compared them side by side did I realize a couple things. First, the prices for the options to buy were ridiculously low, even though the neighborhoods around Franklin Park weren't that downscale. I'd seen that each packet contained an option to buy, but I hadn't noticed that they were all being bought by a single entity, Topalian Place, LLC. That detail meant that one corporation owned the access to what could be very valuable real estate if the Olympic bid came through.

I picked up the phone and called Burton.

"What?"

"Love the phone manner."

"I'm busy here. What is it?"

"Topalian Place. Ring a bell?"

"Nope. That it?"

He could be curt, but rarely was he rude. He must be hot on something.

"Yep. Lamb shanks on the menu tonight."

"Maybe, maybe not." And he cut me off.

I had another thought and looked up the main number of the Record.

"Pedey Thomas," I replied to the mechanical voice inviting me to say whose extension I wanted.

The phone rang with an old-timey buzzing sound, seven times before someone picked it up.

"Pedey?"

"Hold on."

In the background, someone yelled.

"Thomas, will you answer your own fucking phone once in a while?" Pause. "I don't know who the fuck it is. I look like your house boy?"

The handset clattered and I resigned myself to a wait. It was only twenty seconds.

"Thomas. Metro."

"Pedey. Elder Darrow."

There was that silence when someone out of context calls you up or runs into you somewhere other than usual. Pedey, being a reporter, faked ignorance better.

"Yeah."

"Topalian Place, LLC. Ring a bell?"

"What am I, the library? Never heard of them."

"How would I find out who the principals are?"

Pedey's voice hushed.

"Story in it?"

"How should I know? I'm just trying to find something out."

"Corporate registry. On the Commonwealth's web page. Call me back if you find anything good."

And he hung up on me. My day to get cut off.

I found the state's web site easily enough and keyed in Topalian, got back a screen full of information, including box numbers and names of the corporate officers, only one of which I recognized. The corporate secretary was named as Constantine Boustaloudis. I was going to have to call Burton back.

Other than that, I found nothing to follow up on. I shut down the search and brought up my accounting program. Believing Marina was correct that my mental health might improve if I took up another line of work, I needed to calculate the least amount I could take to sell the Esposito that would clear the mortgage and leave me enough to live on for, say, a year, without touching my father's money. The only unknown was what I'd do with the time and the money when I did sell. And the freedom. I'd worry about that then.

41

"OK." Tina Holmes, D-4's in-house interrogation specialist, caught Burton in the hallway outside the interrogation suites. "I put Randisi in the shitbox and the driver in the next one down. No two-way mirror in either one."

The shitbox was the oldest of the interrogation rooms and stank of fear, sweat, farts, old cigarette smoke, and cold coffee. Burton judged, based on his day out on Rinker, that the tractor driver might be a harder case, so he was going to let him stew a while. The fact that there was no two-way mirror meant he could push the limits a little. Audio recordings could always malfunction.

"Thanks, Ti. You want to take a whack at the tractor driver?" Burton glanced at his watch. "In about ten minutes?"

Holmes was a legend at interviews, squeezing information, even confessions, out of unlikely and obdurate suspects. Burton couldn't assign her officially—Martines would balk at using the extra resources, since the two agreed to come in without warrants.

"Campagnelli's his name?" Holmes said. "When you're ready for me to go, knock on your door. I'll be in the hall."

"You know what I'm after, right?"

"How that body got over the water. And who put it on the truck, if possible. Anything else?"

Burton shook his head.

"I'll come in and push them on the stealing afterwards. Little crime, big crime. Let me start talking to Mr. Trick here."

Ti nodded and leaned against the wall. Burton pulled open the door to the shitbox and walked in.

"Trick. Nice to see you again. How's your nose?"

Randisi sat up straight when he recognized Burton, but otherwise did not change the sullen expression. He wore a set of green Dickies work clothes, which Burton took to mean he'd come in right from his job.

"What's this all about?" he said. "I get paid by the hour, you know. I'm losing money being in here to help you out."

"Lose a lot more if the company finds out you're still gambling, am I right?" Burton pulled out a chair and sat. "You comfy here? You want coffee? Or a Coke?"

"Tea," Trick said. "Green tea, if you can do it."

Burton managed not to roll his eyes.

"In a minute. Tell me how that extra body got onto your truck."

Trick locked up. Burton almost smelled burning rubber as the man's brain skidded from answer to answer.

"No idea." He sat back and folded his arms across his chest, resting them on the shelf of his small pot belly. "Never saw the guy until he fell out of the box into the hole."

"Trick." Burton leaned across the table. "We know you, or your partner there, stole the man's watch. We have eyewitness testimony. One of the prisoners you were supervising."

"No way. That was Camp. The backhoe guy. Not me. Someone's out to get me."

"Ain't that the truth," Burton said. "And probably not the first time. But I'm pretty good at getting to the truth of things. So how did you get the extra coffin on the truck? Because I know Campy wasn't there for that."

Trick's eyes rolled up and to the right. Classic. Burton interrupted before the man could lie again.

"I've seen the invoices, Trick. The number you picked up at the morgue? You ended up with one over."

The guard sneered.

"How the fuck would you know that?"

"Because I counted them, Trick. The morning I first came out on the island."

Trick wouldn't know that wasn't a fact Burton could use in court, but he slumped.

"I get an envelope in the mail the night before the run. A little bit of money and an address. P Street, around Fourth."

"Not too far from the docks."

Trick nodded, the soul of cooperation now.

"A little bit of money," Burton said. "How much?"

Trick dipped his head, seeing his payday threatened. He had to know Burton could impound that money.

'Two grand," Randisi said.

"Come on. You'd jeopardize your job for that? A month's worth of overtime, maybe?"

"All right. Seven-five, OK?"

"Odd number."

Trick shook his head, uninterested in the details any more.

"It's what I owed."

"So you stop outside this address…"

"It's a big garage, auto paint shop, something like that. Backed the truck in, didn't watch. Left."

"But you did know you had something extra on board."

He nodded.

"When I started lifting them off. The wood was too new. And the box had been nailed together instead of screwed. Shitty job."

Burton softened his questioning. Trick was on the verge of crying and he didn't want to lose Trick to a lawyer. He'd been surprised, in fact, that the Trickster hadn't demanded one up front. Probably considered himself part of the law enforcement community and thought he didn't need one, that they'd work out whatever it was informally.

"But Trick. Messing with dead people? Seriously? You had to know it was a corpse in the box."

"Already dead, whoever it was. Nothing I did was going to bring him back. I was just doing a guy a favor."

Weak excuse, but then so was Trick.

"And you have no idea who paid you? Who hired the guys to load the truck?"

"Well." He started, then stopped. "This was South Boston, right?

So whoever it was had to have approval."

"'Approval?'"

"You know, like to do things there."

Trick apparently believed in the old criminal territoriality of Boston, where individual neighborhoods worked their turf and the hoods ruled inside narrow boundaries. That mode had fallen apart when Raymond Patriarca went down and Whitey ran, leaving chaos behind. The city wasn't a collection of fiefdoms now as much as a broad plain of possibility, dominated by one or two dukes—Mickey Barksdale chief among them. And Burton hadn't missed the fact that Trick had paid off his gambling debt, which ultimately was Mickey's, by adding the coffin to the truck.

"Tell me about the watch, Trick."

Randisi's doughy face blushed a bruised peach.

"I want a lawyer."

Burton reached back and rapped the door to signal Holmes.

"Of course you do, Trick. But look, putting that extra body on the truck is going to cause you more trouble than lifting a watch off a dead body."

Burton was lying. The extra coffin might only have cost Trick his job, but stealing the watch was a felony and would put him in jail.

"I'm a murder cop, Trick. All I'm interested in is who got you to take the body, try and trace that back to the killer. I don't care about the theft. So tell me."

Lies again. Some days he loved being a cop.

Trick sniffed. Burton had him.

"OK. We took some things, all right?" He frowned. "There wasn't ever very much. Campy saw the watch first."

"And grabbed it."

Trick nodded unhappily. "Seriously. That was it. You don't see me living on a boat in Florida, do you?"

"And that's everything you know about how you got the body?"

"Jesus. Yes." He looked chagrined. "You think anyone important would tell me anything?"

Good point. Burton stood.

"Give me a minute here before you call your lawyer."

As if Trick had a choice. As if Burton was going to save his ass. He met Ti out in the hall, coming out of the other interrogation room.

"I don't really need the tractor guy any more. He give you anything?" Burton said.

"Stole the watch, spur of the moment, sold it to a guy in a bar. Never did anything like that before or since. Never going to do it again. Lying through his teeth."

"Had to be, if Trick wound up with it. He used it as collateral on a debt."

Ti shook her head. Burton grinned.

"Probably just give him probation, anyway," Burton said. "Let him fly. I'll book the Trickster for the watch."

"You're sure?"

Ti looked like she wanted to go back in and take the guy apart with tweezers and an X-acto knife.

"He pissed you off."

"Usual bullshit. He thinks because I'm little, I'm cute."

"Trick's talking."

"K. I'll kick him loose."

"Ti." She looked back at him. "Don't kick him too hard."

She gave him a thumbs up and started down the hall. Burton rolled his shoulders and stepped back into the shitbox to give Trick the bad news. He wasn't going to be going home for a while.

42

Burton did show up for dinner, which I suspected he might. The lamb shanks were a perennial favorite and usually sold out. One of the stray ideas I'd had about what to do after I sold the place was a restaurant, a short-order and breakfast place outside the trendy parts of the city, give people a decent meal for a decent price without everything having to be locally-sourced, artisanal, small-batch, organic, and free-range.

"Constantine Boustaloudis," I said as he buttered a piece of semolina bread. "Isn't that the name of the body you found out on Rinker?"

"Exactly that." Burton used his fork to mash the potatoes and carrots together on his plate. "Why?"

I showed him one of the contract documents from Donald's briefcase.

"There's one of these for maybe twenty-five different properties." I handed him a Google map printout with the properties shaded in yellow. "See where they all are?"

"Franklin Park." Burton put down his fork. "Isn't that where one of the major venues is supposed to go?"

I nodded.

"You know, someone from the BOFF, or even just another developer, would pay through the nose for these contracts. Buy the parcels cheap and either build a couple hotels over there or just rent out the houses for the Games," I said.

"And this Topalian owns all of them? Is that Maldonado?"

Burton was poring over the fine print.

215

"Boustaloudis was the corporate secretary. I asked Markham about them. They're options to buy at a specific price. The holder can assign them to anyone and it looks like Topalian assigned them all to Maldonado."

Burton took a long drink of ale and burped.

"But what did Boustaloudis get for them?" he said. "We checked his family financials. Nothing unusual. But he must have been killed over them."

"And Maldonado?"

Kathleen had thieved her way into a bigger threat than she'd known. Millions at stake. What I didn't get was Randolph wanting the papers for himself now. He'd been Donny's muscle—he wouldn't have the capital to take advantage.

"Weird set of problems," Burton said. "Am I right?"

"The path from Topalian to here? Definitely."

"It might be a motive for Boustaloudis."

"Got another theory?" I said.

Burton picked up his knife and fork, started stripping the fat off the lamb bone. My stomach lurched suddenly. My stomach hadn't quite returned to normal from last night.

"Not so you'd notice. My cases don't usually tend to be Chinese puzzles, you know. They're usually straightforward. Just trying to balance the books."

I nodded and left it at that. It was as emotional as he'd get about what he did.

"For Boustaloudis," he said. "Kathleen. Even for Donald Maldonado. Not that I hold any love for him."

"Tangled."

He looked up from his plate.

"It'll come clear eventually. It won't be what I think it is, and I won't like everything about how it comes out. But it will come clear."

"Hope you're right."

I delivered a pair of pints of IPA down the bar. When I came back, I decided to drop the bomb.

"I decided to sell."

He nodded. "OK."

I don't know if I expected a little more enthusiasm. Or resistance. Maybe I'd overestimated the importance of the Esposito in everybody's life, not just mine.

"Like that? You don't care one way or another?"

"Not especially." His mouth was full. "It's your business, Elder. Not mine."

"Means no more free drinks for you." I gestured at the remains of his dinner. "Having to pay for your meals."

He swallowed some more beer and pushed the empty plate back at me. A blush like a weak sunrise rose through his fair complexion and into his receding hairline. When he'd calmed down enough to speak, the words bore a brutal intensity.

"Look. You don't tell me what to do in my job, right? Who to interview, what leads I should follow. Correct?"

Except for the time Alison Somers died, when I'd been in too deep to care about pissing him off. He'd let me slide then. But the rest of the time, he wouldn't put up with me giving him advice. That was clear as vodka.

"Correct. I wasn't looking for a decision from you. Just trying to judge the general customer desire here."

He played with his butter knife. He was nervous, too. I got it, finally. We'd never burdened our friendship with anything remotely philosophical, psychological, or emotional. We'd drunk together, eaten together, even talked over cases. Occasionally, I had a minor role in something he was working on. But by most definitions, we weren't friends so much as people who happened to travel in parallel orbits. That made me feel sad and heavy.

"You know what?" I said. "Never mind."

Burton looked at me, as if he had words in his throat he couldn't cough out.

It seemed that I'd burdened this little bar of mine with more than it could support: my sobriety, friendships, my entire life outside my mind. If I were going to move forward, I was going to have to leave things—maybe people—behind.

* * *

I hadn't booked any live music in so long, I'd forgotten how much I liked what it did for the place. Burton ordered a whiskey sour, declaring himself on mental health leave. He and Marina had brunch plans at Bar Boulud for tomorrow and it was good to see him unlatch a bit.

My Saturday night crowd was more moderate than usual. The Esposito was attracting more people who eased into their weekends than those who attacked it with both hands, and the trio on the stage, while nothing special, was competent in its niche of cabaret-style instrumentals. They were gliding through an intricate version of "Embraceable You" when there was a clatter at the door upstairs.

Heads turned that way in annoyance—I loved my music-etiquette-aware customers—and a twenty-something young man, thuggish-looking, stomped down the stairs as if the band was playing head-banger music and no one could hear him. Someone hissed. The bass player frowned and faulted.

My newest customer wore a black pea coat over iridescent blue pants, a dark red silky shirt opened to his sternum. The footwear that made such a racket coming down the steel stairs was a pair of pointy-toed, stack-heeled, black tie shoes, what a British pop fan would call winkle-pickers. He strode to the bar with the attitude of a regular and folded his hands on the service area of the bar, where there weren't any stools, then beckoned me down to him.

I held up a finger for him to wait, thinking he was another of those occasional slummers who walked in and expected special service because he had a pocketful of black credit cards. Then he rapped on the bar three times, hard. The piano caught a sour note.

"All right," I said to myself and walked down to see what the idiot wanted.

"Black Jack, straight up. Water back."

I looked him over. He had just the kind of baby face and demeanor the ABC guys sent into bars to ferret out underage drinking.

"Can I see an ID? Please?"

"Forget the drink." His sallow face emitted an ugly dark energy, as if something inside was goading him. "I need to talk to you."

The band finished the tune with a flourish and the between-sets rush was starting. People rose from their chairs to head for the bar. I held up my hand—whatever he wanted could wait.

"Hold that thought. I've got some business to take care of here."

His chest expanded, as if he had things he needed to say right now and he might explode if he didn't get them out. I tipped my head to Burton, who nodded and moved down the bar to get closer to the kid.

I got busy, clicking on the Spotify playlist and filling the drink orders as fast as I could. Locked into the satisfying rhythm of serving, I wondered what I was going to substitute for this feeling of purpose.

It took a hard twenty minutes to pacify the crowd. The bass player was back on stage, tuning his strings, when I walked down to where Burton sat on a stool next to the mysterious boy who needed to talk to me.

"Elder Darrow," Burton said. "Meet Kenneth Boustaloudis."

My eyebrows rose. Burton nodded.

"I'm sorry for your loss," I said.

Kenneth said nothing.

"I can guarantee he's over age, if you want to serve him."

Probably a good idea, in case the savage beast needed soothing. I poured him a generous shot of Jack Daniels and squirted some water into a glass. He tossed off the shot, coughed, and sipped the water.

"What was it you needed to talk to me about?"

"Listen, fuckhead," he said.

Burton slapped Kenneth's upper arm.

"Manners, Kenny. You're not over in Hyde Park now."

Kenny gritted his teeth so hard I thought I heard them crack.

"You've got some papers that belong to me."

Those fucking documents. They were going to be the death of me, though not literally I hoped. I cursed Kathleen in absentia for burdening me with the fruits of her career. I shook my head.

"I have to say, Kenny. I don't know who they belong to any more,

219

they've been through so many hands. I think I'm going to have to get an attorney's advice before I turn them over to anyone. They only came to me by mistake, but I want to make sure I'm doing the right thing with them."

Kenny pulled a revolver from the right hand pocket of his pea coat. I was stunned by the reaction and I felt stupid. I'd never run into anything inside the Esposito that couldn't be resolved with my Little Louisville Slugger and now, twice in one week, I was going to have gunplay here.

"Kenny." My mouth dried up. "Come on. I was joking. You have a problem with me, that's fine. But don't let's get a lot of other people involved, OK?"

He held the pistol as if he wasn't really sure how it worked. While I was trying to talk him down, Burton acted.

He slammed his forearm down across Kenny's, pinning it to the bar top, and with his other hand, wrenched the pistol away. Kenny's finger must have been in the trigger guard because I heard a snap and he took a breath like he was about to scream. Burton slapped a hand over his mouth and pulled him in close to subdue him, as if they were dancing.

The kerfuffle only attracted the attention of the two or three people closest, and as the playlist started into a bop version of "Take the A Train," I looked them off.

Burton passed me the pistol, which I stored gingerly under the bar. Then he removed handcuffs from the back of his belt and secured Kenny's hands.

"Is this about the papers?" Burton said. "Was he doing this for his mother, maybe?"

His mother wanted the papers?

"Could be," I said. "If she was part of the original group that paid for the options. Possession is nine-tenths here, right?"

Burton pushed Kenny in front of him.

"I'll take care of this clown. Tell Marina I'll be back for closing."

"I will."

And he marched Kenny across the back perimeter of the room. The blare of Duke's horn covered the sound of them walking up and out.

I leaned against the back bar, breathing deep to dissipate the adrenaline rush of Kenny's attack and fighting the urge to pull down the Jameson bottle.

The other two members of the trio worked their way back up onto the stage, the audience clapping about as enthusiastically as they deserved. Not for the first time, I realized this quality of band, this size of crowd, was about as good as the Esposito could get. If I hadn't already decided to sell, that might have tipped me over the edge.

On the plus side, the people who'd seen Kenny had been ready to jump in and help. And there was the feel of the music, which I never wanted to lose. At some point, I knew, I was going to have to stop waffling about waffling. Somehow I didn't think price was my biggest question.

43

Sunday mornings rarely found Burton at the precinct, especially if he had to leave Marina to be there, but bringing in Mrs. Boustaloudis's boy last night meant he had work to do. And, truth to tell, Bar Boulud, the bistro Marina had dragged him to, hadn't impressed him that much.

He'd picked up Kenny's pistol when he went back to the Esposito to collect Marina, but she didn't like him carrying his service weapon, let alone a second one, and made him lock them both in a suitcase overnight. And she hadn't been too happy when he sent her home from brunch in a cab, either.

But the nature of what he did was something they were going to have to negotiate if this was going to work this time around. It wasn't a nine to five job—hell, it wasn't even nine to nine.

He pushed his chair back from the computer where he was filling out the arrest report and went to get a cup of coffee. When no one else was here, as on a Sunday morning, he'd break out his stash of Peet's Major Dickson Blend. Bad coffee in the squad room was one of those old Barney Miller jokes. No reason to put up with it at all.

There were more things to worry about than his own schedule, too. What if Elder did sell the bar and she lost her job? She needed to work. Or go back to school. Regaining momentum would take time and energy. And then there was whatever was going on with Carmen. Dementia patients—God forbid it turned out to be Alzheimer's—could hang on for years, and Marina was an only child. For someone who liked things simple, he was putting himself into a complicated situation.

A cloud of fresh cigarette smoke preceded someone up the stairs. Burton was back in his cubicle, tapping away, when Lieutenant Martines spoke from over by the coffee station.

"Someone here?"

Burton heard the clink of the glass pot and winced. Good coffee was wasted on a smoker's palate.

"Here, Loo."

Martines, carrying an oversized mug that Burton was sure had just emptied the carafe, stood in the mouth of his cubicle and stubbed out the cigarette on the sole of his boot. He tossed the butt into Burton's wastebasket.

"Don't rat me out," he said.

"Never."

"You're in here pretty early. What's going on? I was going to talk to you tomorrow morning."

"Mmmm."

Burton offered him nothing. If Martines wasn't any more curious than that, he wasn't going to offer anything. Keeping his mouth shut was never a bad decision, and Martines wouldn't like the added complication of Kenny Boustaloudis.

"How close are you to wrapping up that Olympic thing?"

Burton crushed down the sigh that threatened to surface. There was the dilemma. Martines saw the case as a problem in politics; Burton saw it as the death of a man. He needed to figure out what the kid might have had to do with this before he could say anything more.

"Eh." He rocked his hand back and forth. "Possibilities. Still not enough to arrest anyone."

"Shit." Martines sipped coffee and made a face. "Whoa, that's strong. Really? Not even a prime suspect?"

Burton would have sacrificed one of his theories if he thought it would make Martines happy, but he wouldn't be confident about it and eventually he'd have to prove it. He'd only cloud up what he was charitably calling the investigation.

"Not really. Maldonado was probably the most likely, but he's out of the picture. Obviously."

"Could we pin it on him *ex post facto*?" Martines beat a hasty retreat when he saw Burton scowl. "Never mind. Wasn't there a Maldonado who ran some street dealers over by the Fens a few years back?"

"His cousin Donald. Turned out to be a little nastier and a lot more serious about his business. At least until he got himself shot in the head."

Martines looked baffled. Had he not paid attention to the fact that Donald Maldonado was another entry on his murder board?

"They're connected? Run it down for me."

Burton wanted to sigh again, but retelling the story Martines would know if he'd read the reports was the easiest way to get him out of here. He'd promised to pick up some bagels for Marina at Rose's, though he was never going to stop missing Jack and Marian's.

"Got Constantine Boustaloudis in a pauper's grave."

"Anonymously. Why?"

Burton chafed.

"Hide the crime. So he was probably not killed for his anti-Olympic activities."

"And Mickey Barksdale fits in how?"

"Any connection there is peripheral. This all has something to do with the real estate. Not anything Mickey cares about."

Martines looked as if he wanted to debate that, but Burton didn't give him an opening.

"The whole thing turns on a set of documents. Options to buy a bunch of properties around the Franklin Park area. At below-market prices."

"And Franklin Park, they were going to turn it into an Olympic venue?"

"Right. Boustaloudis was secretary for the corporation that owns them. But they've been through so many hands by now, it's not clear who actually owns the options."

"So there is an Olympic connection." Martines hated the idea.

"Only tangentially. Maldonado got hold of the documents somehow, then this thief—Kathleen Crawford—who got shot on the Frog Pond? She got hold of them."

"So can we soft-pedal the Olympic part?" Martines said. "Because the chief has this Wilder guy running up his ass. Which means the chief is running up mine. The hoi not talking to the polloi."

Burton was pretty sure that didn't mean what Martines thought, but the idea Wilder was getting exercised perked him up.

"Old J. T. What did he want?"

Martines took the cigarette pack out of his pocket, tossed it from one hand to the other.

"Told the chief our inability to solve the Boustaloudis murder was casting a pall over his fund-raising efforts. Did he want the Boston Police Department to be known as the entity that killed the city's Olympic chances?"

Burton snorted. Politics.

"Seems harsh."

"And wanted to know whether we'd found any evidence of Boustaloudis trying to sabotage the pro-bid effort."

"Other than a few pamphlets and Facebook posts? He was mostly talking to people who already hated the idea of the city being in perpetual construction for next five years so a dozen people could get richer. Can you imagine dressage on the Common? Or thousands of tourists trying to drive from one venue to another. In rush hour?"

Martines nodded.

"These guys never believe people don't see things their way. Fucking sociopaths. Being sure of everything is the worst curse I know."

Burton awarded the Lieutenant a point.

"But you and I are here to solve murders," Martines said.

"Which we will. Wilder have anything else to say?"

Martines fitted a Marlboro between his lips.

"Nothing unusual. Veiled threats if we didn't get on the stick. Heavy disappointment in the chief if he didn't make things happen. Usual horseshit. Wilder mentioned you by name, though."

Martines sounded irked, but that worried Burton.

"Really." He hadn't had the sense he'd impressed Wilder on their visit.

"Told the chief if you couldn't figure it out, no one was going to."

"I wonder what he meant by that." Burton could as easily have read it as a challenge.

Martines turned and started down the stairs with his mug. As he disappeared, Burton heard the click and hiss of his lighter.

He pressed the button that sent Kenny's paperwork out and heard the laser printer on the far side of the bullpen click into action.

It bothered him that Wilder was suddenly applying pressure, though it didn't surprise him. Boustaloudis's murder showed no sign of being connected directly to his tiny anti-Olympic effort, mainly because the killer had tried to dispose of the body quietly. It had been sheer bad luck for someone that Connie had popped out of his coffin. Someone who wanted to send a message would probably have made a more public show of it.

Clearly, the focus of the whole mess was the documents. But how Maldonado had acquired them and what benefit killing Constantine Boustaloudis had to anyone was beyond him still.

He walked over to the coffee pot.

"You asshole."

Martines had left just enough in the bottom to coalesce into sludge. Goddamned if he'd make another pot.

He turned off the machine, left the grounds in the basket and the tar in the carafe. Rose's had decent coffee and he'd buy some when he picked up the bagels. He needed to go home to Marina, have a second breakfast, and give his brain some quiet time, a chance to work things out without benefit of the conscious mind horning in.

44

I never expected too much business out of Monday, particularly Monday morning and noon. Even serious drinkers liked to pretend a better week was possible if you took it easy on Mondays. And even though I'd tried to discourage the most degenerate drunks from hanging out, the more presentable ones still came around to contribute to my bottom line, a bit of twisted thinking that I was struggling with. How could I encourage in others what I didn't want in myself?

Kenny Boustaloudis's mad holdup attempt had shaken me. I hadn't talked to Burton about what to do with the documents. I thought about messengering them to Attorney Markham for safekeeping, but I also didn't think there was anyone left in play who cared about them. Randolph wouldn't be back. Kenny was in jail. Kathleen and Donald Maldonado were both dead. The options papers seemed to hold a weird curse, though, and I had the irrational sense that holding onto them would infect me somehow.

I was also still physically shaky from my Friday night slip, and so when the rap sounded on the bar door around ten-thirty, I jumped. It was probably the coffee company. I'd called to have them take the espresso machine back. It was finicky and it wasn't doing much for my coffee intake. I also needed the space. I hoped they didn't send the old witch who'd called me a ballbuster.

I climbed the stairs, trying to ignore my headache, and unlocked the door. Pulling it open was a very short, very wide man in a beautiful black topcoat with satin lapels, wearing a matching homburg hat. His face looked as if he'd boxed at one time, maybe welterweight.

"You'd be Elder Darrow, then." He stated, rather than asked, and when I nodded, pushed inside, forcing me to step back.

He held out his hand, the knuckles of which were gnarled with arthritis, the nails thick and yellow. I updated my first estimate of his age to past seventy.

"I'm here to see if we can come to some kind of agreement."

A brick dropped into the pit of my stomach. Had I found someone else who wanted these bloody documents?

"I'm Murray Carton. I have a little company here in town that builds things."

Yeah, like GE was a little electrical supplier. I closed up like a clam. This guy was not here about any real estate options. This was the man who, according to Pedey Thomas anyway, was interested in the Esposito for its proximity to the proposed Olympic velodrome. The fact that he'd shifted his ass all the way down to the South End to talk to me meant he might want the bar, or the building, more than I thought.

I shook his hand and he led me down the stairs into my own establishment with a distinct air of *droit de seigneur*. He smiled at the Rancilio.

"Any chance I could con you out of an espresso?"

I felt as if I was stumbling along behind a fast-moving parade, with a shovel for whatever the horses left behind. I pointed at the back of the hulking machine, where the water line was disconnected and the power unplugged.

"Sending it back," I said. "Too much work for a bar."

My reactions felt thick and slow. I'd had to work with any number of business and finance types when I set up the bar and they tended to make me nervous. There was a greed gene in most of them, something I felt as a lack in myself, a tendency to focus on self-interest first and always. It made me over-cautious dealing with them.

"I could give you tea."

Carton shook his head, unbuttoned his coat, and perched a haunch on one of the stools, surveyed the back bar.

"How about a little bit of that Woodford's? No ice."

He set his hat, crown down like a cowboy, on the bar. I stepped behind and poured the drink. He took a crisp hundred from his ostrich-skin wallet and laid it on the bar. No sweaty wrinkled money for him. I ignored it, for now.

"I knew your father," he said.

The presumption we might have something in common because of that irked me.

"I'm surprised. He didn't go in for real estate people much. Thought they were mostly chiselers."

Carton's hand hitched a touch as the glass went to his lips, as if my sarcasm were a surprise. Here was another guy too used to people kissing his ass.

"Regardless. I was sad to hear of his passing."

I didn't recall him or his partner Harry Feinberg anywhere near Thomas's funeral or its aftermath. My automatic dislike of this man threatened to run away and I tamped it down.

"What can I do for you, Mr. Carton?"

"Murray, please." He folded his hands around the glass and looked at me with humor in his dark brown eyes. "I'm interested in your establishment here."

"Really." I knew exactly what he meant but I wasn't going to make it easy for him. "How's that?"

"This is an up and coming neighborhood down here," he said equably. "My partner and I were thinking it might be nice to have a foothold in the area."

"I thought your company mainly built things." I was curious how far he'd go not to mention the Olympics, if I didn't bring it up first.

He sighed, the convincing exhalation of an old man put upon by the world.

"I'm getting along in years, Elder. No one understands this until they get there, but at a certain point you lose some of your drive, some of your give-a-shit about fancy new projects and developments. We're looking to create a town square kind of atmosphere, something that will serve the neighborhood, maybe build it into a tighter community."

It was the first time I'd heard someone his age use the language

229

of the millennial entrepreneur to justify his plans. It was a relief to be that certain he was bullshitting me.

"I don't know," I said. "I've just about gotten the place the way I like it. I don't believe I'm ready to sell up yet."

He frowned as he raised his glass again.

"You know, I understand that argument. But you're running this operation on a pretty tight string, aren't you? Between the mortgage and all the money you put into this place? I'd bet five hundred bucks is a big night for you."

His estimate was so close to accurate it was scary, as if he'd been looking at my accounts. For that matter, if he were working with Markham, he may have been.

I poured myself a short glass of club soda and squeezed a slice of lime into it.

"You know, Murray? I don't need a lot to make me happy. I guess I'm lucky that way."

"Well, why don't I see if I can change your mind?"

His confidence that he could irritated me. I waited to see what he would say, but instead he reached into his suit coat and pulled out a folded piece of paper.

"I took the liberty of working this up," he said. "It's a term sheet, not a contract, but I think you'll like the bottom line. It pays off your debt and leaves you with a decent profit on your investment."

I accepted the paper, curious as to why a big cheese like him was negotiating directly with me. Deals like this were usually done at arms' length, through lawyers, with hot coffee, cold drinks, pastries, and a general mutual backslapping camaraderie around the profit margin.

His offer bottomed out at nine hundred thousand dollars, less than the two million he'd offered me originally, but a bump up from the number Markham had conveyed the last time. Which immediately made me wonder if I could trust my attorney. Had Carton raised his offer before? There couldn't be two people vying to own the Esposito.

What Carton had to know, if he knew my family history, was that I didn't need to grab the first offer that came along.

I smiled.

"Murray. Even if I were inclined to sell—and I'm not saying I wouldn't, to the right buyer—even if I were going to, I've been offered twice that for the place. Your offer does include the building?"

Suspicion washed across his face and I wondered if the assumption he and Feinberg had made in the original offer was wrong.

"It does." He tossed off the rest of the bourbon, his eyes watering. "But you know as well as I do, a murder lowers the value of the property. It's almost like the old Esposito, in a way. Isn't it?"

That was egregious—he was trying to unsettle me.

"In fact," he said. "I'm surprised you didn't mention that fact up front."

About as surprised as I was that he didn't mention he and his partner were assembling a block of real estate as a bet on the Olympics coming to town. The people who screamed loudest about other people's integrity were often the ones who had issues with their own.

"Didn't make a difference, actually. Business hasn't slowed down at all."

And if Carton actually did have access to my numbers, he'd know I was telling the truth. The sad fact was that anything out of the ordinary—fire, flood, death—seemed to attract people who wanted to witness it, to tell other people they'd been there. FOMO, they called it: fear of missing out.

"So I take it your answer is no?"

"I'm afraid so, Murray. I'm only halfway inclined to sell the place, so any offer's going to have to be pretty tempting."

"Give me a number, then. A place we can start."

As soon as I did that, I'd be committed to selling to him. It was the old joke about whoredom: the "yes" would establish what I was and then all we'd be doing was negotiating on price.

"Well," I said. "The original offer I had through my lawyer seemed like a fair one. I could live with something like that. Structured correctly."

There had to be tax dodges and profit-sharing fiddles Attorney Markham could come up with. I didn't want Murray to think I expected a suitcase full of cash.

"That's pretty rich," he said. "I guess you're not worried about defaulting on your mortgage? Running into an unfriendly banker?"

Ah, there were the wolf teeth. I stared at him and considered pulling out the Little Slugger from under the bar.

"That sounds like a threat," I said. "Which would mean our negotiation is at an impasse. I'm going to ask you to leave."

"It wasn't intended that way." He stood up and buttoned his topcoat. "Business arrangements can be fickle, is all I'm saying."

"If you want to counter offer, I'd suggest you do it through my attorney. You probably know him: Daniel Markham?"

Murray turned his collar up, jaunty.

"Don't believe I do, Elder." He rapped his knuckles on the bar. "But if you change your mind—let's keep the lines of communication open, shall we?"

He turned his back on me without waiting for an answer and started up the stairs. Ben Franklin's face stared up at me from the bill on the bar, but I couldn't dredge up a bit of his wisdom, anything at all that would advise me how to deal with the situation.

* * *

The espresso machine was gone. The company in the North End didn't send the nasty old woman back, but two bruisers who only spoke Italian. They'd gouged a long furrow out of the plaster wall wrestling the beast up the stairs, and I was repairing it with spackle and a putty knife when Randolph Coyne opened the door.

I looked down to make sure Marina was safe in the kitchen and straightened up from my knees, feeling a twinge in my back.

Randolph was dressed like a man about town, in a gray wool suit with faint purple lines drawing window panes, and a crisp white shirt buttoned to the neck, no tie. The dapper effect was ruined by the bright blue cast on his arm, bulky enough that he hadn't been able to thread it through the jacket's sleeve. When I raised the putty knife, he held up his free hand.

"Please. I need to apologize for everything, past and present. I was only doing a job of work, you understand."

The soldier-following-orders argument, like the ICE people in Texas caging babies and children behind chicken wire. It didn't soothe me.

"I need a much better reason than that not to walk down the stairs and call the police right now."

I snapped the plastic cap onto the spackle container, careful to keep him in my line of sight.

"The 'police' being your friend Detective Burton."

"Talk or leave, Randolph."

I blocked the stairs. He waved his cast at me.

"I can explain everything, if we can sit down, be civilized. I promise you this is a peaceful overture. Maybe even a lucrative one for you."

I scratched my forearm where he'd carved his telephone number, the scars nearly absorbed, then picked up my tools and walked down the stairs. If talking to him would get him out of my life, I'd listen.

"I'll tell you something right now, Randolph." I stowed the knife and plastic container under the bar. "I don't have those documents. I gave them to my attorney until someone figures out who actually owns them."

"Jesus." Randolph smacked his fist on the bar. "You don't want to let them out of your hands."

I stared at him.

"Peaceful," I said. "Good way to start."

He closed his eyes and breathed rhythmically, as if resetting his attitude. It must have been hard for someone who had trained as muscle to change lanes, and I wondered who he might be working for now. He was hustling for those documents, but he knew Donald was gone. And he didn't have the capital or the connections to take advantage of them himself. And I still didn't know that he hadn't killed Donald.

"I only meant that it was an unfortunate choice. I'm trying to effect a reasonable solution for a problem I inherited. I know you've been inconvenienced and I assure you compensation is forthcoming. But the documents—you've looked at them?"

I nodded.

"Then you know they've been assigned to Donald Maldonado."

"Not Topalian, LLC?"

"No. And if you looked carefully, you'd see that I'm the secondary assignee to Donald."

I leaned back against the bar. There weren't any customers yet this morning, and I wasn't going to encourage him by offering a drink.

"You're saying the documents belong to you now? Who wants them badly enough to kill Donald?"

He shook his head.

"Wrong question. My offer is this: one million dollars for possession of those documents, cash money. All twenty-four must be there, of course."

A slash of shock hit me. More money being thrown my way? Two million for the bar, a million for the documents, pretty soon we'd be talking about real money.

"That's a lot of scratch," I said

"For papers that have no value to you personally." Randolph was being earnest, subdued, a chameleon-shift from the man who'd cut a phone number into my forearm.

"Apparently." I was severely tired of the drama around the papers. "I'll be happy to get rid of them."

He relaxed so completely he almost seemed human.

"Maybe we could have a little pop to seal the deal. Is that the Pappy Van Winkle I see?"

"Maybe you should hold up just a minute. You understand that several people have died over these papers. How many of them did you account for?"

"I swear to god, I didn't kill nobody."

I frowned at him, trying to guess if he was playing games with the double negative.

"This trip, anyway," Coyne said, with a smirk.

"Not Donald?"

He shook his head. "I'm not a sniper. I face up to people. My guess is he pissed off someone local."

"What about Kathleen?"

"I chased her for weeks and never caught up with her. Brilliant move, hiding in jail. But Donald liked her—he didn't want me to hurt her."

"Constantine Boustaloudis?" I said.

"Who the hell is that? Look, I only moved north to work with Donald, before he went off the rails."

I didn't know what he meant by that and I didn't care. I cracked the seal on the Pappy bottle and ran it under my nose, poured a short shot, and pushed it over the bar. I ran a glass of tap water for myself.

"Here's how this is going to work, Randolph. You bring me the cash, we'll go to my lawyer's office."

"I hear a condition."

"And I go with you to meet your principal."

I didn't care who it was, but Burton would. Randolph shook his head.

"Sorry, partner. Not going to happen."

I wouldn't have pushed it, except I knew Burton was stymied on the Boustaloudis killing and this could help him out. And, frankly, I wanted to meet with the person responsible for all the aggravation I'd dealt with, get the chance to rain on them a little.

"Nonnegotiable, Randolph. But," I pointed at the glass. "You make it happen, I'll toss in a bottle of that."

He laughed, still shaking his head.

"You are a pisser." He raised his cast. "Apologies for the carving job, by the way. I'm turning over a new leaf."

"Who's your principal, Randolph? I doubt you own the kind of capital to fund a project like this."

He drained the glass, exhaled in pleasure, and set it down on the mahogany.

"Why do you care, Darrow? This gets you out from under and gives you a decent payday. There's no upside to your knowing."

"Except that I like to know things."

"I will bring your money—cash—here tomorrow at nine a.m. We will travel to your attorney's office and you will pass over the papers." He hesitated. "I will make a good faith effort to take you to the person behind the scenes, yes? But it will be under strict nondisclosure. Agreed?"

It was as good an offer as I'd get. I'd try and get Burton to come along, or at least trail us.

"Nine a.m. I may bring a witness."

Randolph shrugged, which made me doubt his commitment to bringing me to the principal.

"Protect yourself," he said. "Once I hand you the money, my only concern is delivering the documents. Anything else that happens, to you or for you, is nothing to me."

45

Burton met with Mickey Barksdale in the Subway in Copley Square, across from Trinity Church. He knew he was behind the curve on this, that he should have done it when Martines started pushing him again. Time to man up and find out the truth, if that was possible. Who'd Mickey kill, if anyone. And why? He made it clear the meeting was mandatory, if Mickey didn't want to deal with some other less friendly branch of the BPD.

Barksdale had the chicken salad, hold the hot peppers. Burton ordered a small tuna. They arranged their chips, napkins, and drinks on a small table by the window. Burton tipped his head toward the square.

"You ever come down to the library any more?"

Mrs. Ward, their fourth grade teacher, used to arrange biweekly visits to the main branch. Burton loved the old building and, as a child, had been awed by the idea of free books for everyone.

Mickey took a huge bite of his sandwich without answering. Stupid question. Gangstering probably didn't leave a lot of time for pleasure reading.

"Better here than somewhere in the neighborhood," Mickey said. "Don't want anyone seeing me breaking bread with the local constabulary."

"Fancy words, Mick."

"Fuck you. Quit the weenie-wagging and let me enjoy my lunch. What do you want from me this time?"

"I'm doing you a favor, Mick. You know they're turning up the heat on this Olympic bullshit in certain quarters."

Mickey nodded, wiped his mouth with a napkin.

"And I told you, Danny boy, my only connection is O'Hanian, at the BOFF. Everything he's doing over there is legal—he's my sister's first cousin, and when he came back from the South, she begged me to find him something that wouldn't end up with him back in Framingham."

"Ah." Burton stepped lightly now. "There's another issue. Trick Randisi?"

"That candy-ass." Mickey's sandwich shed lettuce as he crushed it unconsciously. "Bringing me his nickel and dime shit from grave-robbing and expecting me to pay him top dollar."

"So, one of your guys fenced for him."

"Favor for a friend. I never cleared a hundred dollars on the crap he brought in. And he never made a dent in what he owed for betting, either."

"And getting him to stop so someone could put an extra coffin on his truck?"

Mickey held Burton's stare, but his fair skin reddened.

"No idea what you're talking about."

"Mickey. I've known you since we were six. You think I can't tell when you're lying to me? I know you didn't kill the guy in the box." Mostly because Boustaloudis had died neatly, one bullet to the head. "So where did you get the body to put on Trick's truck?"

Mickey took another bite, chewed, and swallowed, mindful enough of his manners not to talk with his mouth full.

"Seriously, Danny. I do not know. You know how something like this works. Somebody up the line gives an order to someone farther down, who sends it across to someone else. By the time it gets done, Woodward and Bernstein couldn't figure out who wanted it to happen."

"But you're the man at the head of the line, aren't you?"

Mickey's face darkened some more, as if Burton had insulted him. Burton felt his stomach twinge.

"I will say this." Mickey lowered his voice. "Sanford may be able to help you out there. He's told me some strange stories about his boss over there—not criminal, necessarily, but strange."

"The BOFF guy? Wilder?"

"Sanford and I were talking the other night—don't make a thing out of it, he checks in with me once in a while—and he was telling me Wilder has this other guy doing actual security work for him: tall, a hard-ass, dresses like a fag? So why does Wilder need extra security if he's got Sanford O'Hanian?"

Burton took that in along with a swallow Nantucket Nectar lemonade. Did Wilder think he was at greater risk from the anti-Olympic people than he had been? They hadn't been much in evidence. Or did it have something to do with those contracts Elder had? Wilder was a man with serious money, but that didn't mean he had enough. For some people, there was no such thing.

"That helps. Mickey. A little."

Mickey looked around furtively.

"Good. So, the body? Favor for one of my guys. One of his street dealers paid off a debt and gave him a little extra if he could get it done."

Burton felt his case about to take a step forward.

"Street dealer. Someone whose territory might be Cleary Square?"

Mickey nodded.

"The Boustaloudis kid. So, now can you leave me the fuck alone?"

Burton threw him a mock pout.

"Anyone would think you didn't like me, Mick."

Mickey ripped open his bag of Sun chips, scattering them over the table top.

"Sure, Burton. Be a dickhead."

Burton was careful not to say he would leave Mickey alone. He didn't want to set up a false expectation. It was a relief that the talk had produced something, but he wasn't going to lie to the man to make his life smoother.

46

L ate at night, a few silent souls drank at the bar as the clock turned slowly toward closing time. Johnny Hartman crooned in the background—"Lush Life."

"So, Henri made it."

Susan and I sat at a table at the base of the stage where we could talk privately but I could keep an eye on the bar. She sipped a Cape Codder and I drank ginger ale, trying to tell her something, I suppose.

"And you didn't."

"I'm sorry."

She shook her head.

"For now. He's as stable as something like that gets, I guess. They've got him on a drug regimen they've had success with. Extending life. Not curing."

Her eyes were brilliant with tears.

"He could be with us a while longer, then? Months? Years?"

I understood the cruelty of that uncertainty from my own father's death. She shook her head.

"Not years." Her sad look froze my heart. "Best estimate is four to six months."

"So you'll have some time with him."

Which meant I might have some time with her. She'd be staying in Henri's apartment, right down the stairs from mine. I was hoping we'd find a way to cobble something together, a relationship that would move us forward.

She nodded.

"I'm taking him back to Oregon."

She must have seen how I flinched.

"He's dying, Susan. You want to move him?"

"He also has a better idea who I am right now. The dementia's eased," she said. "And I want him to have the right-to-die option, if he wants it."

"And you and I? We go on hold again?"

She rubbed her small hands over her eyes.

"I don't know, Elder. What I do know is that I can't save you."

"The fuck is that supposed to mean? It was one night when I had too many drinks. Nothing worse than that."

Her disappointed look told me I wasn't fooling her.

"We both know better than that. And I can't live with it. Especially now."

"So. That's done, then?"

Her look appealed to me not to be so hard, but I couldn't hold back.

"I will be back in Boston," she said. "When it happens."

When Henri died, she meant.

My anger pushed me up from the table, to be anywhere else than here. I could tell her I was rich, that I'd go to rehab, but that wouldn't change anything. It stabbed me in the heart, but I wasn't what she needed, now or forever.

"Well." I started to get back behind the bar. "All the best."

Burton was standing outside the Esposito's door on Mercy Street when I got there at eight. The neighborhood was deserted, except for a maroon van with a Mass. College of Pharmacy sticker on the back waiting for the convenience store to open and a box truck delivering stacks of newspapers.

I'd spent part of the night awake, feeling despondent, but when I woke up this morning, I'd just been angry. We'd met when I was still a drinker and it hadn't bothered her much then. In the middle of the Alison Somers thing, she'd wanted something from me, at which point I had learned (and apparently forgotten) that Susan Voisine was a woman who did or took what she needed to make herself happy. I felt as if I'd done a fair amount on Henri's behalf over the years, and by extension, for her, and she'd taken that and run.

"You look like someone butt-fucked your hamster." Burton blew on his hands, the newspaper tucked under his arm, a to-go cup of coffee in his hand. "You think spring's ever going to get here?"

I unlocked the door and held it open for him. I'd had coffee at the apartment, but it hadn't cleared my brain or made me want to talk. I hoped he realized that enough not to prod.

"OK. If that's how you feel," he said.

I didn't bother with any of the bar-opening tasks. Marina could take care of them when she got in. I wasn't so sure now I wanted to meet Randolph's principal—what was I going to do, yell at him?—but I wanted to know why and how I'd been dragged into all this. If Randolph refused to take me to him, I was going to pull the plug. The million in cash would be nice, but I wasn't going to miss something I never had my hands on. It might be cathartic to burn the documents that had caused these deaths. Then maybe I'd be able to focus on what came next for me, after the Esposito.

I thumped my ass down on a stool.

"Rough night?" Burton spread his newspaper out on the counter.

"You could say that."

"Check this out." He tapped the headline, in a font only slightly smaller than the announcement of the 9/11 attacks: **Olympic Bid Certain, Group Says**. "You believe that?"

"Literally? Of course I do. Am I not supposed to notice that the power brokers in this city always get what they want? And the little guys get hosed?"

"I don't know," Burton said. "I keep hearing there's a lot of grassroots resistance that's not making the papers. The mayor's started backing away. And not so long ago, pal, your family was part of that power structure."

I wanted to be angry, but I couldn't disagree.

"Doesn't mean we took advantage of it."

As sometimes happens between fathers and sons, I'd found out too late that my father possessed a more ethical approach to his business than I'd given him credit for. He'd been very particular about the projects and people his bank worked with, and that had made him a few enemies. I wished I could have said that to him before he died.

Burton snorted, but didn't extend the thought.

"So what's the program?"

"You're coming along because I think you want to know who the principal is. Don't you think the connection between the documents and Boustaloudis is there?"

Burton sipped from the cardboard cup.

"These things don't always come out the most logical way. But there's a chance you're right. You're thinking whoever it was had Connie killed?"

"Your department altogether. I'm assuming Randolph will come through."

A knock reverberated in the steel door. Burton stepped through the arch into the kitchen. I approved of his caution—he was the one who was armed.

"It's open!"

I folded up the newspaper and turned up the lights.

Randolph strutted down the stairs, wearing designer jeans with a crease and a puffy purple down North Face coat, a square insulated bag over his shoulder.

"Good day to you, Mr. Darrow. How's your amplitude this fine day?"

He was being too friendly, too agreeable.

"Are we visiting your man, or not?"

"Right to business." He grinned and slung the bag up onto the bar. "Take a look inside before you say anything else. I want you to know we're going to do this the right way."

I unzipped the satchel, which was crammed with banded stacks of hundred dollar bills. I flipped through several packets to make sure he wasn't passing me sucker's rolls and to see the serial numbers weren't in order. The money might not be the most important point for me, but I wasn't stupid enough to take marked bills or counterfeit, either.

"Good," I said.

"The papers? I know we're not haring off to your lawyer's office for them."

I picked up the money and started for my office.

"You know the way."

He followed me down the narrow hallway and into the office, where I bent over the safe, shielding it with my body, and twirled the combination. I stuffed the bag inside and pulled out the big folder, set it on my desk.

Randolph grabbed it up and started to count the clipped sheaves of paper.

"They're all here, then." He sounded surprised. "You know, it would be the easiest thing in the world for me to take back that money and keep these. Leave you here."

I slammed the safe door and spun the dial as Burton stepped into the doorway.

"Not as easy as you might think," he said.

Randolph turned.

"And you would be?"

I had to admire Randolph's *sang-froid*. He acted as if he were still in control.

"Independent observer," Burton said. "Kind of like they have at the UN?"

I was surprised their paths hadn't crossed yet. Randolph half-raised his hands, smiling.

"It was not my intention to do that. I was merely making an observation."

I didn't believe him and I doubted Burton did either.

"So, Randolph. The comedy is finished, yes?" I took back the folder. "Are we going to meet your principal or not?"

He nodded.

"He's a little curious as to why you're so insistent, Elder. But he has agreed to. And he has a proposition for you, too, maybe an opportunity to invest some of that cash you just acquired."

I patted the top of the safe.

"Which we will leave right here." I turned to Burton. "I do think we'll take the United Nations along, though. If you don't mind."

Randolph touched his fingers to his forehead in a salute and started for the door. Burton and I followed. I wondered if things weren't coming together a little too easily.

* * *

"Oh, no shit," Burton said from the passenger seat of the Cougar as we followed Randolph's Chevy Volt—I guess even a crook can be planet-aware—off 93 in Milton and onto a country lane called Chickatawbut Road. "I've been here before."

I glanced across. The threads of our separate concerns were starting to weave together. I pulled to the curb outside a modest Cape with dingy white vinyl siding and noticed a maroon van come around a corner and park halfway down the block.

"You're going to love this guy," Burton said. "Looks to me like starting the BOFF wasn't altogether an act of community service."

Randolph waited for us on the bottom step of a sun porch that had been added to the side of the house. We walked up the driveway past a twenty-five-year-old Mercedes wagon with hand controls on the steering wheel.

"Hope you don't mind removing your shoes," Randolph said. "Old J. T. is a little fanatical about his carpets being clean. I guess since he doesn't use them himself."

I saw what he meant when we walked in through the storm door onto the porch and saw a man in a wheelchair facing us, parked next to a small wood stove. I could smell the hot metal from here—it must have been eighty degrees inside.

J. T. wore a heavily-starched tattersall shirt with the sleeves folded back over thick muscular forearms. The wheelchair was old-school, not powered. His eyes protruded like pale blue marbles and the veins across his cheeks and nose suggested he and I shared an infatuation.

"This is the man who's been delaying my project?" The voice reached for thunder, but barely rumbled.

I disliked him immediately. Randolph felt the need for courtesy.

"Elder Darrow, this is J. T. Wilder. He's the chief architect behind the effort to bring the Olympic Games to Boston."

Randolph's loyalties had swiveled easily—he sounded like a loyal middle manager.

"And we will do that," Wilder said. "You saw the *Globe* this morning? We have the full support of the entire city. This is going to be a reality."

The little that I'd heard and what Burton had been telling me was that various neighborhoods were mounting a fairly effective grass-roots resistance to the whole idea, but that the city's traditional media weren't reporting on it very well. Wilder reminded me of the character in Dr. Strangelove who kept yapping about his precious bodily fluids—it was never worth the energy to argue with someone as certain as he was.

"OK." I turned to go. "That's all I needed to know. Burton?"

Wilder rolled his chair to block my way.

"You don't want to hear my offer? I can quadruple the money you just extorted from me."

"Thanks, but no thanks. I wish you the best with your efforts, though."

Not entirely true, but a judicious lie seemed appropriate.

The storm door slammed open behind us. Suddenly it was very crowded on the sun porch. A middle-aged woman in a dark green caftan and a wristful of gold bangles barged in, waving a large silver revolver.

I ducked out of the way as she pushed past. Randolph was trapped between the wall and Burton, who had his weapon out, but only watched.

"You crippled old-fuck bastard!" She screeched at Wilder. "You think it's so easy to steal my life? My husband worked himself sick to make something happen. You think like a rich man, don't you? You waltz in and steal his work?"

The waltz crack seemed unnecessarily cruel, but I don't think it was intentional. Randolph was trying to edge past Burton toward the door, but froze when the woman turned the pistol on him.

"And you! What, you steal the contracts from your own boss, give them to another boss? I should shoot you, too."

"Dorris." Burton's voice was as gentle as a mother's. "You can't do that, Dorris. Think about Kenny. He's not going to make it without your strong hand on his back."

"Kenny." She made a spitting noise. "He's the reason Connie sold the papers in the first place. Kenny stole the money from his dealer boss—Connie saved his life."

Her gun hand wavered. Randolph ducked behind Burton.

"And he killed Constantine," she said.

Wilder eyed her as if she were a snake.

"No, Dorris," Burton said. "And you know that, don't you?"

She slumped, anger draining away with the truth.

"I know," she said. "But what did he expect, the fool? Tying up all our money in that stupid real estate? What was going to be left? You can't eat paper. Or houses. I got mad with him."

I was confused, but Burton seemed to understand what was

247

happening, and that was good enough. Apparently, she'd killed Constantine Boustaloudis.

A crackling from behind got my attention. I turned and saw Wilder stuffing the papers into the burning stove. They went up like dry tissue paper.

"No," Dorris screamed, and fired in his direction.

The bullet smashed into Wilder's cheek, below the eye socket. If he wasn't dead on the spot, I was Mary Poppins. And I wasn't.

I wanted to drop to the floor, curl up, and roll into a corner. Randolph took advantage of the stunned lull to slide out the door. I didn't hear his car start, but those electric vehicles are quiet.

Dorris sat down hard on the floor, as if the one shot was all she'd had energy for. Burton relieved her of the gun.

"Well," I said to him. "So much for all that."

The fact that I'd gained a million dollars in exchange for what was now a pile of ashes didn't escape me, but like any good Yankee, I wondered what it was going to cost me to keep it.

"Well, this shoots a hole in the Olympic movement," Burton said. "No pun intended."

"Nice one. What else do you need from me?"

"You know what? It's probably easier if you weren't here at all. For any of this."

I could see how that made sense. "How did you get here, then?"

He shrugged. "I'll think of something."

I knew he would.

"Done and done." I headed for the sun porch door. "Good luck."

* * *

Driving back to the Esposito, I thought about the loose ends Burton was going to have to tie up for me, the answers I didn't have yet. The BOFF effort to bring the Olympics to Boston was likely to fall apart without J. T. Wilder's money and influence, not to mention his megalomania, but I didn't feel too bad about that. I loved my city too well to see it carved up and built over for a temporary benefit to a few greedy people.

My cell phone buzzed as I parked the Cougar in the alley by the loading dock behind the bar. Private number. I shut off the engine and answered.

"Elder Darrow."

"Mr. Darrow. Good morning. Murray Carton."

I rolled my eyes. I hadn't given a second of thought to selling the bar to him since I'd talked to him. "Murray. How are you?"

"Hey." His voice sounded upbeat, but I detected a hint of strain underneath. Either that or I was just one thing on a long list he had to handle today and he was in a hurry to check me off.

"You see the paper this morning, Elder? Things are looking a little rosier than they were a few days ago. Which is to your good, my friend."

I rubbed my face with my hand, fighting an overwhelming urge to tell him to go fuck himself, so I could open up my bar and get back to work. One of the things I wanted Burton to explain to me was who had killed Kathleen. Her loss still hurt, strangely, and it seemed that she'd been on the periphery of most of this.

"On my way in to work, Murray. How about saying it out loud?"

Pregnant pause, a long offended breath.

"I don't think we need to get personal, Elder. I'm ready to increase my offer for your property."

"Is that so?"

I climbed out and leaned on the roof of the car. The sky was a clear bright blue and the air crisp and windless, the best kind of late winter day I could imagine.

"Is so, my friend. Let me tell you what I have in mind."

"Let me tell you what I have in mind, Murray."

It hadn't occurred to me, even after inheriting from my father, how liberating it was to have enough money not to worry about pissing anyone off. The cash in the Esposito's safe alone freed me up for all kinds of foolishness, if I so chose.

"The full two million dollars you offered originally. No loans, no tax dodges, deferred payments, nothing. Cash in my attorney's hands by five PM today. I'll fax him a power of attorney and you can sign everything in his office."

I was making a large bet, both on Carton's greed and my hope that the Olympic bid would fall apart and leave him holding the bag. Maybe he knew something I didn't, but I didn't care any more. I was jumping off the cliff and sewing a parachute on the way down.

"Done," he said. "You don't want to be there at the signing?"

"Daniel Markham is the man you need to satisfy," I said. "You bring him the cash, he signs for me. That way I don't have to see you again. I can be out of here in a month."

Murray huffed a pleased laugh, as if he hadn't expected it to be so easy.

"All right, my friend. Pleasure doing business with you."

"Can't say the same, Murray. But have a good time with the bar. Cheers."

I thumbed the phone off, locked up the Cougar, and went off to open up the Esposito, my bar for only a little while longer. I'd have to let Marina know, but my chest felt as if a hundred pound barbell had been lifted away.

48

Burton was smoking a panatela from the box he'd bought at L. J. Peretti to celebrate solving the Boustaloudis mess. Lieutenant Martines's office was a yes-smoking zone again, the Loo having given up his latest attempt to unlatch the nicotine monkey.

"I told my bride, Daniel," he said. "I told her with my addictive nature, I was always going to be hooked on something. It could be booze, or dope, or other women."

Burton felt expansive enough to fake some empathy.

"And she said?"

"She caved."

Burton shook his head.

"That's bullshit."

Martines gave a stiff laugh.

"Yeah. You're right. She said I could smoke anywhere but in the house."

"Compromise," Burton said. "It's a beautiful thing."

He exhaled and regarded the lengthening ash on the end of his cigar.

"Which appears to have been the problem with the Boustaloudis couple."

"He'd been buying up those options for years? Before there was any talk of the Olympics?"

Burton nodded.

"Nostalgia trip—he wanted to preserve the Franklin Park where he'd grown up. And immigrant wealth-building. You see what goes on with the banks in Greece? The Greeks don't trust them for shit."

Martines shrugged. He always said he never read anything in the papers but sports.

"But when Kenny tries to steal from Mickey Barksdale, Connie sells the options to Donald Maldonado," Burton said. "And Dorris figures the family's lost its wealth."

"And offs the old man." Martines tapped his cigar into the ashtray. "She's claiming he beat her, but that's seriously *ex post facto*."

"And Kenny, using his temporary good graces with Mickey B., gets the body disappeared and it all looks good, until Connie pops out of the box."

"Do we have a case we can take to court, though?"

Burton nodded.

"Statements, physical evidence. A confession from Kenny. The gun she used to kill her husband. We have her for Wilder, regardless."

Martines stubbed out the butt as if he didn't like the taste, fired up a cigarette.

"He going to make it?"

"Questionable. And the BOFF already withdrew its bid. The scandal didn't sit well with the national committee."

"Like I give a shit," Martines said. "So who did Maldonado? Dorris?"

"Kenny. Dorris wanted him to prove he wouldn't roll on her."

"His own mother. Nice family, huh?"

"Dorris figured Maldonado screwed Connie over when he bought the options, bought them cheap."

"What I don't get is how your buddy Darrow got his hands on them."

Martines didn't want the answer to that. It might taint the case against the Boustaloudis family. Burton had made an executive decision not to muddy things with Elder or Kathleen Crawford.

"No idea, Loo. Can't help you there. All I know, we solved what we were supposed to solve."

Martines looked at him suspiciously, then made his own decision, and nodded.

"Good enough. You're right. We don't need anything more."

49

I listened to Burton tell me the version he'd given his boss and approved of his leaving me out of it.

"Whole thing seems unbelievable now. A little sad, though. Old J. T. didn't make it, you know."

Burton nodded, spooning up some of Marina's bean soup.

"His body was so fucked up from being in a wheelchair so long, it couldn't cope. So, goodbye Olympics, unless someone else steps up."

I shook my head.

"Tide's turned on that. The neighborhoods rose up in arms even more, once the details of the proposal came out. Lot of lies and hand-waving. One thing I don't get—what was Donald Maldonado doing in Boston? Icky Ricky's business here was less than zero."

"Best guess, according to our financial forensics guys? He bought the options figuring to either sell them at a profit or do some real estate development on his own. He was trying to get a foothold in the city."

"Don't think your pal Mickey would have liked that much."

Burton ate more soup, ignoring that.

"So do we know why Kathleen was killed? Or who did it? Was it Donny?"

Burton put down his spoon, hearing the catch in my voice. Wes Montgomery spun his guitar out in to a skein of notes in "Road Song" in the background.

"Best guess?" he said. "Randolph, as part of getting the documents back. And he's been immunized. With the Feds. Good luck getting

253

any answers out of them."

"They can shield him from a murder charge? That's fucked. So what else does he know that they could care about?"

"Yes they can. And who knows? Though I've heard chatter about gun-running from down South to up here. Whisper 'organized crime' to the Feds and they wet themselves."

I drank some club soda. The urge to drink hadn't returned after Susan and Henri hied off to Oregon yesterday, but it was too early for me to crow. Susan had made it clear she didn't want me there to say goodbye.

I took away his soup bowl and brought him a fresh beer.

"So now you're the BPD's star again."

He shook his head.

"That never lasts. And I've still got the one unsolved."

Kathleen. I was surprised by how quickly my grief over her death faded, though I felt guilty about that. My brief time with her had been a try at breaking some of my self-built strictures, getting out of old patterns, but all it taught me was how I needed structure, stability, and peace in my life.

"Couple months, you're going to have to find a new place to drink," I said.

Burton raised his eyebrows.

"You really selling?"

"Money's in the bank, papers all signed. I'm out of here the first of June."

"Marina?"

"Ask her yourself. She wouldn't tell me, but I think the plan is culinary school."

Burton looked chastened and I kicked myself. Marina's news should have come from her.

"Talk to the woman," I said. "That might have been one of the ideas on the table."

"And you? What are you going to do?"

"Shit if I know. I'm not in a big hurry to find out, though."

Burton looked as thoughtful as I ever saw him. Then he stood up and headed for the kitchen.

"Better go ask," he said.

* * *

He'd left this morning's *Globe* on the bar. I unfolded it, wondering what I was going to do with all my free time this summer, besides catch up on my sleep and read some big books. Having three million dollars, all liquid, didn't generate as many crazy ideas as I thought it might. I'd have to be careful with the cash in the safe anyway, unless I wanted tax trouble.

The front page headline was not as much of a shock as the font tried to make it be: **Hub Olympic Bid Rung Up**. The *Globe*'s headline writers always tried a little too hard.

But with Wilder's death and some pressure from the national committee, the BOFF was disbanding. Sanford O'Hanian, a spokesperson for the group, cited the organization's deep grief at the passing of its founder, but Burton had told me Wilder wanted the options for the properties because he didn't think he had enough leverage for the bid to succeed.

The phone under the bar rang.

"Esposito. This is Elder."

"Mr. Darrow. This is Harry Feinberg."

Murray Carton's partner. I guessed what was coming.

"We were wondering, in light of developments, whether you might be interested in retaining ownership of your establishment."

"You must take the *Globe*, too," I said. "No. Our deal is done. You were the ones who pushed for the quick sale."

Pedey Thomas unearthed the rumor that Carton and Feinberg had no intentions of developing the parcel, just flipping them on to greater fools. I felt no sympathy.

"All we'd have to do is unwind the contract," Feinberg wheedled. "And you keep, say, half a million, for your trouble."

I wasn't tempted for more than a second or two. I didn't always make the best decisions, but once I'd made one, I didn't waffle.

"Appreciate the offer, Harry. But I don't think so. Maybe you can find someone to run the place for you."

If he hadn't done so many deals in his career, I guess he would have been angry with me, but real estate developers probably had to be hard: some deals worked, some didn't. And when one didn't, you cut your losses and moved on. Much as I felt about the Esposito now—it had served its purpose.

"First of June, Harry. Have a good time with it."

There was a certain amount of satisfaction in chalking one up over the developers, but the only open question I had, and I saw no way I was ever going to get a definitive answer, was who'd killed Kathleen Crawford and why. I didn't buy Burton's guess.

50

Burton sat in his cubicle at D-4, looking at a picture on his phone of Marina in a chef's hat, brandishing a knife. She'd texted it to him when she found out she'd gotten into the Culinary Institute.

He was putting off the voluminous paperwork required to explain all the crazy things that had happened in the last few weeks. At the very bottom, he could only make a logical argument for why he felt so good. He'd never been driven by a profit motive—if he had, he would have gone to Tufts Dental, like his mother had dreamed. But this was the feeling he'd gone into police work for, the satisfaction of explaining to living victims of a killing who the people who died were and why they were murdered. This last missing piece was bothering him, but he couldn't see how to fit it into the story. Kathleen Crawford had been executed at the Frog Pond and he had no evidentiary links to her death. Inquiries to the Feds resulted in a denial from Randolph—no surprise there—and he had no indication that anyone else had a reason to do it.

The other disturbing fact was that he and Mickey Barksdale were heading for a collision. He'd finessed the confrontation this time, but he wouldn't be that lucky forever. Mickey was too strong and too malevolent a presence in the city. Not to mention that the loss of the Olympic bid had probably cost Mickey money and goodwill.

He finished up the last form and pressed the key to route it to the Administrative section, dusted his hands together dramatically, to no audience. Elder hadn't seemed too broken up by Kathleen's death. Burton even considered whether he might have killed her, but Elder was not a burst-of-passion guy. He would have spent so much time weighing the pros and cons, he would have talked himself out of it.

Burton cleared the top of his desk, stood up, and shrugged on his coat. Working this case gave him some comp time to burn, and he'd promised to take Marina to New York for some shows after the Esposito shut down.

He shook his head. The place hadn't been around in its current form more than a few years, but he'd gotten used to having it. And hanging out with Elder from time to time.

That relationship was going to change and he wasn't sure how. He hoped to Christ all the free time didn't drag the man back to his former pastime of drinking himself to death—with the money he had now, it wouldn't take any time at all.

When his phone rang, he thought about ignoring it. He planned a nice thick corned beef sandwich from that deli in Brookline, a couple of beers, and a long nap in the afternoon peace of his apartment.

"Detective Burton? Frank Aschult. The Marine Patrol officer?"

Burton frowned, wishing he could forget that boat ride out to Rinker. Was Aschult trying to double down on Burton's promise to commend him?

"Yeah. What's up?"

"I picked up this woman at the dock, wants to go out to Rinker? Says she wants to pray over some graves?"

"So?"

"Well, first of all," Frank said. "I don't give fucking tours. And she looks like one of those women that tied me up that day, when you were out here? Did they ever catch them?"

"Big woman? Weepy, kind of? Sad sack face, like an unhappy bulldog?"

"Close enough," Aschult said. "I had to take away her weapon and she didn't fight me too hard, thank god. Big as she is, she could have caused more trouble. She's sitting in the stern of my boat, in handcuffs. You want her or not?"

"What for, for crissake?"

"She says she wanted to go back out to the island to pray for

Nina, that she was sorry for what she did. Wasn't Nina the other one, the woman who escaped with her?"

Burton felt the charge, the sense he was about to find out the answer to the last unexplained questions.

"She had a weapon? A .22?"

"Yep. Why?"

"Hold her there," Burton said. "I'll come out and get her."

In a weird way, it made sense that the woman—Alberta was her name, he remembered now—was the one who killed Kathleen. Knowing Kathleen, she'd abandoned Alberta as soon as she could. Which made Kathleen's ending more fitting than anything to do with thievery or blackmail or valuable documents. She hadn't had the ability to be loyal to anyone or anything but herself. She'd fucked Elder over good, and apparently hurt this Alberta woman enough to make her take vengeance. Burton could never in good conscience cheer the death of any person, but he was constantly reminded in his work of the ways in which karma rolled around in a big old circle.

About the Author

Richard J. Cass is the author of the Boston-based Elder Darrow Mystery series.

The first book in the series, *Solo Act*, was nominated for a Maine Literary Award in 2017. The second book in the series, *In Solo Time*, is the origin story for Elder and his friend, Boston homicide detective Dan Burton. *In Solo Time* won the Maine Literary Award for Crime Fiction for 2018. *Burton's Solo* continues the story of Elder and Burton and the Esposito Bar and Grill.

Cass's short fiction has been published widely and won prizes from *Redbook, Writers' Digest*, and *Playboy*. His first collection of stories was called *Gleam of Bone*. He blogs with the Maine Crime Writers at https://mainecrimewriters.com and serves on the board of Mystery Writers of America's New England chapter.

He lives in Cape Elizabeth, Maine, with his wife Anne, and a semi-feral Maine Coon cat named Tinker, where he writes full time. You can reach him on Facebook at: Richard Cass – Writer or on Twitter at: @DickCass.